THREE FACES OF JENNIFER

AN ARNIE & ZELLIE COZY MYSTERY

Eric Small

ERIC SMALL BOOKS
St. Augustine, Florida

Disclaimer: This is purely a work of fiction. Any resemblance of any character or any situation in this book to any person or situation is unintended and purely coincidental. The characters and places, other than nationally known entities which are also used fictionally, are figments of my imagination. Middletown, New Jersey is a real place, as are Monmouth County and the neighboring towns such as Rumson and Lincroft. Many of the depicted streets actually exist, but the town descriptions are intended to provide general geographical information only, not as completely accurate portrayals.

Eric Small Books
P.O. Box 840003
St. Augustine, FL 32080
www.ericsmallbooks.com

Three Faces of Jennifer - Eric Small -- 1st ed.

For my late father – We shared a love of words, but I am at a loss to find ones suitable to express how much I miss you.

Acknowledgments:

This book would not be possible without my wife Denele's unwavering love, support and encouragement, and her many helpful comments and suggestions during the writing and editing process.

I greatly value and benefit from the love, support and encouragement I regularly receive from my family – my mother Sally, my brother Steve, and my sister Nancy, as well as from my late father Richard, whose love of books and reading had much to do with my own love of words.

Thank you to Nanny, my late grandmother. I wish I could thank you in person for your love and support, and the wise words, history, and a few words of Yiddish that you shared. You loved mystery novels. If only you were around to read these.

Thank you to Middletown, New Jersey for its excellent sense of humor in tolerating multiple fictional murders in that great town. It was an excellent place to grow up, and remains a nice place to live.

Thanks to Rik Feeney (RickFeeney.com) for permitting me to use his cover design for Brazen Gambit as a model for *A Tale of Two Freddies*, upon which I modeled this book cover.

Author image used by permission from Lifetouch Portrait Studios, Inc.

Licensed cover art:

ID 96996781 © Vector Moon | Dreamstime.com

ID 5871136 © Rui Vale De Sousa | Dreamstime.com

ID 154201107 © Chipus | Dreamstime.com

ID 125253559 © Alexandra Ryzhkova | Dreamstime.com

ID 126974306 © Rashad Aliyev | Dreamstime.com

CHAPTER ONE

Beelzebub was back. I spotted her departing figure from a vantage point down the street. A casual stroll morphed into a nervous trot, as I hastened to determine the nefarious reason for her visit. Zellie kept pace at my side, as we closed the gap between us in order to discover the newest mischief committed by the ever enigmatic and always dangerous Jennifer Marquette.

I turned to Zellie with a cautionary hand raised. Her brow creased, she nodded. With a gentle touch, and surgical precision, I pulled on the exterior screen door. As no explosives or other dangers manifested, I pried the door open and beheld a note taped to the inner door, in Jennifer's unmistakable handwriting.

It contained two short sentences and a phone number. Zellie peered over my shoulder and we both viewed the scrawled "Please call me as soon as possible. I need your help."

"You won't call her, will you?" Zellie asked.

"I don't intend to," I said, not knowing why I had hedged like that instead of shouting no, no, no at the top of my lungs.

Zellie studied me. "You're thinking about it."

I sighed. I couldn't put one over on Zellie if I tried.

I told the truth. "Maybe," I replied, as we walked inside the house and shut the door. "I guess I am, even though every fiber of my mind and body are telling me it's foolish and maybe even dangerous."

I should explain. My name is Arnie Fischer. Zellie Morgan and I have known each other for our whole lives and are partners in the unlicensed A to Z Detective Agency. After a whirlwind romance, that lifelong friendship and partnership culminated in our recent engagement.

Jennifer Marquette was my first love, and I guess you never quite get over that first infatuation. She and I had not seen each other for many, many years when she reappeared in my life, only to cheat me in a stock swindle, and disappear. She'd later reappeared in a way best described as part of a criminal enterprise that Zellie and I unraveled during our very first case. We'd thought she was in jail, but here she was again, like a recurring nightmare.

Zellie stated the obvious. "She's trouble. You know that."

"She saved our lives once," I pointed out, referring to our first case.

"I guess that's true, sort of. I mean, she might have had another reason for doing it, and she's the one who put us into danger."

"She wasn't the only one," I said.

"I suppose so, but Arnie, why are you defending her? She's caused you nothing but misery."

"I don't know. There's a kind of desperation in this note, don't you think?"

"That's her customary opening act."

"Yeah, it is. Okay, I won't call. But I doubt she'll give up," I said.

Zellie grimaced. "No, not a chance."

That determined, we went into the living room and sat down. We had lots to think about, and exciting things to plan. We discussed finding office space. As our last attempt at securing a new place of business had gone up in flames, both literally and figuratively, we needed a new idea.

"We can call Melissa, I suppose." Zellie said in a voice which suggested she'd rather clean the bathrooms. I knew the reason for her reluctance. Melissa was a local real estate broker, among other vocations, who'd helped us in our previous search for office space. And we loved her, we really did. But her efforts had disastrous results, although neither of us blamed her. But still.

"I have a better idea," I said, after a silent consideration and rejection of the Melissa idea. "Let's take Rupe up on his offer to find us space in one of his buildings."

"It might be expensive," Zellie warned. "He owns lots of premium space. We're more lowbrow."

"That's a little harsh, isn't it? We've solved two cases."

"Neither one of which involved real, paying clients," Zellie pointed out.

"The first one sort of did, and we still have most of the reward money from that one."

"We do, don't we?"

"Yup, and it's just dying for us to spend it. Anyway, it won't hurt to ask."

"I guess not," Zellie said. "Call him."

He answered on the first ring.

"Arnie, you simpering simpleton. To what do I owe this annoying interruption of my delightful ride in my Rolls Royce in the south of France?"

"Rupe, you grandiloquent gasbag. You're not in the south of France, you're in Middletown, New Jersey, and you don't own a Rolls Royce. You own an old Chevy just like...." I trailed off, then continued. "I used to own."

"Impressively alliterative rejoinder, my good man." Rupe dropped the pretense of an affectation. "Arnie, I'm sorry about Matilda. She was a fine car. And maybe after some time has passed, you'll look for a new one."

Rupe referred to my vintage 1966 Chevy Impala, dubbed Matilda, destroyed during our last case. Rupe had a similar vehicle, albeit in an inferior model year of 1965.

"Thanks, but I'm not ready to go that route yet."

"If you do, I'd suggest you avoid the 1966. The 1965 is far superior."

"Your expression of sympathy is boundless, you know that?"

Rupe just laughed. "What's up?"

"As our potential office went kaput, Zellie and I thought we'd take you up on your suggestion that we occupy space in one of your buildings. We'd prefer a slum property. We have little money allocated for the purpose, having no clients and all."

Rupe chuckled. "Cheap office space, I get it. I don't suppose you'd consider a subsidy, or investment in your business? No, I didn't think so. As it happens I have something that might fit your budget, although you haven't told me what that is."

I gave him a figure, and he whistled. I'm pretty sure it wasn't about the sheer size of the potential rental I'd proposed.

"I think that will work," he said. "The space is right here in Middletown, and is just fine for your purposes. If you call Jared at the rental office tomorrow morning, I'll have it set up." He gave me a number, I thanked him, and we exchanged a few more pleasantries before I disconnected.

I turned to Zellie. "It looks like we're all set. We can look at the space tomorrow."

"Great," she replied. "No dead bodies, and no criminal landlords."

"I think I can guarantee the second one. But not the first. We'll check that out for ourselves."

"Did he describe the space?"

"Nope. Just that the price is right. I think we can trust him it'll work for us."

"What now? We don't have a new case, and we can't view our new office until tomorrow morning, and I know we don't want to have the inevitable long drawn out discussion about wedding plans, if we will have a big or small one, justice of the peace, elope to Las Vegas, et cetera."

"I think we can postpone that, at least for today," I said in haste. "Let's take a day off. Just the two of us. No visit to Audacious Bagel, and no electronics of any kind," I added, switching my cell phone off, and putting it in the little drawer in the coffee table.

"I'm in," Zellie said, pulling out her phone and sliding it in the drawer next to mine. "What should we do?"

"I'd suggest a visit to Holmdel Park, but that would involve driving, and a car is pretty much full of electronics."

Zellie nodded, then reminded me of a park walking distance from our homes.

"We should go to Fossil Creek, you know, in Poricy Park."

"Good idea. We haven't visited it since we were kids."

"I still remember the fossils. Old shells and rocks and things. Our teachers told us the fossils were thousands of years old."

"That's what they said. They might have made it up."

"Who cares? It'll be fun just to visit it again. And we can use the exercise. We drive everywhere now."

"Why not?" I said. "Let's get going." I took Zellie by the hand, and we went out the door.

I stopped short. "Oops, I need to go back in for a second."

I returned moments later, and we were off on our big adventure.

CHAPTER TWO

Holding hands, we walked out of the neighborhood, a short distance up the street, and past our old elementary school to the entrance to Poricy Park. As we had not visited the place in about forty years, we took a few moments to get our bearings.

"A little different from back in the day," I observed.

"They made it a lot more formal."

"If you mean they put a sign up, I guess I'd agree, but it otherwise seems unchanged."

We walked into the park, if you want to call it that. It comprised a wooded area with a narrow creek running along one edge. Fossil Creek, we'd called it back then, and the name remained the same, I noticed on a small sign. We walked over to an embankment and peered down at the creek. Almost at once, I lost my footing in the soft soil, and slid unceremoniously down the hill, landing in the shallow water butt first with a splash. Zellie slipped and landed next to me.

Covered with mud, we looked at each other and burst into uproarious laughter.

"What now?" I asked when we calmed down. "Are you up for a little mud covered exploring?"

"No question," she replied, setting her jaw. "It's just a little mud."

I reached out and embraced her. "Now it's a lot of mud," I said, causing her to break out laughing again.

"Let's walk along the creek," I suggested. "Maybe we'll find some fossils."

She grasped my proffered hand, and we strolled as best we could along the side of the creek, taking care to avoid protruding rocks. Once in a while, Zellie stooped down to pick up one of the many fossils scattered in the shallow water. They resembled old rocks more than the petrified trilobites I'd seen in museums. But you knew they were very, very old.

"This is nice," I said after a while. "Quiet, peaceful and alone with my sweetheart."

"Mmm," Zellie said, leaning in close to me, and snuggling into my shoulder as we continued to stroll along the stream.

I leaned down and kissed the top of her head, and we stopped.

"Maybe we should find a flat, grassy area," I ventured, as Zellie looked up at me with those beautiful eyes.

"A private one," Zellie agreed, looking down at her clothes. "With a little pond."

"We could wash this mud off."

"And go for a swim," she said.

"Among other things," I added.

"Among other things," she agreed.

We left the creek and headed up the same hill we'd slid down a short time ago. Highly motivated to find the specified idyllic spot, I led the way to an area in the park I thought I remembered from long ago. Intent on my task, I neglected to look down at the thorny brambles and protruding tree roots as I walked, and tripped over a low-hanging branch and fell into a nearby prickly bush.

"Ow, ow, ow." I muttered as I extracted my scratched limbs from the bush.

Zellie was solicitous, almost Clara Barton-like in the loving care and attention she gave in administering quality first-aid. She demonstrated this by doubling over with laughter at my predicament. Looking at my scratches, she started up again, with the gasped observation that if I'd tripped after skinny dipping, my arms might not be the only appendages with scratches.

I couldn't help it, I forgot about my minor injuries, and laughed along with her. "Our grassy bed would be poison ivy, too."

That led to another round of us cracking up, and we looked at each other. I spoke first. "Let's get out of here."

"Fossil creek day is officially canceled."

Taking Zellie's hand, I turned around to head back through the brush toward the park entrance, and promptly tripped over a big log beyond where I'd fallen into the bushes. We tumbled down together into a large pile of leaves. I had little chance to consider my recent bout of clumsiness, when Zellie whispered in my ear.

"We're not alone in here."

I understood. An unknown critter shared the pile of leaves with us.

With a finger to my lips and my other hand pointing away from the lump in the leaves, we slid away, and out of the pile. Standing up, we looked back at where we'd fallen, and saw nothing moving.

"Let's go," I whispered, but Zellie shook her head.

"There's an elementary school right near here," she whispered. "What if that thing is rabid? We should call Animal Control."

"If it's rabid, we should at least move away from it," I said.

"Good point."

We moved back a distance and kept staring at the leaf pile.

"It's still not moving," I said after a respectful silence. "Should I poke it with a stick or something? We just assumed it was a critter, but before we set off alarm bells and panic a lot of schoolchildren, maybe we should check it out."

Wrinkles appearing on her forehead, Zellie replied, "I don't know. I know I started this and all, but maybe you were right to begin with. Maybe leaving is the best option."

"Look, maybe we can prevent something bad from happening, without too much risk. You stand farther back, and I'll take a very long stick, and just tap it a little, not enough to make it angry, but enough to get its attention so we can verify that leaving is okay." I pointed to a long thin branch on the ground behind us. "There, just the thing," I added, picking it up.

"Arnie, wait. This is a terrible idea. Let sleeping dogs lie, and all."

"It's okay, I'll be careful. Stand back." Extending the tip of the long branch toward the leaf pile, I tapped on the lump. Nothing. I tapped just a little harder. Still nothing. "Maybe it's dead," I said.

Zellie's response was sensible. "We should leave."

"One more thing I can try."

"No, please stop. We tried, it's enough."

Too late. I used the top of the branch to clear off some leaves covering the lump, revealing a human foot.

CHAPTER THREE

"Oh crap. Not again. Why can't we get clients the normal way?"

"We're not licensed, we can only get the non-paying kind, remember? And anyway, it's not a client."

We stared at the foot silently for a while. Finally, I spoke again.

"Maybe he's just sleeping." I said it like a kid telling his dad, "maybe they'll have ice cream."

Zellie looked at me. "I don't think he'd be sleeping under a huge pile of debris. And we don't even know if it's a man."

We looked down again. "We need to clear this off him. Or her," I added.

"We need to call the police." Zellie responded. "We shouldn't touch anything." She reached for the mini purse hung around her neck. "Oops. No phone. No tech day. We need to find someone with a phone."

"Or someone who thought having one for an emergency might be a good idea," I said, hanging my head.

"You didn't."

"Well, yes, I did. But in my defense, I turned it off. See?" I showed her a blank screen.

"Oh, I suppose it's a good thing you did. But you're lucky we found a dead body, so that there was a real need for it." She paused and giggled. "Did I just say we were lucky to find a dead body?"

"Yup."

"Okay, I'm giving you a pass on your prevarication."

"Wait a minute. I didn't lie to you, I just wanted to be prepared. Like a Boy Scout."

"You're no Boy Scout."

She had me there.

"Just give me the phone, Mr. Boy Scout."

"Why you?"

"Um, because you have a history with the cops."

Right again. And not a good history. They hated me. At least the local cops did. I handed her the phone, which she switched on, and tapped out 911.

While we waited for the police, I turned to Zellie and gestured at the leaf pile.

"We agree that we're not looking into this one, right?"

"I didn't say that. We might conduct a few inquiries to satisfy our curiosity, but he or she is emphatically not a client."

"Okay, good. It's settled."

We waited in silence, but braced for my twin nemeses to arrive. We expected Officers Madison and Dunston, they of the crackerjack investigative squad employed by the Middletown Police Department. In fairness, they could be fine officers, but they had bad attitudes and hated me.

We were happy when two different people showed up. The officers behaved professionally, addressing us as Mr. Fischer and Ms. Morgan. A refreshing change from "Fischer and "who's the bimbo?" preferred by Officer Dunston. They introduced themselves as Detective Johnson and Officer Yang, and took charge, carefully brushing the leaves away to disclose a very dead man, about six feet tall, or long in his present state, and weighing about 200 pounds. He had full, bushy dark brown hair, a thin mustache, and a bullet hole right through his forehead.

Upon inquiry, I explained how we discovered the body. As we had nothing further to add, the officers took our contact information and gave us a polite, but firm dismissal.

***

We returned home. After a much-needed washing up, we sat down in the living room to reconnoiter.

"We didn't count on regularly finding bodies when we started this business, did we?"

"No, we didn't. We intended a nice, safe detective agency. Lost puppies, a misplaced hula hoop, stuff like that."

"Hula hoop? Even if we had the ability to time travel to the 1970s to find a hula hoop, how do you lose one of those things, anyway?"

"I lost mine on a vacation to the Cape."

"Okay, we'll take a trip to the Cape and see if we can find it. I bet it's still there, right next to your lost roller skates."

"You can wear your bell-bottom pants on the trip," Zellie giggled.

"No cell phones or internet."

"We'll play my Beatles album on the eight-track."

We continued like that for a while, then Zellie turned serious. "You know, we may have strayed a little from the original business plan, but..."

"We had no business plan."

"No, I don't mean that. We had no plan or preparation of any kind. But we had the 'find stuff' thing."

"Sure, what about it?"

"Why not go back to it? I don't know about you, but I think our first two cases might have put us in a teensy-weensy bit too much danger."

I thought about that for all of one second.

"Yeah, just a little," I said with an involuntary shudder at our multiple close calls. "What do you have in mind?"

"A return to our roots. Go back, I mean start limiting our cases to finding stuff."

"Might be a little boring, after our previous adventures," I said.

"I can accept a little dull, if it means not regularly putting our lives in danger."

I thought about it for a moment. "It might solve our licensing problem, too. Who will care if we don't get involved in police matters?"

"And it might give us more time to plan a wedding," Zellie added, holding up her hand and looking at her engagement ring.

I looked up. "We haven't discussed that much."

"I know. But we need to."

"Do you want a big wedding?"

"I don't know what I want. What about you? I had a wedding. To a jerk, but it was a wedding."

"I know. I was there. Witness number two, remember?"

"I remember. I must have known even then that my fiancé didn't warrant a big wedding with a white gown and all."

"Do you want it this time?"

Zellie paused for a moment, then looked me squarely in the eyes.

"If ever there was a person to get all gussied up and wear a long, flowing white gown for, it's you."

"I feel the same way, sweetie. Not about the long, flowing gown thing, but the person. Should we go for it?"

"We might be a little old."

"I don't think you're ever too old."

"It would have to be small."

"Very," I agreed.

"Just a few close friends and family."

"Right. Just a couple of friends, and your parents."

"And yours. You can't exclude them."

"Oh, I don't want to do that. They're good people. Just a little... reserved, that's all. Not great party types."

"We'll talk about it some more."

"Good."

I glanced at my watch. "Let's get something to eat. I'm starving."

"Me too. What a day!"

We threw together a makeshift dinner, then watched a movie on TV, during which we both fell asleep, then woke up and went to bed.

CHAPTER FOUR

My phone rang the next morning while we were drinking coffee in the kitchen. I answered and listened for a few moments.

"Okay, we'll be there. Thanks."

I looked at Zellie. "Rupe. We're to meet his butler at this location." I handed the piece of paper on which I'd scrawled an address.

"His butler?"

"Oh, you know Rupe. I'm guessing an intern, or someone in his office."

She took the paper and looked at it. "It's right on Route 35. Do you know where this is?"

"Not a clue."

"We're supposed to meet him at nine o'clock. We'd better get a move on."

I gave an exaggerated eyebrow wiggle and wink, Groucho Marx style. "Maybe we should shower together to save time."

If I expected Zellie to blush, or to get a rise out of her, I'd be disappointed. She was too fast on the uptake.

She reached over and patted my thigh. "We're in a rush, honey. No time for that this morning. You'll just have to soap your own jewels today."

Yup. Typical Zellie. I chuckled and held up my hand. "Okay, okay, all business. Separate showers."

We efficiently bathed and dressed and headed out to meet Rupe's "butler."

I drove Zellie's car, as I'd not yet bought a new one. She held her phone, which was squawking directions, and sending us to a small strip mall right off Route 35. I parked, and we looked at the seven stores lined up in a simple row, all with parking spaces in front. We didn't know what Rupe had in mind with this, unless he was renting us one of the storefronts. But we had no idea which, as they all seemed occupied. And we didn't even have a description of Rupe's assistant. Our questions were soon answered when a familiar face popped out of one store, which bore a big sign reading "Cinnamon Buns."

Rupe. In person. He waved us over, and we exchanged greetings.

I looked up at the sign. "I don't want to ask. The sign looks like something Delilah would wear to trick me into making some sort of suggestive remark."

Delilah was our favorite waitress at Audacious Bagel, or AB as it was known. She studied business at night, and wore double-entendre shirts as marketing gimmicks.

Rupe looked up at the sign and laughed. "No, it really was a bakery. Specialized in cinnamon buns. But it could be your new office. Come on in." He put his hand on my back and ushered me inside, with Zellie following.

A faint cinnamon scent greeted us when we entered.

"Pleasing aroma, am I right?"

Zellie and I glanced at each other, then collectively at Rupe.

"For a bakery, yes," I said, for both of us.

"Show a little imagination, you two. I didn't reach the pinnacle of real estate tycoondom without imagination."

"No, you inherited a bajillion dollars from your grandmother. And tycoondom is not a word."

"Correct on both counts, my good man. But seriously, I can have my renovation team in here to make the space look more like Sam Spade than Betty Crocker in no time. One of my companies owns the whole shopping center, and a vacancy is not good for business. Having you two in here would be doing me a favor. Just keep it maintained, and pay the utilities you use, and I'll waive any rent."

We both knew that this was a load of baloney. He could, and should rent it to another bakery, or boutique, or something other than a detective agency for no rent, and I told him so.

Rupe looked at me.

"I want to help my friends. As you so indelicately put it, I have a bajillion dollars. How much more do I need? And I would add something, good sir. You understated my inheritance by referring to the almost paltry sum of a BAjillion, when in fact, it was a GAjillion. Please take note."

"Oh, I will, Rupe. I won't make that mistake again. And anyway, I thought we were meeting your butler here today."

"Are you kidding? I don't have a butler. A valet, assorted footmen, maybe, but not a butler."

"You don't have any of that stuff."

"True. Hey Zellie, look at this." He gave me a wink, as he pointed Zellie toward a long string in the back of the store. "It's an attic. I know how you both love attics." Rupe referred to our last case, where an attic played a pivotal role.

He pulled on the string, and Zellie and I cringed. A pull-down ladder emerged.

"See, no bodies. I hope you aren't disappointed. I know how you like corpses."

Zellie assured him it wasn't a problem. Then I told him about our discovery of the body yesterday.

"Again? What's the matter with you two? Are you going to take him on as a client, too?"

"Yes, again. Nothing is wrong with us, just bad luck. And emphatically, no."

"That's a relief. I'm all in favor of your detective business, but Sarah and I think you get involved in risky, dangerous cases. And as the raging capitalist that I am, ones that don't pay you anything."

"Don't worry," Zellie said. "We're working on a plan to make this business a low-risk moneymaker. And it begins right here. Thank you. This place is perfect as our new office."

Rupe looked pleased. "Great, let me know what renovations you want, and I'll have my team get it done in the next couple of days. We'll go right ahead and remove the large baking ovens. Once we do that, we'll turn the rest of the space into something more like an office."

"Sounds good. We'll leave it in your hands."

"Yes," Zellie agreed. "But if it's okay, could we leave a small kitchen and that little oven?"

"Sure, we can do that. I'll have them wall it off, so your clients don't see it."

"Great."

With that, I shook Rupe's hand, and Zellie gave him a hug, and we went our separate ways.

Before we drove away, I told Zellie "Good idea keeping the kitchen. We get hungry a lot, and we can save money preparing our own food."

"That's the idea. Also, I can bake cookies."

"Ooh. I love cookies. And one thing I insist on."

"What?"

"We leave that Cinnamon Buns sign up there." I pointed to it.

"Okay, sure. But why?"

"I just like it. And it might bring in business. Everyone loves cinnamon buns."

"So much so that the previous occupants went out of business," Zellie said dryly.

"We don't know that. Maybe they just moved to a bigger location."

"I suppose. Okay, the sign stays. But I'm getting fancy lettering stenciled on the door."

"Done."

We drove home, and predictably, all we could talk about was the new office.

"Nice of Rupe," I said.

"He's a gem, for sure," Zellie agreed. "Maybe we should get him a present."

"Like what? Gold cufflinks? I bet he has fourteen pairs he never uses."

"As opposed to you, who has one set you never use."

"Rich people get to not use stuff more than we get to not use stuff."

"It's all stuff, anyway. I have a different idea. How about free lifetime investigations?"

"Free illegal investigations. Just what he needs."

"There's that licensing thing again. We should do something about it."

"Isn't our current idea that the police would ignore that problem if we stopped finding bodies and putting ourselves in mortal danger while interfering in their investigations?" I mused out loud.

"And showing them up in the process."

"And that."

"All we can do at this point is open up in our new office, with no private investigations wording anywhere. Maybe they won't notice."

"Okay, it's decided. Free lifetime 'finding stuff' for Rupe."

I called Rupe and told him the good news. We spoke for a few minutes and I disconnected.

"He's very pleased about our gift," I told Zellie. "After joking about us finding his baseball that I lost down the storm drain."

Zellie smiled. "He still hasn't forgiven you for missing his throw that day. Did he have anything else?"

"After our nostalgia trip, he told me he might have something for us in the near future, but on a strictly paying basis."

"You told him we wouldn't charge him, right?"

"Yes, but you know Rupe. Some nonsense about needing a business deduction resulting in a win-win situation. We get income, he gets a deduction."

"He's making that up, you know."

"Of course. We just won't bill him. Anyway, he asked whether we wanted to go back to 'Operation Cinnamon Bun' to supervise his crew in remodeling our office."

"He moves fast."

"He does. You up for it?"

"You betcha. Let me fix my hair and put on some fresh lipstick and we can go right away."

When we arrived back at our new office, Rupe's crew was already at work. We spoke to the foreman for a moment, but he didn't need much direction. As usual, Rupe had handled everything. We retreated to a bench in front of the place to watch. As we did so, a knockout gorgeous woman wearing a form-fitting red dress and a voluptuous figure approached us. She flashed big blue eyes and flicked her long strawberry blonde hair at us before she spoke.

"Are you the new owners of 'Cinnamon Buns?' she asked in a voice tinged with a foreign accent, the origin of which I couldn't place.

I kept my composure. Um, no, I didn't. My jaw was agog, but I remained speechless.

Zellie glanced at my catatonic state with a glimmer of annoyance, but she responded politely to the woman.

"We're moving in, but not as a bakery," she said.

If the woman noticed my ogling, she said nothing. She just responded to Zellie in a normal voice.

"Oh, what a shame. Not about you," she added in haste, "I just mean I love great buns. And those were wonderful."

I found my voice and managed a weak, "Do you work around here?" I asked it with a glance at Zellie, and a fervent desire to not have it sound hopeful. This would not go well for me at home if this lady worked nearby.

"Oh yes," the woman said. "That's my shop right there. Looks like we're neighbors."

I might have imagined it, but I thought I heard Zellie say "oh crap" under her breath. I couldn't be sure, and the woman didn't seem to notice. Zellie's too confident to worry about a pretty face.

She was at her personable best, chattering away with our new neighbor, Sasha, about the other tenants of our little shopping center, and getting the lowdown on the various personalities.

I injected a periodic pleasantry into the conversation at what I thought were opportune times, and eventually Sasha stood up and said she needed to get back to the boutique.

"Stop in any time for a cup of coffee," she called to us over her shoulder, and went back into her shop.

"Nice lady," I remarked as she disappeared from view.

"Very nice. And I'm sure you didn't notice her incredible figure and movie star good looks," Zellie replied.

"Oh, is she good looking?" I asked with a smile and a pantomime of innocence. As unobservant as a brick, that's me.

Zellie punched my arm. And not lightly either.

"Ow. What was that for?" But I knew.

"Oh, for being a... guy, that's what."

I started laughing, and Zellie joined in. Can't keep her down for long. Not that she was morose about it, anyway. Sasha seemed like a nice person, which was much better than having a jerk next door.

"So, what now?" I asked. "Should we take Sasha up on a cup of coffee?" I added with an exaggerated wince at an imaginary second blow on my arm.

"I don't think so," Zellie responded with an eye roll and an indulgent smile. "Why don't we check with the renovation team to make sure they're on board with our design preferences, then get some lunch. That cinnamon bun smell made me hungry."

"Me too."

So we checked with the foreman, and it appeared that everything was proceeding smoothly and according to plan, so we headed out to Finnegan's Pub for sandwiches. Upon arrival, I waved at my old friend Sam, who stood imperiously behind the bar, presiding over his empire, as the hostess seated us nearby.

I know it seems like Zellie and I know everyone in town, but it's not true. We frequent places where we know people, and Finnegan's was no exception. I met Samuel Coleridge Finkelman many years ago, when we both waited on line to take the SAT's in high school. We weren't close now or then, but we remain friendly acquaintances. Sam was a savvy businessman, having morphed the original Sam's Falafel Shop, with its wonderful food and wildly unsuccessful business plan into Finnegan's Pub, which appeared to spew money like a geyser.

Sam stopped by our table while we waited for our sandwiches, and plunked down two tap beers, poured to perfection.

"How are my favorite detectives?"

"Good," I answered. "We're opening up an office on Route 35. Of course, we have no current case, and no license."

Sam waved his hand dismissively. "Minor issues. If I let the little stuff get in my way, I'd still be the proprietor of Sam's Free-Range Chicken House."

"I don't remember that one," I admitted.

"See? That's what I'm saying. Anyway, gotta get back to the bar. A plethora of potentially drunken patrons just arrived. Keep at it, guys."

We snarfed down our sandwiches and beers while we strategized. Okay, we chit-chatted about nothing in particular.

"This is fun, but we need a business plan." Zellie had drained the last vestiges of her Guinness and turned all serious on me.

"Do we? That sounds so... formal, so corporate."

"Oh, I know. We never intended something like that, and I don't mean we have to turn our business into IBM. But how are we going to get clients? We can't just wait for them to fall in our laps."

"That's worked pretty well so far," I said with a smile. "Although the last one almost fell on our heads, not in our laps."

"It did, didn't it?" Zellie cracked a smile. "But it wasn't a paying client."

"No, we couldn't get payment, he being dead and all."

"Right. We need the living kind, with the big, fat wallets."

When we returned home, we sat at Zellie's kitchen table and talked about ways to drum up business.

"We have an office now, with very tenant friendly rent, and very few expenses."

"Zero rent is the definition of tenant friendly," I agreed. "Rupe's a peach."

"He is for sure. He also said he might have some business for us, but we shouldn't wait for that. Should we advertise?"

"I don't want to, and we still have that nagging problem of no license."

"Right. But we've already recast our business in a way that might not require a license."

"We sure did. A lot safer, and I don't think the State of New Jersey would mind."

"Should we change the name of our agency?" I asked.

"Maybe we should. The A to Z Agency name isn't a legal thing. We never formalized it. We can change it at will."

"Okay, how about A to Z Tracking? We can advertise that we track stuff down from A to Z."

"A to Z Tracking it is. I told Rupe's foreman that we'd let them know what lettering to stencil onto the front door, so why don't you call him?" She handed me a piece of paper. "Here's his number."

I called, and received assurances that he'd take care of it at the very end of the renovation, which he expected would occur by the end of the day tomorrow.

"Rupe's people work fast," Zellie observed. "I'm very excited."

"Me too," I assured her.

"Arnie. I'm very excited."
"Oh!"

CHAPTER FIVE

As we sat at the kitchen table drinking coffee the next morning, my phone emitted its familiar sound. I looked at the caller ID, and it said "Unknown Caller," so I ignored it and put the phone back in my pocket and kept chatting with Zellie. We both had errands to run, but I still had no car, and automobile shopping was the last thing I wanted to do that day. We agreed that Zellie would drop me off at the car rental place and do her errands, and I would see about getting a short-term rental. We'd meet up later, with plenty of time to check out our new office together.

While I waited at the rental place, I checked my messages and saw one missed call and one voicemail. I listened to the message. Jennifer. Calm and businesslike. A new persona for her, I thought. In the past, she'd been demonstrative, like a stage actress projecting her words. A very passionate woman, no question. But evil to the core. I checked myself on that. I didn't think she was evil. Just misguided, another person faced with a myriad of choices both good and evil, and choosing the wrong path. Or maybe guided into the wrong path. Anyway, someone to avoid.

So naturally, I stepped outside and called her back. I have no idea why. Men do stupid things, or so I'm told. All the time. Jennifer answered right away, in the same businesslike tone.

"Thanks for returning my call," she said, in a normal voice suggestive of the conduct of routine matters.

"I'll admit a level of curiosity. Why aren't you in jail?"

"I will explain that, and a lot more, when we meet."

"We're not meeting. You know that."

"I knew you'd say that. But I have some important things to share with you and Zellie, and I'm hoping that you change your mind. And I will offer you conclusive proof of my good intentions when we meet."

"Why not now?"

"You will understand when I see you, I promise."

"Your promises have had little value."

"That's true. I can't help that now. But you and Zellie could benefit from a meeting, and you have nothing to lose."

I gave a derisive laugh. "Are you serious?"

"It's just a meeting, Arnie. In a public place, but for reasons I will tell you, the conversation must be private. No chance of anyone overhearing. So outside somewhere. You pick the place and let me know. But please, get back to me today. If I don't hear from you, I'll assume you don't want to meet, and I'll leave you alone. I promise."

And then she hung up. Whoa, that's new, I thought. I can just do nothing, not even tell Zellie, and she'll go away and leave us alone. Well okay, great. I'm done. I'm not getting involved with that con-woman ever again. That decided, I went back inside, signed a few papers, and headed out to run my errands driving a Chevy Malibu, the quintessential standard rental car, severed from the fleet of identical automobiles. Another sheep taken from an enormous herd. I pulled my ovine companion onto Route 35 and completed my list of errands in two hours. Then I called Zellie, and arranged to meet her for a late breakfast at AB.

When I arrived, Zellie already sat at our usual table, chatting with Delilah. I checked out her shirt and was disappointed to see her wearing a standard-issue AB T-shirt.

"No provocative shirt today?" I asked.

"Not today, but I wonder why you stare at my boobs before you even say hello."

"But, but... you started it," I managed, and Delilah cracked up, while Zellie nearly fell off her chair laughing. They got me again. I must have a big sign on my head saying "Gullible." We chatted for a few moments, then Delilah skittered off to fill our orders. I had resolved not to tell Zellie anything about calling Jennifer, and to let the whole thing go. So naturally the first words out of my mouth were "Jennifer left a message this morning, and I called her back."

Zellie gave a long, long sigh, and an intense gaze. I assumed she was gauging my sanity, or lack thereof. I started to add an explanation, but she held up a single finger. I was grateful it was not her middle one. I guessed she needed to process the bombshell I'd just dropped, so I sat in silence. A very uncomfortable silence. Zellie and I can sit together in companionable quietude. This was not that. I couldn't tell whether she was angry or sad, maybe a little of both.

"What possessed you to call her?"

"Her message was different this time. It sounded calm, not stage managed, sad almost." I pulled out my phone. "Here, listen for yourself."

Zellie waved it away. "I believe you. But she always acts that way. Sweet and nice to begin with, but wily as a fox. What does she want this time? To get back together with you, because of her undying love? Information? A stock investment?"

That last one hit me where it hurt. I held up my hand. "Okay, I get it. She's a snake. But don't you wonder, as a detective with an inquisitive mind, why the heck she's not in jail?"

Zellie pursed her lips and fidgeted in her seat. She sighed again.

"I do," she said. "But that's just curiosity. How will a meeting with Jennifer benefit us?"

It was a good question. And one I had no answer to.

"I don't know," I admitted. "But is there any harm in hearing her out?"

"Jennifer's a con artist. Need I say more?"

She didn't. Involvement with Jennifer always ended in misery of one sort or another.

I held up my hands in mock surrender.

"Okay, okay, I get it. She's trouble."

We chatted about other things, then headed back to Zellie's house.

***

I remained unconvinced that we should let it go. We'd come out on top in our last involvement with Jennifer, and a big part of me knew that it would be a profound mistake to contact her again. But Jennifer was a narcotic, and I knew I couldn't resist hearing what she had to say. I resolved to call her again. Zellie didn't approve, so I needed to wait we were apart. As if I'd willed it, the opportunity soon presented itself.

"I need to run a few more errands," Zellie announced.

I looked up, and acted nonchalant. "I didn't finish mine, either."

"Okay, see you a little later." Zellie gave me a quick kiss and was off.

I made my call and Jennifer agreed to meet in an hour. I headed out to our designated meeting place.

I spotted Zellie right away. Dwight Road is not a superhighway, and Zellie had owned that green Honda for almost ten years. I pulled over on the shoulder and walked back to her car, eyebrows raised.

"What's up? You left before me." Okay, I knew why Zellie followed me. The jig was up.

"I knew that look you gave this morning, and you couldn't be more clumsy in your effort to conceal your intentions. You're meeting Jennifer. You didn't invite me, so I tagged along."

"Invite you? I was..."

"Sneaking around, trying to arrange a clandestine meeting."

"Um, yeah."

"Mind if I come along?"

"I'd like nothing better. Let's return one of these cars back home and go together."

So, the full membership of A to Z Tracking went to meet Jennifer. I kidded Zellie about her tailing expertise, or lack thereof, and she retorted that I was awful at being a sneak.

"I'm sorry I tried to shut you down on this. I know it's important to you," Zellie said.

"I shouldn't have tried to do it in secret."

"I hate to tell you this, but you didn't. Honestly, you have the worst poker face. I could tell right away that you were hell-bent on seeing what was up with Jennifer."

"Don't you want to know, too?"

"I do. Hence the elaborate scheme to follow the suspect to the meeting place."

Well, let's hear what she has to say," I said. "And don't worry, my default position on anything she suggests is a resounding no way, no chance, no, no, no."

***

We met Jennifer in Holmdel Park. She sat alone on one of the many benches scattered around the park. Other than a pair of teenagers tossing a Frisbee several yards away, we were the only people within view. Jennifer stood up as we approached. She greeted us quietly, without a scintilla of her trademark over-zealous and fake enthusiasm. This was a different Jennifer, but I was acutely aware of her acting ability. She was a chameleon, and I intended to exercise extreme caution. I didn't worry about Zellie being taken in by the new Jennifer. Zellie's body language resembled a tiger, poised to pounce.

Jennifer didn't waste time on any preamble, nor did she ask us to sit down. Obviously, she intended to have a quiet conversation with the three of us standing in a huddle. That was okay with me. I didn't intend to stay long. My plan was to hear her out for a limited period, reject anything she proposed, and leave with my curiosity satisfied.

"This won't take long," Jennifer said. "Either you're in or you're out. If you say no, I promise to leave both of you alone forever. No unannounced visits, no calls, nothing. I think my proposal will interest you, and I'd prefer your participation. I think it will work better with you in. If not, I'll find a different way. But before I tell you what this is all about, I want you to call this number. It's a personal reference. Given our history, I figured you'd insist on one. A down-payment on my credibility."

I looked at Zellie, who shrugged, so I made the call. To my utter shock, the operator answering my call identified the organization I'd called as the Federal Bureau of Investigation. I gave the operator the extension Jennifer had given me, and a familiar voice answered.

"Special Agent Marilyn Magnuson. How are you, Arnie?"

"Um, very surprised."

"I bet you are. Quickly, what Ms. Marquette will propose is legit. But don't forget for a second who she is, and the ultimate nature of her character. She's a viper. She may listen for a time to the music we're playing, and her fangs may be something less than they once were, but don't trust her. You understand?"

I assured her I operated under no illusions, heard her out on a general outline of what Jennifer would propose, and rang off. I pulled Zellie aside and a few paces away, and explained what I was told, including Marilyn's non-specific pronouncement that she might even help us get our license. Jennifer waited while we had our private conversation, a picture of serenity.

"It looks like they flipped her," I whispered to Zellie, referring to prosecutors cutting a deal with a criminal defendant for information about bigger fish, in her case, some very dangerous members of the New Jersey mob. She'd received her freedom, with supervision, and was essentially a confidential informant for the FBI. Unlike Marilyn, who had her cover blown while taking down the mob in our first case, Jennifer's remained intact, although she still had some very dangerous enemies in the criminal underworld.

As I explained it to Zellie, Marilyn had told me that besides her information, Jennifer had valuable skills that the FBI could use.

"Oh, that's just great. Ripping people off is now a skill set. That's just perfect. We're turning this down, aren't we?"

"Don't worry, that's what I think as well, but we should hear the specifics, shouldn't we? I mean, what if we can help the FBI stop a group of innocent people from getting scammed?"

"By working with the quintessential con-woman?"

"Who better to know their tricks."

"You said Marilyn told you not to trust her."

"And we won't. But no harm in hearing her plan."

***

"First, some background," Jennifer said. "The FBI has identified a group they believe plans to prey upon retirees. They've targeted an investment advisor who manages retirement funds. The scam is sophisticated," she added, looking straight at me. "Hence the benefit you could bring to this, Arnie. You know the securities business inside and out."

"Maybe not so well," I muttered. "Not well enough to avoid getting scammed by you."

Jennifer ignored my remark and continued. "With your investment knowledge and Zellie's people skills, and your unusual and well-honed investigative techniques, you both could help with what I have in mind."

"What is it, already?" Zellie snapped. "Out with it. We're hearing you out, but you haven't told us anything. And you promised it would be short. And anyway, why are we hearing this from you, not the FBI?"

"Okay, okay. Fair enough. I'm beating around the bush. This is new to me, too. To answer your last question, the FBI is letting me design the operation because I'm good at it. And you can call them anytime. I'll keep them fully informed. It's a condition of my release. And I want to stay out of jail."

"What's the plan, Jennifer?" I said it quietly. "Enough of the preamble. Let's hear it, so we can reject it and get on with our lives."

"I don't think you'll reject it after you hear it, but here goes. We'll blow up their plan from the inside and out."

She gave a general description of how she'd set up the operation. And to our joint surprise, Zellie and I agreed to take part. Saving people's life savings? How could we say no? But we had a few more questions.

"What is our role in this?" I asked.

"Just do what you always do. Investigate these people. Ask questions. Try to find out the truth. You're good at that. Don't act. Leave that to me. Treat it like it's a real case, because that's what it is. There are people trying to cheat ordinary folks. Take the few clues I've given you and run with them. I'm guessing we'll end up in the same place, but if you identify different con artists than the FBI has identified, that's fine. We're just interested in protecting people."

My throat constricted, and I hissed "You've never said or done anything remotely resembling protecting people. It's hard to believe even the FBI could convince you to follow an honest and decent path. Which side are you really on?"

Jennifer just looked at me. "I don't know. I've depended on a specific set of abilities for so long, I doubt I can do anything else. But to be clear, this time I intend to use those abilities to do some good."

"Why should we trust you?" Zellie demanded.

Jennifer looked Zellie straight in the eyes. "Oh, you shouldn't. Assume I'd screw you in a second. And the next time you see me, treat me like an enemy. Don't trust a single thing I say or do."

"Including now?"

"Look, do your own research. If you think the case is worthy, go for it. If not, don't take it on." That said, she walked away.

We stared at her departing figure.

"Whoa." It was all I could manage.

"She's a force to reckon with. Are we really doing this?"

"Let's do what she said. Do our own research and decide on whether to take on the case. Isn't that what private investigators do?"

"Maybe the first question should be how we get paid," Zellie said. "Is this yet another unpaid investigation?"

"We're still not licensed. We can't take payment, anyway. We're trackers, not investigators."

"What are we tracking?"

"Evildoers."

"Of course."

CHAPTER SIX

We headed back to our new office to see how the work was progressing.

"Look over there," I said when we arrived. I pointed at the door where a workman was stenciling something on the window.

We strolled over, and watched as he put the finishing touches on gold lettering that read, in beautiful calligraphy, "A to Z Trucking."

Beaming with pride in his workmanship, he asked us what we thought. I complimented his skill, but gently pointed out we'd asked for it to read "A to Z Tracking."

"What? No, it says right here... just what you said." He put his head in his hands. This is embossed. We'll need a new window. He pulled out phone to make a call, and Zellie put her hand on his arm. Wait on that, Paul."

I watched Zellie and knew what she intended. We both hoped that the whole "tracking" stuff would give way to a window with "Private Investigators" on it. We left the Cinnamon Bun sign alone. So why not leave the trucking reference as our own private joke?

"No need to change it," I said.

"Oh, no. Mr. Farnsworth will be furious. He's very particular."

"I'll talk to him," I promised.

"Well, okay, I guess. It will take a little while to get a replacement window, anyway. But if he tells me to fix it...."

"You'll do as he says."

"Good. Thanks."

Zellie smiled as he walked away. "I like it. We're in the cinnamon bun trucking business now."

"We now have two separate subterfuges for our real private investigation business. So much for our honesty first policy."

"We're not changing that one bit. We didn't plan on either of them. They just happened. Serendipity."

"We might as well look inside," Zellie said. "Let's see how the renovation is going."

We walked in and looked around. They had almost completed the work, other than painting.

"I'm glad you're here," Lou, the foreman said to us, a hand extended. We shook. "What do you think?"

"It looks fantastic," I replied, as Zellie echoed her pleasure.

"What color are you going to paint the walls?" Zellie asked.

"That's up to you."

Zellie gave a quick response.

"Pale yellow."

"What she said," I agreed with a smile.

"Pale yellow it is." He produced a book with what seemed like hundreds of little paint chips in it, turned to the shades of yellow section, and handed it to Zellie.

"As soon as you let me know which one you want, we'll begin. Oh, I almost forgot." He produced another, smaller book for our perusal. "Carpet colors. The boss already selected the type and grade. Don't worry, you're getting a very high quality."

As if we'd worry. We were getting the place rent free, and now Rupe was requiring the use of much better materials than a converted cinnamon bun shop warranted. We took the two books, promised to let him know right away, and stepped outside to sit on an adjacent bench to look them over.

"We should hold these up on the wall and look at them for a couple of days, just to be sure…"

My expression must have resembled something like acute dismay, because Zellie stopped short, and smoothly continued.

"But we don't have time for that. We can't keep Lou waiting, can we? Let me see… hmm… not this one, not that one, no, no, maybe, let's see what else… um… how about that one?"

"Looks good to me. It's pale yellow."

"You didn't look. They're all shades of pale yellow."

"I did so look, and I like it."

"Okay, good. Now the carpet."

That process went much the same as the first, but we settled on a carpet style and returned the books to Lou with our choices.

"Excellent selections," he said. "And very prompt. We can have all of this done by… say tomorrow afternoon."

"I was sure he would have said almost anything we chose was great, but all I said was "Wow. Thank you."

We bid him goodbye and headed over to AB for lunch.

We sat down at our usual table, and like a lightning bolt, Delilah appeared, wearing a T-shirt with two eyes on her chest and the inscription "You Can't Stop Looking."

"I'm not touching that one," I said.

"Of course not, Arnie. You can look, but no touching."

Okay, she got me again. Zellie poked my arm in amusement, and I laughed at my own discomfiture. "Okay, okay, turn around, let's see it."

The back of her shirt read "At Our Beautiful Bagel Presentations."

We ate our bagel infusions greedily, while talking about our new case.

"We are taking it, right?" I said.

"Oh, I guess so. But let's at least do some of our own research first. Even Jennifer said to do that."

We left a tip on the table, paid the cashier on the way out, and headed home.

Zellie turned on the computer and went right to work. "We have the name of an investment advisor," she said. "And not much else."

"That's a good thing," I speculated, pulling up a chair.

"How so? And maybe don't get so close, or we won't get any work done."

I sighed, but put a little space between our pressing bodies.

"Limited information to begin with means we draw our own conclusions, without being biased by pre-existing facts and ideas."

"True enough," Zellie said. "Look here." She pointed at a profile of Bertrand Sterling, with the lofty title "Chief Executive Officer, and Senior Wealth Manager, Goldback & Sterling, LLP."

"Sterling and Gold," I muttered. "Convenient wealth management names."

"Or made up ones," Zellie said. "Our first impression?"

"A little too coincidental, for sure. We'll check them out. But we have no other facts. We don't even know if they're the con artists or the ones being conned. We need to learn who their customers are, pronto."

"This could be interesting."

Jennifer knew we'd be hooked. We were definitely on the case.

"We might as well start by looking into Bertrand Sterling's background. It's the only information we have, so let's see what kind of person he is."

Zellie tapped a few keys, which resulted in a long list of items, including dozens of people named Bertrand Sterling; Pound Sterling; the definition of a sterling reputation; and other cyber detritus one can count on in typing a name into a search engine.

"Oops, too broad," she said, and limited the search to Bertrand Sterling of Goldback & Sterling. A picture of Mr. Sterling rewarded her. He wore a coat and tie, and his shoulders seemed to burst almost through the fabric of his dark blue blazer. His stern oval face and bushy eyebrows completed a very serious expression, like he'd snap your pelvis if you tried to take a single dollar away from one of his clients.

"Looks very... um... tense," I said.

"He's pretty burly, isn't he?"

"Built like a linebacker. Not exactly mean looking, but still...."

"An immovable force."

Together, we read the short biography included in the Goldback & Sterling website, which included Ivy League college, an MBA at a reputable business school, and almost twenty years of wealth management experience. The firm's principal, Morris Goldback, founded the firm in the 1970s and had retired a few years ago, leaving Bertrand Sterling as the senior member of the firm.

Further searches yielded a few articles written by Sterling, and a company blog that seemed to include his regular posts. A brief survey suggested that they comprised snippets of ordinary investment issues, and tax matters. We found no complaints, and nothing incendiary about him or Goldback & Sterling that would raise any alarms, or merit further inquiry.

"There's nothing here," Zellie said.

"I know. So why did Jennifer start our inquiry there?"

"Are they the people targeted for the con?"

"Maybe. We need to look deeper. Anyone can create a website and blog these days. I think even I could."

"My, aren't we getting technologically brave," Zellie teased.

"Well, maybe I could with a bit of help from someone who had a clue. But you get what I mean."

"I do, and you're right. This is not the end of the search. It's the beginning."

CHAPTER SEVEN

Bertrand Sterling sat at his desk in the Goldback Building. He stretched, yawned, and looked out the window. He had a marvelous view of Calabash Park from his corner office, and the sun shining through his window should have cheered him, but his lugubrious demeanor revealed no pleasure. He stared morosely for a few moments, and then abruptly picked up the phone and made a call.

"It's a go," he said into the mouthpiece. He listened a few moments. "Yes." He hung up without saying another word.

Sterling held his temples with the palms of his hands.

"This is my life?" he asked the empty office, dropping his hands and looking around at the diplomas and assorted pictures adorning the walls of his office.

"Sometimes I think Morris got the better deal."

At that moment, someone knocked on the door, and it opened a crack.

"Did you call me, Mr. Sterling?"

Sterling looked for a long moment at his pert associate. A beat too long, but too late now. Crap.

"No, thank you, Cindy. Just thinking out loud." About getting you into bed, he thought, but brushed the lecherous feelings away.

"But don't go anywhere. I need something." Same feelings. Have to stop this. Maybe get an ugly male associate, instead of the five foot two, beautiful woman standing in front of him.

"Please look at the financials in this file and give me your thoughts." He handed her a red folder, and she glanced at one chair in front of his desk and back at him.

"Not here," Sterling added. "Go back to your desk and take some time with it. Give me your impressions in, say..." he looked at his watch... "an hour. Thank you."

She took the file and turned to exit his office, while Sterling watched her pretty butt until the door closed. Amorous feeling aside, Sterling held a genuine interest in her analysis of the financials.

***

"Maybe we should look at the Goldback and Sterling staff," Zellie suggested. "That might yield a clue. Maybe one of them is even the potential culprit."

"As good an idea as any. We're just flailing at this thing, anyway."

"I know. It looks like a wild goose chase. But we have to start somewhere."

"How did I let Jennifer talk me into this?" I mused.

Zellie pursed her lips. "You're a sucker for tall, beautiful brunettes?"

"What?" My head lurched toward her as I tried to see if Zellie was kidding. I didn't detect any seriousness, but no smirk, either.

"No, that's not it," I said. "I much prefer beautiful mid-sized blondes."

"Nice save, fella. To be clear, she talked both of us into it. And it wasn't her, it was Marilyn, and more to the point, a desire to stop innocent people from being bilked."

"Right. Now I remember. We have a good reason for our aimless quest for justice."

"Yes, we do. Now let's get started looking into Bertrand Sterling's staff."

"Okay, where do we start?"

Zellie pointed at the G&S website home page, and pulled down a staff directory.

"Whoa, it's a miracle. Look at that!"

"Okay, okay, enough with the hyperbole. How about we start with this person?" Zellie pointed to a name, and I read it out loud.

"Cynthia Diamond?" I read. "Gold, Sterling and now Diamond? This has to be bogus, from top to bottom."

Zellie nodded. "Too much of a coincidence. Let's see, what's her job?"

"Financial Analyst in the Office of the CEO," I read on the screen. I was enjoying leaning over Zellie's shoulder, touching her cheek as I did so. "Is there a picture?"

Zellie clicked the mouse. "Here you go. Whoa!"

"Yowza," I added. "She's a looker, for sure. I bet it didn't matter to Sterling whether her name was Diamond or Smith, or cubic zirconium."

"No, I doubt it," Zellie said. "I wonder if she's the con artist."

"I suppose. But isn't it pretty dumb for a con artist to use an obviously bogus name?"

"That's a good point. We don't know enough to draw any conclusions."

***

Cindy closed the door to Bertrand Sterling's office and carried the folder to her desk. Twirling a lock of her hair, she stared into space. Her boss was a lecherous old fool. But she had to put up with the harassment. She'd agreed to do this job, and she'd see it through. Sterling had never even checked her credentials, which she'd fabricated, including the bogus Diamond last name. He'd thought it cute. As cute as the rest of her, he'd said with a leer. The comment ticked Cindy off, but she had said nothing, and Sterling hired her on the spot.

With a sigh, Cindy opened the folder and leafed through the pages. A few spreadsheets with long lists of numbers along with an executive summary. She read that first, and... holy crap!

Her eyes cut back to the spreadsheets, and she scanned the numbers in each. "Oh great," she muttered. The narrative summary didn't even touch the surface of the problem, but the numbers showed it to be much worse. What to do now? She couldn't give Sterling her true analysis, although she wondered why he'd given it to her. He might be a lecherous cretin, but he was not stupid. What was his game? Was he testing her?

Cindy decided not to rush. She looked up to the sight of a tall, pretty, fifty-ish brunette entering the office. The woman chatted for a moment with Sterling's executive assistant, who ushered her into Sterling's private lair, um, office.

* * *

"So what else does it say about her?" I asked, peering at the screen. "Maybe her CV is true, and she just used the name to get a foot, and um... the rest of her in the door."

"Put your tongue back in your mouth, Arnie. And I'm guessing her curriculum vitae is just as fake as those... um... her... name."

"You were going to say boobs."

Zellie laughed. "Guilty as charged."

"Are you sure they aren't real? I'd be happy to investigate."

"I'm sure you would, but I think I can safely say that the answer to that burning question is not material to our case."

"No," I said, getting serious. "Looks like the rest of the stuff on there is a load of malarkey, too. Yale University, Harvard Business School, and an internship with the Federal Reserve. Um, I don't think so."

"I agree. You don't join a small outfit like Goldback & Sterling with a resume like that. More like a big Wall Street firm."

"Is she our criminal mastermind?"

"It's hard to say, especially because we don't know what we're supposed to be finding out. And there's no sign of Jennifer yet."

"It can't be that easy, anyway. It's always complicated when Jennifer's involved."

"She's the mistress of mixed messages, that's for sure." Zellie's eyes wandered.

"What's bothering you?" I asked. "Other than the usual angst when dealing with the maelstrom that is Jennifer Marquette."

"I don't know whether it was a good idea getting involved in this. Why are we needed? We don't want innocent people scammed. That was the hook to get us to agree. But can't the FBI just investigate and shut down whatever operation they've targeted? Where do we fit in?"

"We know nothing." I admitted. "We signed on the dotted line without reading the fine print."

"Jennifer has an enormous capacity to make us crazy. Why not just give us the details up front?"

"Because she's up to something," Zellie replied. "She has her own agenda about this, no question."

"And we walked right into it. Again."

"That's about the size of it. Let's put all of this aside and visit our new office."

I brightened. "Let's go. I'm sure they've completed it by now."

***

Bertrand Sterling watched his potential new employee enter his office. For a moment, he remained sitting at his desk, just eyeing the curvaceous brunette who graced his doorway. He viewed her tall slender figure, long dark hair and pretty face with approval. She was not young, but that didn't matter to him. Well, not much, anyway. He guessed she was about fifty, but nature had treated her kindly. She could pass for forty. And her extensive resume suggested a brilliant woman with a choice of jobs.

He decided that was his first question, as he rose and extended his hand. They shook hands, and he gestured to one of the guest chairs in front of his desk.

She sat demurely and gave an expectant look in his direction.

"I appreciate you coming in today, Ms. Love," Sterling said.

"The pleasure is mine, sir. To speak to a financial legend is an honor. To work here would fulfill a longstanding dream. And please call me Ruby."

He knew her name was Ruby; it was on her resume. He also knew that it was a load of baloney, just like Ms. Diamond out there. And

Bertrand Sterling, for that matter. The weird thing was Morris Goldback was his given name, one he held onto for his entire life.

He looked at Ruby Love, or whatever her real name was. He knew she'd just presented him with a giant pile of cow chips and an enormous calling card.

"I don't think we need to discuss this any further. You're hired."

***

"What do you think?" Rupe's foreman asked.

We had just entered our new office and viewed it from the entryway. Honestly, my jaw had dropped. The place–our place–was flat out beautiful. No question, Rupe had spared no expense in transforming the former cinnamon bun bakery into an office fit for a Wall Street law firm. It sported a reception area, two private offices, a small glass enclosed conference room, a bathroom, and yes, a gleaming kitchen area with brand new appliances. The rooms were empty. We needed to get office furniture right away.

"It's fantastic," Zellie exclaimed, as she wandered around the rooms, pointing out the outstanding paint job, the skilled workmanship of the doorway, moldings and tile-work in the kitchen and bathroom.

"Yes, it's great, thank you so much."

"You're welcome. But the one to thank is Mr. Farnsworth. He told us to create an A-grade space for you, and to spare no expense."

"Oh, we'll thank him in person. But you and your crew are something special."

"Much appreciated, sir." He nodded at Zellie. "And ma'am."

He stepped outside, motioned to a remaining member of his crew, who joined him at his truck, and they departed.

I looked at Zellie, and we hugged.

"We need some furniture."

"Also, to set up electric service, phone service, internet, and a million other things we have no money for."

"Oops."

"Good grief. A beautiful office, rent free, and we can't afford it."

"We can pay the bills at least for a little while from the remaining reward money."

"We don't need phone service. We can just use our cell phones."

"We'll get second hand furniture at Goodwill or a used furniture store."

"We'll steal our neighbor's wi-fi. That's what most people do, right?"

"We're not stealing wi-fi."

"No, we're won't do that. But I'm sure that guy who moved into the house next door to mine has hacked into my cable somehow."

"Just a little paranoid, are we?"

I laughed. "Nah, I'm not like that. We'll figure out how to get up and running. But there's one thing we have to do right away."

"What?"

"Call Rupe."

He answered on the first ring and dispensed with the usual pontificating.

"What do you think?" he asked, in a voice which suggested that he already knew what we'd think.

"It's fantastic," I replied. "Your crew is top-notch, and whoever designed that layout is a real artist."

He met my comment with laughter.

"What's going on? Why the giggling?"

"She didn't tell you, did she?"

"Didn't tell me what?"

I looked over at Zellie, who I could tell was acting innocent. Of what, I didn't know.

"Zellie designed the whole thing, up to and including the window dressings. Everything. Although, I understand you helped pick out wall and carpet colors. My crew is great at executing a plan, but the client supplies the plan. You're the client."

"I stand by my comment. It's fantastic. And thank you, for your enormous part of it." I looked over at Zellie. "And I'll figure out a way to thank Zellie for shouldering the design burden. We'll occupy as soon as we get some furniture and set up utilities, et cetera."

"I guess they haven't arrived yet," Rupe said.

"Who? Clients?"

"Oh, the clients will come. I may send you some. No, I meant the movers."

"What movers? We have nothing to move."

"I arranged for delivery of some of our surplus office furniture. It may not be in the best condition, but it should help you get started."

"Rupe, you've done enough. We have to pay for it."

"Look, if I thought I could make a profit off of the furniture, I would have done it. In fact, I started with the idea that I could gouge you for it, especially when you're in this maudlin appreciative state, but Sarah would never forgive me. It's going to the dump, or to you. Take your pick."

"I choose us," I said, without hesitation. "Thank you."

"Don't thank me yet. The stuff is hideous. Gotta go, take care," He hung up.

"We're getting furniture, too," I said to Zellie.

"We have to figure out another way to thank him for all this, beyond free investigations."

"I know. We'll think of something. But what do you give to someone who has everything?"

Zellie looked pensive. "Maybe we just did," she said. "What better gift for a wealthy person than to share the wealth with his friends?"

I nodded. "I guess we wait for the movers."

Zellie took my arm. "Let's sit on that bench."

We sat and waited. It wasn't long before a big moving truck pulled up, and a heavy-set white man with a bald head and a thin goatee, hopped out of the cab. Another man dismounted and stood behind him.

"I'm looking for Arnold Finger, or Zesty Morgan," the bald man said, looking at us.

"Um, could it be Arnold Fischer or Zellie Morgan?" I inquired as politely as I could muster.

"That's what I said. Is you them?"

I resisted the impulse to reply "we is them," and offered a milder "That's us, sir."

He looked down at the clipboard he held. "Sez here outside delivery," he told the other man. "That means we dump it right here. Let's get started."

The other man opened the back doors to the truck and started removing a few desk chairs.

"May I see that?" I asked, pointing to his clipboard.

He pulled it towards his chest, as if to hide its contents.

"I assume you'll need a signature on it anyway," I added.

The man sighed and handed it over.

"It says inside delivery. Our office is right there. We'll show you where to put everything."

Zellie pulled me aside while the two men unloaded the truck.

"Good thinking," she whispered in my ear.

"Self-preservation," I replied. "Those desks look heavy."

＊＊＊

Sterling watched that perfect ass as Ruby Love, or whatever her real name was, exited his office. Even his lecherous self couldn't get motivated to enjoy the sight. There was something very hard about that woman. He couldn't put his finger on it, but she was up to something. So was the other precious gem in his employ, Cindy Diamond. But Ruby Love struck him as tough as nails under that gorgeous facade. He sat for a long time thinking about it. Maybe they were in it together. Whatever "it" was. Or maybe one or both of them were cops. Well, if they were local, he'd find out. If they were Feds, well that might be a little more difficult, but he figured he could flush them out.

He didn't think they were law enforcement. He knew they were up to something. But bogus names suggested they wanted him to know they weren't what they held themselves out to be. He couldn't figure that out. Unless... they knew about the true workings of Goldback & Sterling and wanted in. A piece of the action, in a manner of speaking. Well, if that was the case, they'd make their move at some point. And he'd be ready.

* * *

The men placed each piece of furniture where Zellie directed, and I slipped the head guy a couple of bills, and thanked him. We stood in the doorway and stared at our new, fully furnished office, albeit without wifi, or even the ordinary desk paraphernalia like pads, paper, pens, inboxes, outboxes–you can't have one without the other.

"We have lights," Zellie observed, looking above at the industrial type florescent lights on the ceiling.

"And electricity," I added, flicking the switch. "Does our lease includes that?"

"We have no lease. We have a dear friend helping us out."

"Right. We need to get a paying client so we can stop mooching off of Rupe."

"Yes, we do. But it will have to be as trackers. We have no license to do private investigating."

"I know. I'm hoping that Marilyn wasn't yanking our chain when she made that vague promise about helping us get our licenses if we went along with this Jennifer craziness."

"We're doing this because it's the right thing to do, trying to prevent any more elderly people being scammed, aren't we?"

"Of course. Helping people is good. If we can help ourselves — even better."

"Twice as much helping," Zellie said, laughing.

"Double the altruism."

"Let's get to work. I claim the office on the left." She walked in and sat down at the empty desk, with bare walls surrounding her.

"You look good in there," I told her, as I walked into my new office, the one on the right.

I sat down at my empty desk and immediately leaned over and pounded on the wall.

"What?" Zellie shouted from her side.

"Aside from our vacant offices, have you noticed anything else that might be a problem?"

Zellie walked into my office.

"Maybe the fact that all we've done is to erect a wall between us?"

"Bingo. How is this going to help?"

"Maybe we should work in the conference room and use these offices for another purpose."

"That might work. We could bring your laptop in here. Let's think about how to restructure this place so we can use it better and mostly do things together. That was the point of the business."

"Okay, let's head home. We can get started tomorrow."

CHAPTER EIGHT

When we returned home, I fired up my aging, but eminently reliable desktop computer. Zellie much preferred her laptop, but, as you might have guessed, I'm a little slower to adopt new technology. As if a laptop computer is new, but I like the big screen and the comfortable keyboard and mouse. Call me old-fashioned. Everyone else does.

Anyway, this time I had a jump on Zellie, technology speaking. And it was a rare occasion, so I intended to play it out as long and elaborately as I could.

"We need more information on Goldback & Sterling, correct?" I asked Zellie this in the most formal way possible.

"That's the mission, spymaster," Zellie said, with an expression that said she'd humor me, and play along with my performance.

"We need to speak to EDGAR," I said, trying hard to say it casually, as if I would introduce Zellie to an acquaintance.

"Who's he?" Zellie asked. "Some low-life snitch you met on the internet? Tell me you're not meeting random losers on the internet."

"Oh, he's no loser. More like a corporate guru, a veritable orb of useful information."

"So how are you going to speak to him? On Facebook? Or maybe Skype? No, that can't be it. You don't know how to use either of those things."

"Hey, wait a minute. I may not have a Facebook page, but I know about it, and I used Skype at work."

"When someone else set it up for you, pointed at the screen, and told you to speak."

"Um, yes. But still. Oh, the heck with it. You made your point. I'm not savvy. But I know EDGAR, and you don't." I resisted the temptation to stick my tongue out and say nyah, nyah, na, nyah, nyah. I beckoned at the computer screen.

"Take a peek."

She looked. It was the search engine for the SEC. And it bore the name EDGAR.

"What does EDGAR stand for? It doesn't say."

"Earnest Descriptions Guaranteed American Results," I said.

"Really?"

"Not a chance. I have no idea what the acronym stands for. I'm sure we could find that out, but it would be another piece of useless information to clutter our brains. The name is not important. One cannot overstate its value as a repository of extensive financial and biographical information on public companies. There are other financial related sites, too."

"This is great," Zellie said, as she clicked the mouse.

"Are they listed? This one only works for public companies. But they might be public. Not in the same way a multinational corporation would be, but still with shares sold to the public."

"Well, let's see," she said, entering the desired name in the search box.

"Presto," I said.

We couldn't say from the information on the screen that the business was bogus, or a confidence game of any sort, much less one parting folks from their hard-earned money. But it didn't look good.

"GS ASAP," Zellie read, looking at the bottom of a long list of companies under the Goldback & Sterling entry in EDGAR. "Goldback Sterling American Senior Annuity Plan, a wholly owned subsidiary of Goldback & Sterling, Inc., itself a subsidiary of Goldback & Sterling, LLP."

"Complicated business structure," I observed. "Not uncommon for a big multinational company, but we're not dealing with that here. By itself, it doesn't mean anything sinister."

"Wouldn't a corporate structure maze like that make it harder for people to sue them, if they committed a fraud?"

"Yes. Much harder. The idea is to shield the parent company, and its officers and directors."

"We need to look further at GS ASAP."

"Fast," I said with a grin.

***

Cindy pored over the financial information in the folder Sterling had given her. Assorted spreadsheets containing some very interesting data on an annuity business of a subsidiary of Goldback & Sterling, Inc. She did a few calculations and compared the information in one set of figures with the other and gave a low whistle. She did a furtive glance around to assure herself that her verbal slip went unnoticed, then began furiously checking and rechecking her math. No question, she thought. It was only part of the story, but she knew her hunch was right. She needed to verify it. The information was of great value to her other employer, but only if it was unquestionably accurate. The risk was too great otherwise.

Cindy considered what to do next. Sterling had given the file to her in paper form, so she couldn't just download it to a flash drive. She could scan it, but she didn't have a scanner at her desk. And she wanted a copy. She surreptitiously removed her phone from her purse and quickly used its internal scanner to copy the documents. It wasn't ideal, but it got the job done.

Having accomplished that, she stood up, picked up the file, and strode over to Sterling's office, advising his executive assistant, Lois Carver, that she wanted to give him an oral report on the financials he'd given her.

Lois looked at her. "He will want a written report, Ms. Diamond," she said, not unkindly.

"I assumed so, but to prepare it properly, I think I need some additional documents."

Lois sighed. "I've worked for the man for ten years. And it hasn't been easy. But I've stayed. The pay is good, and so are the benefits. But he's not an easy man to work for."

Lois paused and looked Cindy over.

"Someone who looks like you will do okay with him. Anyway, I'm just trying to help you. He gave you only part of the documentation for a reason. He wants your analysis, but doesn't want you to see the big picture."

Cindy was about to inquire further, but the door to the inner office opened suddenly, and an angry Bertrand Sterling stood in the doorway.

"Which one of you is responsible for this?" Sterling brandished a single piece of paper, waving it under the noses of Cindy and Lois as he bellowed his imperious inquiry. Lois responded first, in a voice that could calm Mother Nature during a hurricane.

"Exactly what are you referring to, Bert? From your tone, I assume you aren't trying to determine which of us deserves your effusive praise, but is instead an effort to assign blame. As such, we are entitled to know what in tarnation you're talking about?"

Sterling looked at Lois, his mouth agape. All the fury left him. He looked down at the paper he still clutched.

"Someone has not labeled this properly," he said. "It should bear both the file number and the account title right here." He pointed to a spot at the top of the page.

"Of course. Silly me. Just an oversight, Mr. Sterling. I'll take care of it right away," Lois spoke in a soothing tone as she took the paper from his hand.

"See that you do."

Sterling turned and headed back to his office. But before he entered, he turned.

"Um, thank you Lois."

"Think nothing of it."

When he had closed the door, Cindy waited a moment to be sure he wasn't coming out again.

Satisfied that he wouldn't return, she leaned down and in a conspiratorial voice, whispered "It was my screw-up. You didn't have to take the blame. But thank you. And that was impressive how you handled it."

"Handled him is more like it. I'd say his bark is bigger than his bite, but he can bite hard, too. You don't get to where he is without some toughness. But he shouldn't direct the venom at his allies, like us. He knows that he overreacted to a silly mistake, hence the belated thank you. That was his version of an apology."

"You called him Bert after he yelled at us, and Mr. Sterling when you agreed to fix the problem."

"I've known him a long time. He has no problem with me calling him Bert. I think it's more appropriate in a business setting to call him Mr. Sterling. But if he acts like a child...."

"You treat him like one," Cindy finished for her.

Lois nodded. "Better get back to your office. This is not the time to give him an oral report on something. Write it up and wait for a strategic time. He doesn't like surprises."

***

"So how do we go about it?" I asked. "We're not turning up GS ASAP as a public company, so we only have the information we just looked at, which doesn't amount to much."

"What did you do to research companies' financial information at Mort?" Zellie asked, referring to Mortal Securities, the now-defunct financial firm where I'd worked until shortly before all kinds of bad things happened there, as those of you who remember our first case know.

"Relied on detailed and exhaustive research conducted by super-smart twenty-five-year-old associates with MBAs. Can we do that here?"

"Do we have any of those in our detective agency?" Zellie asked, with an indulgent smile.

"Um, no."

"Then we're out of luck there. But you must know how to do the research yourself, right? You rose like a rocket at Mort. Weren't you one of those young whippersnappers yourself?"

"Not really. I started on the floor, with all the other new people. And I was a little older than most of them. I don't have an MBA, so I was less qualified, too. I just worked harder, took advantage of the information the smart guys put in Mort's databases, made some smart or lucky recommendations, take your pick, and made the partners a lot of money. That impressed the bosses, particularly the firm's founder, who took me under his wing. Long story, but the upshot is that I never did great financial research."

Zellie gave a faint smile. "I think you did just fine," she said. "And more apropos to this case, demonstrated exceptional skill in assessing financial information. From what I can see, we need that skill to figure out whether Sterling is a crook."

I nodded. Once we obtained more data, we'd need to figure out how it fit into a criminal enterprise.

"And I have a few tricks up my sleeve. All we need is a certain brand of vacuum cleaner."

Zellie looked at me like I'd just proposed enlisting the help of space aliens.

"Huh?" is all she managed.

"A Hoover, to be precise," I added, enjoying the confusion I'd wrought. "Let me explain."

"Please do," she said. "Because I'm ready to call the men in white coats. We need financial information, and you propose cleaning the carpet." She looked down. "Which could use a good scrubbing, now that you mention it."

"Hoovers dot com," I said. I gestured at the computer. "Type it in."

Zellie complied, and we viewed a big screen announcing "D&B Hoovers."

"It's a Dunn & Bradstreet database that also provides corporate information, like the names of principal officers and contact information, company profiles and industry analysis, and more."

"Edgar and Hoover. Interesting names for investigative tools," Zelllie mused.

"I don't think J. Edgar Hoover had anything to do with either of these," I said, quickly picking up Zellie's thought process.

"No, I wouldn't guess so," she said. "But this is a gold mine. We'll surely find what we're looking for here."

"It will take some work," I warned. "I don't think we can just type in a question and get an answer."

Zellie wasn't listening anymore. She already keyed in a few things, muttered something, typed in something else and muttered again.

I inched away. This was Zellie's skill set, and she was best left alone to do her work. If she had questions, or something to report, she'd let me know.

I had another idea. Years in the securities business had yielded many knowledgeable contacts in innumerable businesses, and I knew of one offhand that had particular expertise in annuities. While Zellie was doing her research, I made a few calls, got some interesting general information, and set up two appointments for us.

I strolled back to the computer area, where Zellie remained hard at work. She seemed to be flipping back and forth between EDGAR and Hoovers and jotting things down. She whistled softly while she worked, and I could hear faint strains of a Bruce Springsteen song.

I leaned over and kissed her on her temple, and she took my hand absently while continuing to look at the screen, then looked up at me.

"How did you do this all day?" She asked.

"Dry stuff, huh?"

"Dry doesn't even begin to describe it. Imagine the most arid desert climate in the world, multiply it by three, and maybe it approaches...." She pointed at the screen. "This stuff."

"I heard you whistling Born in the USA while you looked at it, so it couldn't be that bad."

"With apologies to the Boss, I changed the words in my mind to 'Bored in the USA.'"

"That makes more sense. Did you find anything useful?"

"Yes. There's a wealth of information here, but I don't have the skill set to assess it. That's your department."

I glanced at her notes. "I can do that," I said. "But by itself, that won't tell us how it fits into a possible scheme to defraud."

"We'll figure that out together," Zellie said.

"Yes, we will. And I know someone who might provide some expert assistance. Did I ever introduce you to Bart Singletary?"

"No. I don't think so."

"Bart's an odd bird. I think you'll like him, if you can ignore his, um, peculiarities."

"I ignore yours, don't I?" Zellie teased.

"Bart's a little different. You'll see. We have an appointment with him tomorrow morning. Oh, and he's an insurance agent, so prepare for a sales pitch. He knows we just want information from him, but he won't be able to resist."

"I can't wait." Zellie's tone suggested a preference for a root canal.

I ignored her negativity. "We still have a few hours left before calling it a day. Let's arrange for internet service for the office, then go out to an early dinner and a movie."

"We're banned from all the local theaters."

"For talking too much. Strike that. Let's get an early dinner and watch a movie on Netflix."

I called the cable company, and they offered a promotional first year price, which I accepted.

"By the time the promotional fee expires, we'll have an active business," Zellie exulted.

"Sure, we'll be rolling in the cash," I replied with only a smidgen of doubt in my voice.

Our mission accomplished, we discussed restaurant choices, finally settling on The Frog's Pajamas, a local eatery specializing in what they described as eclectic cuisine. And yes, it was Zellie's turn to choose the restaurant. I'm not that adventurous.

"What does 'eclectic' mean," I asked. "And what's with the name?"

"Haven't you ever heard the expression 'it's the cat's pajamas,' meaning it's excellent?"

"Um, yes. Something your ninety-eight-year-old aunt might say. But what does Frog's Pajamas mean?"

"The same thing. They're just not cat people," Zellie said, stifling her laughter. "And 'eclectic' means food you won't like."

"Oh great. Like desiccated goat spleens on a bed of chilled couscous?"

"Yes, excellent culinary creations like that." She pointed at the online menu. "Or a New York strip steak."

We had a nice dinner and came home to watch a movie. True to our custom, we yakked all the way through it, and Netflix didn't mind a bit. Exhausted after the long day, we went to bed early.

CHAPTER NINE

I awoke to the smell of bacon, which is a fabulous way to wake up. I threw on a robe and followed the pleasant odor to the kitchen where Zellie was tending a frying pan.

I kissed her on the cheek, grabbed a cup of coffee, and sat down at the kitchen table.

"Are you ready for a scintillating insurance pitch?" I asked with a smirk.

Zellie glared at me, but only for a moment, and only to make a point.

"Anything for the cause, oh gallant soldier," she said. "I head into battle against the demons of boredom with a heavy heart, but a ferocious spirit."

"You practiced that," I accused.

"Maybe."

"Anyway, it won't be that bad, I promise. Bart is a character. He makes insurance fun, if you can believe it. And he knows we're there for a different purpose. You'll get the show without the heavy sales pitch. Maybe. Um, I doubt it, but as you said, anything for the cause. And there's no one who knows more about the annuity business than Bart."

"If you say so. Hand me that plate. No, not that one. The one next to it."

I handed her the plate, and she heaped the first batch of bacon on it, then scooped some scrambled eggs from another pan and split it between the two plates on the table.

"Ta da! Breakfast."

"Thanks, sweetheart."

As we dug in, Zellie asked what time we had to leave for our appointment. I looked at my watch and told her we had forty-five minutes to get ready.

We made it to Bart's office in Lincroft with about thirty seconds to spare. A receptionist greeted us. She sat at a desk which had a nameplate proclaiming her as Natasha. She was about twenty-five years old and had shoulder length green hair.

"Nice hair color," I commented.

"I know, right? I had purple hair before, but the boss suggested green, and it was like, a totally great choice. Anyway, he'll be out in a moment. Five, four, three, two, one."

At the exact moment her countdown ended, the door to the left of her desk burst open, and none other than Bart Singletary jumped out. I say jumped, because that's what he did. Leaped into the room, like a diminutive Olympic broad jumping garden gnome.

I pretended not to notice, which was hard, because I had an enormous giggle welling up in my chest. I glanced at Zellie, whose mouth was agape. No words came out.

Bart was about five feet tall, and weighed about two hundred pounds, much of it muscle. He wore a blond wig on his bald head. A wig, not a toupee. And his attire was 1970s polyester leisure suit all the way. He looked like a short, heavy-set lounge singer. I almost expected him to ask me where I'm from, and then break out into a rendition of Dream, the Impossible Dream.

I extended my hand. "Bart, good to see you. Irrepressible as always."

"You too, Arnie. I like to keep things interesting. It's not always easy. I'm in the insurance business, for crissake."

He looked at Zellie.

"Where are my manners?" I said. "Bart Singletary, this is my partner and fiancée Zellie Morgan."

"Fiancée, huh? Congratulations. But he's not good enough for you, my dear. He's a rotten scoundrel. Now me, I'm a sweetheart." He laughed. "Of course, only a scoundrel would say something like that." He looked at us for a moment.

"You look good together. My best wishes, I mean that. Now come inside to my office, and we can visit the exciting world of annuities."

We sat on the sofa in a small seating area next to Bart's desk. Bart plunked himself down into a big, overstuffed easy chair. His keen eyes gazed at us for a moment, giving the impression he was assessing what we needed. Which was a little dumb, because I'd told him over the phone. But Bart wanted to make an impression. No doubt learned it in insurance school, or at Harvard Business School, where he'd earned his MBA.

"For a new couple like yourselves," he began, "I recommend a whole life insurance policy. Builds equity and insures against the unexpected demise of one of you. Better yet, we'll call it a key employee plan, and you can deduct it as a business expense."

"Bart," I started.

"You're thinking that in your business, there is a greater possibility of, shall we say, leaving this world than in some other lines of work? No problem, a term policy would work, too."

I held up my hand, palm facing Bart, but he kept on talking.

"I know, I know. You came here to learn about annuities. Good idea. That is a very realistic alternative for retirement planning. And a good idea to incorporate that into your business plan."

"Bart, stop. Please."

He grimaced, and adjusted his wig, which had turned askew, making him look like Alfred E. Neuman on steroids.

"I was doing it again, wasn't I?"

I nodded.

Bart turned to Zellie. "I have this tendency to get too excited about my work. I am aware that the insurance business can make most people yawn. So I overcompensate sometimes and don't let people get a word in edgewise. I think I'm afraid they'll make excuses to leave if I don't hold them here."

"Is that the reason for the outfit?" Zellie asked.

"This? Why, is there something unusual about it?" Bart said it completely deadpan.

Zellie looked at me, then at Bart, who'd burst out laughing.

"Yes, it's theatrics. Don't worry, I'm mostly sane. Right Arnie?"

"Oh sure. Like Woody Woodpecker."

"Exactly like him. Anyway, enough of this. You guys want insurance, and I do think it's a good idea, you call me, okay? Now let me give you the skinny on the annuity business and my understanding of certain types of people who might misuse a legitimate retirement tool to line their own pockets."

***

Jennifer idly fingered the papers on her desk. Her thoughts were miles and years away, harkening back to simpler times. Before she became... a person of many faces. She'd transformed into so many roles in the last twenty years, she'd lost count. And once again, she was playing a part in a theatrical production of her own construction.

Oh, the planning of this caper involved others, but she had remarkable latitude in its development. Surprising, because she knew they didn't trust her. Hell, she didn't trust herself, so why should they? One thing was certain — she intended to use that freedom to accomplish something beyond what they'd contemplated. Jennifer looked down at the papers. While she pondered, she'd doodled all over them, and had rolled up the sides. She was good with numbers, always had been. And she knew just enough about finance to fool some bright people, and she included Bertrand Sterling in that category. But she was also sure that Sterling didn't care one iota about her financial abilities. He'd hired her even though he knew her credentials were a crock of spoiled soup, and her name right out of central casting. He had a scam in mind, and he no doubt figured someone with no scruples could be useful. Jennifer knew she fit that description perfectly.

***

"That's what we want to know," I said, and Zellie nodded.

"Most of the major insurance companies offer annuities, and they're legit. They may or may not be a good retirement choice, and there is risk involved, although they kind of downplay that. But they're entirely on the up and up."

"What about GS ASAP?" Zellie asked.

"The name implies urgency. What do you think?"

"That they rush people into deciding. Buy now, before it's too late and you lose out on an outstanding deal."

"Ding, ding, ding. Give the lady a prize. That's exactly right. One should decide on a retirement investment, or any financial product only after careful thought and research. Except anything I try to sell you."

Zellie smiled at him. "We'll take the careful consideration advice, thank you."

"Well played, my dear. Arnie, you got yourself a smart one."

"I do," I agreed. "But tell us more about GS ASAP."

"Morris Goldback was a prince. A good guy, old school. Maybe cut a few corners here and there, but he did nothing blatantly dishonest. And he didn't bilk little old ladies."

"But he retired," I prompted.

"Yes, and Bertrand Sterling became the CEO. Bert's cut from a different cloth. Big bucks fast, that could be his motto. The firm is a wealth management company. Not that high-falutin' securities trading gig you had going at Mort. Smaller scale, and more personal contact with clients.

"With a few exceptions, we had only institutional investors," I agreed.

"Right. But Sterling deals with individuals. He convinces them to buy products, like annuities. His firm recently acquired a major player in that market."

I leaned forward. "Which one?"

"Horsehead Global," Bart said. "Remember them?"

I did. One of the many companies we dealt with while I was at Mort. And how I met Bart. I turned to Zellie to explain.

"In my early days at Mort, the partners occasionally sent me out to gather what they called empirical research. That meant I was a glorified gopher, but I didn't mind. It got me out of my cubicle and gave me some hands-on education about the various businesses. In those days, you paid for subway fares using tokens. They gave me two subway tokens and an address and told me to interview the specified person and report back."

"And one of those people was Bart," Zellie guessed.

"Nope," I said, as Bart and I both giggled.

"We met in an elevator in a building in mid-town Manhattan."

"We were stuck together in an elevator," Bart clarified.

"For two hours," I added. "Two long, aggravating, wildly entertaining hours with a certifiable lunatic."

"That would be me," Bart said, as if there was any doubt.

"How did it happen?" Zellie asked. "Were you asked to interview Bart?"

"No. I never talked to the original guy. By the time the elevator started up, he was so backed up with other appointments, he had to reschedule. I went back to the office empty-handed. But I'd gained a valuable, albeit mostly crazy colleague."

"Again, that's me. Very valuable." Bart said.

I ignored him. "Bart worked for Horsehead Global Insurance. That's how I learned about the company."

"I thought it was legitimate, even with the mob sounding name," Bart said. "And maybe it was. I learned a ton about legitimate insurance products during my time there. I couldn't say for sure it is anything other than an upstanding insurance company. Anyway, it had a large annuities business, and its acquisition made Goldback & Sterling a major player in the market."

***

"This is a crazy investigation," Zellie remarked as we left Bart's office.

"How so?"

"Usually you see a crime. Then you look for clues, examine evidence, check out online and other sources, interview suspects and identify the perpetrator. Here, we don't even know if anyone committed a crime."

"We can't even call Sterling a suspect, much less interview him," I agreed. "We only think he might defraud people. We have no evidence that a fraud has already occurred."

"I know," Zellie said. "How can we even talk to him? We have no reason to make an appointment."

"True. But I wonder...."

"What?"

"Just the germ of an idea. Let me think it through."

"You told me this morning that we had two appointments, but only told me about Bart," Zellie said as we got into the car. "Where are we going next?"

I flashed a grin. "It's a surprise."

"Is it related to the case?"

"Absolutely not."

"Very mysterious. But okay. Lead the way."

I headed south to Asbury Park, where I pulled up at an office building a few blocks from the beach. I took Zellie by the hand and we walked into the building and took the elevator to the top floor. We exited into a foyer where a glass-walled reception area awaited. On the door, embossed in gold script were the words "Felicity Amour, Wedding Planner to the Stars."

Zellie took one look at the door, looked at me, and broke into hysterics.

I couldn't help myself, I started laughing, too.

"We're not stars," Zellie gasped. "But someone named Felicity Amour never met one, anyway."

"She has an answer for that," I said, pointing at the small print under the name on the door.

"Where everyone is a star at their own wedding," she read out loud. "Well, that explains it. Where did you find this person?"

"I know Felicity," I said. "And that's her real name. The Amour part of it is not. Her real last name is Lebowsky. I met her through a friend at work who'd hired her for his wedding. He thinks she's great and said her strong suit is helping people figure out what type of wedding they want."

Zellie leaned over and kissed me. "That's very sweet. No harm in hearing what she has to say," she added, and pushed open the door. I followed her, and we identified ourselves to the perky woman sitting at the desk in front of us.

"Felicity is expecting you," the woman said, and we followed her through a door next to the desk.

A woman with a brunette ponytail greeted us.

"Arnie," she said with the exuberance that one might reserve for an old friend. I'd only met her once, but her behavior, which included a warm hug, suggested otherwise.

"And you are Zellie. I've heard so much about you, I feel like I've known you for years." She took Zellie's hand in both of hers, and held them for a moment, then gestured at a small seating area in the corner of her office. We sat down together on the loveseat, and Felicity plopped down on the edge of one of the straight-back chairs, leaning forward.

"How can I be of service?" she asked with shining eyes focused on both of us.

"Well," I started, "We're engaged, and want to figure out the details of our wedding."

"Can't decide between big and small, who to invite or not, and whether to just run away together and get hitched?"

"That's it," Zellie said. "Except that we've already decided on small. Just a few friends and our parents."

"I think I can help with that," she said. "I'm a wedding planner, which requires advanced degrees in psychology, sociology and business administration. I have all three, if they gave out doctorates for on-the-job experience. Simply put, what feels right to you, who do you want involved in the process and what do you want to spend?"

"That about covers it," I said with a smile.

"We love each other and want to get married," Zellie said, and I clasped her hand.

"You already have the important part. I can help with the details."

***

After departing from Felicity's office, with the bright sun shining above, we strolled the few blocks to the beach, and the venerable Asbury Park boardwalk.

"Let's get a hot dog, and sit and talk," I suggested.

Zellie nodded, and soon after, wieners in hand, we plopped own on a long wooden bench facing the beach.

Between bites, we deferred further thought about the wedding and discussed the case instead.

"We've gathered about as much preliminary information as we can without talking to the principal players in this little drama," Zellie noted.

"We need to talk to people inside Goldback & Sterling," I said. "But how?"

"Should we pretend to be prospective clients?" Zellie mused.

"That won't get us access to anyone other than a salesman."

"True. We need something else, but what?"

"Maybe we could say we're journalists writing a story about what makes a financial firm successful."

"That's not bad," Zellie said. "It would appeal to Sterling's ego. I'll bet he'd be happy to talk about himself. Men love to do that."

"You know I'm sitting right here next to you, right?"

She snuggled up against me. I'm very aware of that," she replied, placing a hand on my thigh.

We sat for a while, then headed back home to work out the details of our plan.

CHAPTER TEN

"**I** like the idea of us as journalists," Zellie said, after we settled in at home. "But we've become sort of famous around here. Will they believe us?"

"We're not that well-known. Maybe by name, but not necessarily by sight."

"We could use assumed names, I suppose," Zellie mused.

"Maybe we could be investigative journalists instead of feature writers. I think I'd like that."

"How could we explain that any better?"

"It's a natural fit. Investigative journalism is a type of detective work."

"Maybe." Zellie sounded doubtful.

I persisted. "We're not licensed detectives, so we need some other source of income. It's a perfect answer if anyone asks, or if some pesky governmental authority tries to shut our detecting down."

"It's not a bad idea," Zellie admitted. "But who'd hire us? It's not like we have journalism degrees, or experience as reporters."

"A lack of experience or authority never stopped us before."

"True enough. Yet another field in which ignorance triumphs over education."

I disregarded her cynical tone.

"First thing to do is get jobs as investigative reporters," I said.

"Sure," Zellie said. "With no journalism degree, reporting experience, or frankly any skills, we'll just leapfrog over the massive throng of qualified wannabe investigative reporters, most of whom have labored in the trenches reporting on Cub Scout picnics, high school proms, and the big game just to get a chance at doing some real hard-core news."

"Um, when you put it like that, maybe the journalism idea isn't such a good one." I paused. "Unless...."

"Uh, oh, what unsavory scheme is that pea-brain of yours cooking up?"

"Hey, was the pea-brain comment necessary?" I asked in mock anger. "Oh, the heck with it. Peas are very intelligent little vegetables. And I have a good idea."

"Okay, oh great and exalted legume. Out with it."

"We don't need to be real reporters. And as you so pessimistically pointed out, we have little or no chance of getting one of those jobs, much less two. We just need press credentials to support our fake journalist identities."

"I don't think forging press credentials is a great idea. We get caught doing that, and it's goodbye ever getting PI licenses."

I looked at her for a long moment. "And it would be morally reprehensible."

"That too. What do you have in mind?"

"Prateek."

"You think he'd go along with this craziness?"

"No harm asking. We can't give him all the details. But we can promise him an exclusive on whatever public information comes out of it. And he's a good guy."

"Are you sure we won't be putting him in a difficult position? They don't dole out press credentials like advertising flyers. There's a certain prestige to having them."

"I know. We'll promise to only use them when dealing with Goldback & Sterling and its subsidiaries, unless he gives permission otherwise."

Prateek Chowdhury was a college friend of mine, and the editor-in-chief of the Monmouth Clarion-Gazette, a prestigious newspaper and media outlet with an extensive readership in the tri-state area.

Upon Zellie's agreement, I called his office and made an appointment for the following day.

***

The Clarion's main office was in the Ironbound section of Newark, New Jersey, about a forty-minute drive from Middletown. Zellie and I parked nearby and walked a short distance to the main entrance. We passed through security and took the elevator to the ornately decorated reception area of the office of the editor-in-chief.

"Wow," Zellie said, looking in the glass-walled area. "This is not what I expected."

"This looks nothing like the loud, frantic newsrooms you see in the movies, with everyone yelling at once, and the grizzled old editor stopping it all with a single raised hand of authority," I agreed. "Looks like Prateek is a big cheese."

Zellie nodded. "A rare Brie or finely aged Camembert, I'd say." She pushed open the door, and I followed her in.

We introduced ourselves to the receptionist, a thirty-something man with a crew cut and a look of quiet efficiency. He consulted an electronic tablet and cleared us for takeoff, I mean, entry into the inner sanctum of the exalted editor-in-chief.

A dark-haired woman inside the doorway escorted us to Prateek's office, where the man himself dispatched the woman with a nod, and he rose to greet us, his piercing, cobalt eyes upon us, intelligently assessing all possible reasons for our visit.

"Arnie, Zellie, nice to see you," he said, extending his hand. "To what do I owe the honor of your visit?"

I'd thought better of giving specifics to the secretary with whom I'd made the appointment, other than to say I was an old college friend, and hoped he'd see me. He'd agreed, or we wouldn't be here.

"We need a favor," I started, and Prateek reflexively looked at his watch.

"Look, I know you're busy, so I'll be quick," I hastened to add, and I told him what we needed.

"I love you and Zellie," Prateek started. "Well, Zellie anyway. But we don't give out press credentials like candy bars. Our credibility is the only currency we have. We can't trifle with it. I'm sorry, the answer is no. You'll just have to find another way."

"I didn't want to use this card, Prateek, but use it I must. You owe me."

"For what?"

"I introduced you to your wife."

Prateek started laughing despite his obvious intention to remain stoic.

"You didn't introduce us. You were chatting Desiree up at a party, and I walked over and started talking to her. You had designs on her, but she only had eyes for me."

"See? You admit it."

"I'm admitting nothing. But as a special favor to Zellie, I'll give you credentials for a single, special assignment, only usable for your so-called feature story on Goldback & Sterling, and the Clarion-Gazette will own one hundred percent of both the feature, and any news that comes of it."

I looked at Zellie, and she nodded.

"Done," I said, "Subject to any reporting we might have to do to law enforcement entities."

"Agreed," Prateek said, rummaging around in his desk drawer, and handing us two press passes. "You're officially reporters. You can get your photos taken downstairs. And bring me back a great story."

"Now get out of my office. I have real work to do." He smiled as he said it, and added a request for a future social get-together as we departed.

Press passes clutched in our hands, we headed downstairs to the newsroom to get our pictures taken. The scene allayed my earlier disappointment at not seeing the bedlam depicted in the movies in an instant, as we entered the pandemonium that served as the Clarion-Gazette newsroom. People rushing around, narrowly avoiding bumping into each other as they passed, with everyone yelling, and pointing, and acting like kids run amok on a playground.

We stood and watched the chaos for a while, uncertain of where to get our photographs, and just to take in the marvelous scene. I stopped a slower moving passerby for directions, and he pointed to our destination, before quickening his pace, as if recognizing that I'd caught him acting like a tortoise.

Our photos taken, and our press credentials complete, we exited the building and located a cute bistro for a late breakfast. After an amiable repast, we headed back to Middletown. En route, we decided to go to our new office.

We settled into the conference room. I sat across from Zellie, who peered at her laptop.

"Who should we interview first?" I asked.

"We have to do something before that," she responded.

I tilted my head like a dog saying "huh?"

"We have to figure out who to approach with our cover story of a feature article."

"Don't we just contact their publicity department?"

"No. As a former public relations maven, I will tell you that's the last thing we want to do."

Again, the head tilting, so Zellie continued.

"I always found it more desirable and effective to set the parameters in advance for the interviews. If someone pitched an idea to me for an article or interview, they already had a fixed concept from their editor or producer they wanted to effectuate.

"Kind of like an investigator or prosecutor determining guilt before looking at the evidence. Everything thereafter conforms to the original assessment, resulting in overlooking facts that don't fit the original theory."

Zellie laughed. "A little hyperbolic, but not a bad analogy."

"More to the point, it made it harder for you to spin it the way you wanted."

"Yes. We want to set the agenda. And the best way to do that is to approach someone, ideally Sterling himself, about the concept. That will make the publicist react to an already existing idea. We get Sterling to ask us to write about him." Zellie said.

"Oh sure. He's just going to call two fake journalists up and ask them to interview him."

Zellie pulled out her press pass and toyed with it between her fingers.

"We're legitimate, as far as this story goes. And reporters for a well-regarded media enterprise."

"True enough," I acknowledged. "But how do we get him to ask us?"

"In the time-tested way people transact all business. Either on the golf course or in a bar."

"We're taking up golf? Or worse, drinking?"

"We're not doing either one. We're figuring out where Sterling goes to hoist a few after work and sending in a ringer to engage him in conversation. At some point, the idea of a feature article will magically come up, and Sterling will have your cell phone number."

"Who do you have in mind?"

"I have a few ideas. I need to do a little research about Mr. Sterling's personal life. I'm thinking a beautiful woman. That always works for professional men."

"You've done this before?" I asked, incredulity creeping into my voice. Although I should know better. Zellie did this kind of thing for a living, and she was outstanding at it.

"Maybe once or twice," she said with an unmistakable twinkle in her eye.

"How do you know which bar Sterling frequents?"

"I made a few quiet inquiries. Sterling is a public figure. People know him."

"You've been busy," I observed. I thought about who Zellie might have in mind as her ringer. Delilah? Marla? Melissa, I doubted it. Not Sarah. I had no idea, so I asked.

"Sasha," Zellie said.

"Who's... oh. Our new neighbor."

"You might have noticed that she's beautiful."

"Um, sure, I guess in a..."

"Gorgeous way. You can say it, Arnie."

"We don't even know her. And she has her own business. Why would she help?"

"Turns out that she's an aspiring actress."

"How do you know that?"

"Because we've been talking every day on the phone. I thought it a good idea to get a little background on our neighborhood. Who's coming and going to the various places in our little shopping center, who the various proprietors are, things like that. She's very nice, and frankly perfect for our little ruse."

"I don't know," I said. "She fits the bill as a woman who'd attract a man, for sure. But can we trust her? And should we involve a relative stranger in something that might be dangerous?"

"I don't think there's any risk on either front," Zellie said, rhythmically twirling a lock of her hair like the tapping of a musician preparing to go on stage. We were entering Zellie's area of expertise, and she was getting ready to perform.

Zellie stopped fidgeting. "There's almost nothing Sasha needs to do. She sits at a bar, waits for the inevitable approach by Sterling, works the conversation around to publicity, lets him ask her if she knows any friendly journalist types to do the feature, and extracts herself gracefully from his clutches."

"What if she can't escape from him?"

Zellie just looked at me.

"It's a public place, and she's probably very good at keeping men at bay," I said, and Zellie nodded.

"She might not convince him," I warned.

"She'll do just fine," Zellie said with confidence I did not share. But I kept my mouth shut.

* * *

Sterling looked at his watch. Twenty after five. He opened the door to his office and peered outside. Not a soul in sight.

"I bet the Sahara is more populated than this place at 5:01," he muttered.

He decided to get a drink at Lightning (Fast Moving and Dangerous), his bar of choice. Good booze and pretty, but gold-digging women. Let them try. As long as they gave as much as they hoped to get.

Entering the crowded bar, Sterling spotted a curvaceous woman standing alone near the door, and he approached with what he thought was a hip demeanor.

"Hello beautiful. How can someone who looks like you be alone?" he asked.

"Get away from me, you old jerk. I'm not alone, she added, as a tall, muscular man approached with his hands clenched into fists.

Sterling put up his hands, palms facing the couple.

"My mistake. No harm intended."

The two glared at him as he scuttled away. He headed towards the bar where much to his delight, a gorgeous woman with long strawberry blond hair and a perfect figure, sat on a stool, nursing a glass of white wine. He slid into the empty spot next to her and ordered a Black Label on the rocks from the approaching bartender.

With a small measure of trepidation resulting from his immediate past rejection, Sterling ventured a slight turn of his head, and a simple "Hi."

The woman turned and said in a slight foreign accent, "Hi yourself."

Encouraged by the absence of hostility, Sterling plunged ahead by introducing himself.

"No clever line?" the woman inquired.

"I can come up with one if you'd like," Sterling said. "But you strike me as someone who'd hate that."

"I think most women hate that. My name is Sophia."

CHAPTER ELEVEN

As we sat eating breakfast in Zellie's house the next morning, her phone rang. She picked it up, listened for a few minutes, congratulated the other person on a job well done, gave her thanks on both our parts, and disconnected.

"Sasha?" I inquired.

"The very same." Zellie laughed. "Or Sophia, as she called herself to Sterling."

"She moves fast," I observed.

"When I told her what we had in mind, she couldn't wait to get started. That woman is a natural."

"Did she tell Sterling about us?"

"My understanding is that Sterling asked her if she knew any journalists who might give his business favorable treatment."

"How did she do that? I know you hoped that would be the result, but I didn't expect... I mean... I didn't know... wow."

"You didn't believe me," Zellie said sweetly. "We did that stuff all the time in the public relations business. You need the right people for the job. But that's what I meant by Sasha's natural ability. I could see that right away."

"So we can expect a call from Sterling?"

"Sasha can't guarantee that, and I didn't ask. All she had to do was get him to ask her for our names and your cell phone number, and the name of our publisher. The rest is up to Sterling."

"Why my cell phone number and not yours?"

Zellie patted her hair and turned up her nose in mock superiority. "Do you really think I'd give out my cell phone number to a complete stranger?"

"Heaven forbid," I said. "I better start answering all calls in a terse 'Fischer,' at least until I know who's calling. 'Arnie Fischer, intrepid reporter' would be a little over the top. Right?" I know I sounded hopeful.

Zellie smiled. "Just a smidgen."

***

Sterling sat at his desk the morning after his visit to the bar. He tried to conduct business, but he couldn't stop thinking about Sophia. She possessed outer worldly beauty without question, but her accompanying intelligence had surprised him. He looked down at the phone number she'd scrawled on a piece of paper. A couple of journalists she'd claimed could do a favorable feature story on him and his business. He wasn't so sure about that. But he could use some good publicity, in view of Goldback & Sterling's recent venture into the annuity business. That business couldn't make a profit without the public knowing it existed. Sophia had given him a blank look when he told her what he did for a living. She'd never heard of him or G&S, much less its subsidiary. He recalled that her eyes lit up when he mentioned wealth management. Another gold digger, he thought. But she'd turned him down flat on his request for her phone number.

He fingered the scrap of paper, and wondered if the two reporters she'd mentioned were legit. He had raised the issue, not her, so that added a measure of credibility. She'd done nothing other than tell him of her lack of familiarity with Goldback & Sterling. He'd told her that he had publicity people who he guessed weren't very good if no one knew about his business. He couldn't recall the rest, but he remembered saying something unflattering about the media, and she'd gotten mad and said she knew some people in the business who were very honorable. He'd asked her for their names, and she'd told him, and given him their contact information. She wouldn't give him her own number and had departed in a huff.

Sterling decided to call. No harm in talking to the reporters off the record. And at least part of him, heck maybe most of him, thought calling them might lead him back to Sophia. And he very much wanted to spend the night with Sophia.

***

My phone chirped, and I looked at the caller ID. Private caller. I almost never answer those, but this time I decided to. I'd earlier received a call from Pradeep's administrative assistant that Bertrand Sterling had contacted the Clarion office to verify Zellie and my status there, and as promised, they'd affirmed it. So I expected my private caller was none other than the man himself.

"Fischer," I barked.

The caller identified himself as Bertrand Sterling, of Goldback & Sterling, and expressed his understanding from our mutual friend Sophia that I was a feature reporter for the Clarion. I smiled inwardly at his characterization of "Sophia" as his friend, but listened without comment. He requested that my colleague and I meet him at his office the following day to discuss our doing a feature article on his company.

"We don't write articles on request," I said.

Sterling hastened to tell me he didn't mean that, but that he thought his business might be an interesting subject for our readers. He added that he'd make it worth our while.

"I hope that wasn't an offer of money, Mr. Sterling. We do not countenance financial incentives."

Zellie was watching me and could only hear my side of the conversation, but she was almost beside herself with mirth. I looked away to avoid cracking up along with her.

"No, no," Sterling said, pulling me back to the conversation. "I just meant we could talk over a nice lunch, say at Cardamom. My treat."

Cardamom was a chic and very expensive bistro in Rumson, a few towns over from Middletown.

"Okay," I said, putting as much reluctance into my voice as I could muster. "We have to eat, and no harm listening to you telling us all about the interesting…" I sighed "… finance business."

I disconnected, and Zellie greeted me by clapping.

"A wonderful performance, and I thought Sasha was the actress. You have acting chops yourself."

She turned up her nose in affected snootiness. "We do not countenance, shall we not deign to say the word, freaking bribery?" And she started laughing again, as I took a bow.

"We're getting a free lunch, and we have him right where we want him," I said.

"You got Sterling to beg for an interview. You learn well, grasshopper."

"I acknowledge the wisdom of the maestro," I replied.

"We need to prepare for the meeting," Zellie said, shifting to all business mode.

"It's not even the interview," I replied. "It's just a luncheon to discuss whether we even want to do a story."

"I know." And we must prepare for the actual interviews, if and when they occur." She eyed me with suspicion. "We can't just wing it."

I acted hurt that she would ever consider that I'd do any such thing, but we both knew preparation wasn't my strong suit.

Zellie didn't seem to notice my defensiveness, plunging ahead with her plan for the lunch meeting.

"We should continue to show reluctance, at least for a short while. And we need to establish the ground rules right away. Access to his senior staff, ability to interview anyone at all within the organization. And no publicists. Involvement by his paid mouthpieces is an absolute deal breaker. We should tell him we'll walk out if that's a condition."

"What's wrong with publicists? You were one."

"Any good publicity agent would want to write the story him or herself in the most favorable way possible to the client, under our bylines."

"I get that," I said. "But why do we care? Our aim is to get access to Sterling and people within his organization. The story itself doesn't matter."

"Two reasons that I can think of offhand. One, we promised Pradeep a real story, with luck, a scoop to justify the huge favor he's doing for us. Two, if Sterling involves a publicist, he or she will want to control access to the employees to only those with a favorable impression of the company. We want to avoid as many limitations as possible. There are other reasons, but those will do."

I held up my hands in surrender, but couldn't resist saying one more thing.

"Boy, you hate publicists."

"Not true. I respect them. And I love them when they're on my side. It's only the adversaries that I know enough to address with care."

***

We met Sterling the next day for lunch at Cardamom. We knew what he looked like from his picture on the company website, but we pretended otherwise. We were sure he did not know us by sight. Sterling had evidenced no recognition of our names, and we'd decided to not assume aliases.

Upon our entry to the restaurant, we consulted with the hostess, who pointed to a man sitting alone at a table near the front. We'd seen him already, and studied his body language before he realized our presence.

An impatient man, I surmised, accustomed to people jumping at his command, with little tolerance for tardiness. He glanced at his watch several times, and his chest heaved in a clear sigh at the temerity of the two journalists keeping him waiting for all of six minutes.

As we approached his table, he rose with his hand extended. He gave me a firm handshake and turned to Zellie, who I could tell was afraid he'd try to kiss her hand. Instead, he gave her a firm handshake, and we sat down.

He turned to the waiter who'd noiselessly appeared at this side, and ordered a Black Label on the rocks for himself. He turned to us with a questioning expression, and we both demurred.

"Are you sure? I'm buying. And I don't trust people who won't drink with me."

"I think mutual suspicion is more exciting," Zellie responded with a flirtatious flick of her hair.

Sterling leaned in Zellie's direction. "No question about it." He waved the waiter away.

Having provided Sterling with another attractive reason to work with us, we listened to Sterling's pitch for a feature article over a delicious lunch. As Zellie expected, when we showed interest in taking the project on, Sterling tried to impose conditions, including the involvement of his publicity team. We shot that idea down immediately with the explanation that anything interfering with our creative process was unacceptable to us as serious journalists, and that our editor would not permit any such meddling. But what really convinced him was Zellie pointing out the questionable publicity value of even a very favorable feature if it read like a publicist's statement.

"No one would believe it, trust me," she said.

"You told me not to trust you," Sterling said, sporting a broad smile.

"I did, and don't," she replied. "But you know I'm right about this."

Sterling nodded. "I've read many publicist statements. They sound like the hedging of a lawyer defending a client he doesn't believe."

I glanced at Zellie and hoped I'd silently conveyed "don't say it, don't say it, swallow your pride on this one." Because I was certain Zellie's publicity statements read like Sinatra's music sounded.

To my relief, Zellie just smiled.

As predicted, Sterling also wanted to limit our access to only certain employees, and expressed the need for client privacy. At our protest, Sterling gave in on the access issue, and we agreed to only access client information with names and personal information redacted.

At the end of the luncheon, I told Sterling we'd discuss the feature with our editor, but that I expected to secure his approval.

"The next communication from us will be a request for information, and a list of employees we will want to interview," Zellie added, as she picked up her pocketbook and prepared to leave.

"I hope to speak to you earlier than that," Sterling said, looking straight at Zellie, as if I were no longer standing there.

"Oh, that won't happen," Zellie said, and we left the restaurant.

***

"Well played, flirting with him in the beginning, and shooting him down at the end," I said as we walked to the car.

"Oh, I know his type. He's mostly after Sasha, but giving the wolf another proverbial sheep to hunt never hurts. It gives him even more reason to cooperate with us."

We returned to the office to plot our strategy. Almost the moment we pulled into the parking lot, Sasha trotted out of her boutique and followed us into our front entrance.

"How did it go?" she pressed.

"Whoa," Zellie said, hands up in defensive posture.

"I assume you were waiting for us to get back. Were you looking out the window, watching?"

"Maybe," Sasha replied. "Okay, yes. Business was slow, so I hung out near the door to wait for you for the last half-hour or so. But I'm dying to hear what happened."

"And you're entitled to hear it, given the help you gave us." Zellie said. "Why don't you go into the conference room and sit down? Would you like a cup of coffee or tea?"

"No, thank you. I need to get back to the shop. But take your time getting settled. I didn't mean to ambush you like that."

Zellie put her pocketbook on the conference room table, and I dropped the fake file I had carried to lunch, and we filled Sasha in on the day's events.

"He didn't mention you at all," Zellie assured her when she inquired. "He did when he first called, though, using you as a reference. But I doubt he's forgotten you," she added.

"He's not as creepy as some guys who I've had to deal with in the past," Sasha said. "He's one of those guys who lives for the chase. He thinks his money can buy anything and anyone."

"He hit on Zellie right in front of me," I said.

"That's the guy I met." She rose, gave her thanks for the update and walked out.

CHAPTER TWELVE

"Who should we interview first?" I asked after Sasha left.

Zellie pondered for a moment. "Let's start with a few of the lower-paid workers. We can get their view of what's going on, and follow up with the official story later. That might give us a baseline to better target our inquiries of the senior staff."

I nodded. "That's where I started. In the corporate version of steerage. I'd add something to that, however. We should pick employees with at least a few years' experience at the company. The newest ones are still drinking the Kool-Aid doled out by management. Sucking up to your bosses at least in the first few years is an integral part of getting ahead in business, and a great American tradition."

Zellie looked at me with a curious expression. "Is that what you did?"

"Yes ma'am." I replied. "I'm very patriotic."

Zellie smirked. "And I thought you rose through the ranks from hard work and financial acumen."

"That too."

"Okay. That's where we'll start as soon as we get the employee list and contact information from Sterling. Or rather, from his 'girl,' as he put it, the misogynistic creep."

"What a weasel," I agreed. "Hey, let's add a newbie to the interview list."

"I thought you said...."

"I know," I interrupted. "But maybe they give the new employees a sales pitch to give in the new annuity business that the veterans don't receive."

"Good thinking."

I started to ask when to expect the information from Sterling, when my phone dinged. I took a glance and proffered it to Zellie. An email from someone named Lois at Goldback & Sterling, with an attachment.

"Quick," I said. "He wants that feature."

"He wants a glowing one," Zellie said. "And we'd better give every sign that he will get one, or he'll cut off our investigation before it gets started."

"True," I said, as I opened the email attachment. "Good news. It's not a virus. It would be nice to print this out, rather than look at it on my phone. When are the cable people coming to get wi-fi in here?"

Zellie looked at her watch. "Today. I'd forgotten all about it. Somewhere between 3:00 and 5:00 pm."

***

Sterling examined the stack of papers on his desk. Examining the first file folder, he paused. The annuity business. He needed to talk to his marketing people to see how much business they'd generated, and to Cindy Diamond about the actuarial figures she'd compiled. Also, he would speak to the new employee, Ruby Love. She'd hinted about her willingness to do almost anything to get ahead, and he had a special project for her. He hesitated for a moment. He'd have to figure out a way to sample that delicious bowl of fruit. So many gorgeous women, so little time. Sterling began humming the Sean Kingston song, "Beautiful Girls," before pressing the intercom button for Lois.

"Tell Cindy Diamond to report to this office," he barked.

"You mean 'please call Ms. Diamond and request her presence at her earliest convenience,' I assume?"

"Yes, yes, all that. Just do it, Lois," he said. "Please," he added with poor grace.

"Very well, sir. I will contact her using the very device you used to reach me."

"One of these days, Lois...." he started, but she'd already hung up.

***

"You asked to see me, sir?" Cindy inquired. She felt the usual discomfort of waiting while Sterling looked up and down at her, positively leering. Cindy felt a compelling desire to punch him in the mouth. But she needed the job, although not for the obvious reason. Her other employer wanted her in the exact job she held, and pleasing that employer was her main objective. So, she'd put up with Sterling's crap, at least in the short run.

"Did you bring the actuarial report for the annuity business?" Sterling asked Cindy's breasts. At least that's where he looked when he posed the question.

Cindy ignored the direction of his gaze, telling herself that having Sterling preoccupied with her curves made him more vulnerable.

"Right here," she answered, in as perky a voice as she could muster.

"Good, sit down and tell me how the more purchasers of these annuities we have, the more money we make."

"But sir, the actuarial data..."

"Are you deaf? Did you hear my question?"

"I did," Cindy responded, her temper rising to a dangerous level. She had to control it. Getting fired, even by a cockroach like Sterling, was not an option.

"Then give me an answer."

Cindy knew she couldn't tell him that the actuarial data he'd requested, and the number of purchasers, were different measures of profitability. Cindy gave the only possible answer.

"Yes. More purchasers, more money."

"Good, thank you. Leave that file here and go back to your office."

Completely flummoxed by Sterling's bizarre behavior, Cindy rose to her feet, pivoted, and departed. She felt his eyes on her backside all the way to the door.

***

"Let's interview this guy first," Zellie said, pointing to a name.

I peered at the screen. "Roger Danish. Why him? And his name and the cinnamon odor around here make me want a pastry."

"Me too," Zellie said with a laugh. "Three reasons. He's a relatively new employee, he is low on the totem pole, but his job description puts him at the center of the firm's marketing effort."

"Exactly what we want."

"Yes." Zellie switched her screen back to the list of questions. "These should do fine to start," she said. "And the questions will lead to others, and we can drill down to a clear picture."

"Okay, let's do it." I picked up my phone and made the arrangements. "Nine o'clock tomorrow morning in a conference room at G&S."

At that moment, a buzzer sounded, signifying someone's entry into the office.

Zellie rose and looked out at the front foyer.

"It's the cable, um, person," she said. "Good timing. We can get that done and get some dinner."

The cable person was a woman built like a fireplug. She had a tool belt on, and a coil of cable sprung out of one pocket. She wore a sunny smile, and I liked her on sight. Flashing an ID evidencing her employment by the cable company, she surveyed the office.

We discussed the location of each outlet, which turned out to be unnecessary.

"This place is pre-wired," she said after eyeballing the various rooms. "Super easy to install. I'll finish this in a jiffy." And with that, she busied herself setting up our cable internet.

"You guys want TV, too?"

"No TV," I said, and Zellie nodded. Television at home, not at the office. A ballgame or an old movie was our sole use of television.

***

Upon our arrival the next day at Goldback & Sterling, a good-looking fifty something woman named Lois Carver ushered us into a conference room. Ms. Carver exuded competence. After inquiring whether everything met our expectations and was satisfactory for our interviews, she departed.

I glanced at Zellie, and her eyes mirrored my thought. This was the woman who sent the e-mail, the one Sterling referred to as "his girl."

"What a creep," I muttered.

Zellie did not respond, instead rose and extended her hand. I looked over my shoulder to the sight of a stocky man sporting wire-rimmed glasses and a wide, toothy smile. He looked about twenty to twenty-five years old. He also had his hand extended. I rose, and we shook. He quickly moved to do the same with Zellie.

"Roger DAH - nish," he said.

"Good morning, Mr. Danish," I said, attempting to emphasize properly the first syllable of his name.

"My name is Arnie Fischer, and this is my colleague, Zellie Morgan. Thanks for coming to talk to us today."

"As if I had a choice," he said, with no change to that broad smile.

"Do you have a problem talking to us?" Zellie asked.

"No, I don't. But if I'm in here, I'm not selling anything. No sales, no income. The life of someone making a living solely on commissions. But I do pretty well," he concluded.

"Business is good?" I inquired.

"The best I've experienced. The company is spending serious dough on advertising the new annuity business."

Lucky break, I thought. No need to guide the conversation to the issue. Roger raised it himself.

"How do you know who to sell to?" Zellie asked. "Do you call people randomly and give a sales pitch?"

Roger laughed. "You can relax. We are not the people calling you at dinnertime. Absolutely no robo-calling. I promise. No, the calls come to us. Each of us in the sales and marketing department sit in a desolate, undecorated cubicle containing nothing but a chair and an old-fashioned wired telephone. We answer calls all day long. The night crew answers them after seven pm. It's a round the clock and round the world operation."

"You have international customers?" I asked in some surprise.

"Sure we do. And we like to call them clients, not customers. Don't ask me why, orders from the top. The advertising is on the old-style airwaves..." he eyed us for a moment... "um, television, radio, newspapers, things like that. But our primary effort is on social media." He paused again.

Zellie jumped in. "We may be dinosaurs, but we do understand."

Roger smiled. "Caught me being snarky. I better control that impulse. Almost all of our current and future clients are over fifty. Not that I mean that's old. I mean, um, well....I'm just getting in deeper and deeper trouble here, aren't I?"

"Yup," I said. "But no worries, we're writing it all down. Every single word is pure gold. It will make great copy for our article, won't it Zellie?"

Suppressing a smirk, Zellie nodded vigorously and pointed to her notepad. "It's all right here."

"No, hey guys, please don't write that," Roger pleaded, craning his head to read Zellie's notes upside down.

"I don't know," I hedged, enjoying every second of his discomfort.

"No, please. I could lose my job over that."

"You might persuade us to forget you ever said it," Zellie started. "But we're journalists. We need to write something. What can you tell us that might not be the standard company line?"

"Off the record?"

"Sure. If you give us a juicy avenue to explore that doesn't involve you, we'll have no reason to write about you at all."

"Other than as a very articulate salesman for the company's products who loves his job, and who only told us what management wants us to hear," I added.

"Um, that sounds good. I think I have something."

"What do you have?" Zellie inquired.

Roger leaned forward conspiratorially. "There's a script they give you to say to the prospects, and you get fired if you deviate at all." Roger sat back and folded his arms.

"That's it?" I said it incredulously and looked at Zellie. "We have all we need from him. Let's just write about his disdain for elderly clients."

Zellie nodded. "You can go, Mr. Danish. Thank you." We stood up.

"Wait, wait, I can give you the script."

"We have the script. It's part of the prospectus. You've offered us nothing we don't already know, other than employees getting fired for going off script. That's strict, but not uncommon in the industry. Lawyers write the prospectus, to make sure the company complies with its disclosure obligations under state and Federal law."

"What if I know something not necessarily in the script?"

We sat down. "Out with it," I said.

"They tell us something not in the script."

"What is it?"

Roger fidgeted in his seat. "It's just, well, I don't think they mean it the way it will sound. I don't want you to get the wrong impression or anything. I think the product is good, or I'd quit right away. I can only sell what I believe in, and I'm all in on what we're selling."

"What, already? Stop stalling." I was losing my patience.

Zellie looked more serene. "It's okay, Roger," she said. "We understand you're acting with the best intentions. But if we're going to write an article, we'll need something to write. You understand that, right?"

Roger looked grateful for Zellie's kind words. Another example of honey trumping vinegar.

"They tell us to push harder when the prospective client is elderly." he blurted. "But they only tell us that because those folks have a more urgent need for the annuity," he added, with evident distress.

"Did they define 'elderly' for you?" Zellie asked.

"Older than you."

Zellie smiled. "Good to know I'm not considered elderly at my advanced age."

"No ma'am. You're hot for an older woman."

"Better stop now," I warned. "You're treading on thin ice."

"I just meant, um, it was a compliment."

"It's okay," Zellie said. "I took it that way. Is there anything else you can tell us?"

"I think I've told you more than I intended already."

We shook hands and headed out.

CHAPTER THIRTEEN

"Who's next on the hit list?" I asked Zellie as we walked to the car.

"How about Barbara Newton?"

"Who's that? I don't remember her name."

"The sales supervisor. I think it's a good idea after Roger's revelation."

"You remember her name from the list?"

"Yes, but only because I sifted through that department with particular attention."

"Great memory for an old lady," I teased.

"Watch it, buster. And I'm a hot old lady, according to Roger."

"I sort of liked the little miscreant," I said.

"Me too. He's charming in a Barney Fife kind of way."

"So, we follow up on his comments about the elderly with his supervisor."

"That's the idea. But with a light touch. We don't want to throw Barney, I mean Roger, under the bus."

"Let's break for lunch, then we can tackle Ms. Newton."

"Suits me. Where to?"

"How about Jimmy's?"

We ate a good lunch at a local eatery known for salads, wraps and burgers. In case you are wondering, the salads and wraps were for Zellie. I had a burger. While we ate, we figured out a game plan for Ms. Newton, and I called G&S to set up an interview for after lunch.

* * *

Ms. Newton was a statuesque bottle blonde with sharp features, a steady jaw, steely blue eyes and a demeanor reminiscent of Uma Thurman in Kill Bill. In short, not a woman to mess with.

She shook hands with us with an iron grip, and positioned herself in a chair facing us, leaning forward in a semi-aggressive position. Given her height, it was an impressive effort at power placement, as she towered over us without standing.

Zellie and I both had familiarity from our prior jobs with people like Ms. Newton. I refused to let her intimidate me, and I looked over at Zellie, who had set a firm jaw of her own, prepared to do battle.

I expected Zellie to start with something formal, like 'state your name,' but she asked politely if Ms. Newcastle had any tips for us in figuring out the corporate structure and the just- launched annuity business she'd heard so much about.

Ms. Newton, who'd appeared prepared for an interrogation by the evil scourge of journalism, sat back in her chair.

"That I can do," she said, her guard still up, but with some dents in her armor. "I assume you've received the organization chart?"

We nodded.

"Have you seen the prospectus for the annuity business?"

We nodded again.

"Okay. Forget them."

"Huh?" escaped from my mouth.

Ms. Newton laughed. "I don't mean that literally, but those are very dry, fixed representations of the business, which is quite organic."

"What do you mean?" Zellie asked.

"A corporate chart is a nice outline of the different positions within an organization. But it will never show the interplay of individuals within a dynamic organization like G&S. In the same way, a prospectus for a financial product is not prose, it's a legal document, written by attorneys."

She paused, waiting for us to give her an obligatory cringe at the mention of lawyers. Zellie remained stone-faced. I formed an expression that I hoped sufficed, and she seemed satisfied.

"That said," she continued. "The sales staff must adhere to the script. Management is very particular about that, and we fire anyone who deviates."

"So, what's the interesting part not in the prospectus?" I asked, growing more and more confused. I looked over at Zellie, who wore a befuddled expression.

"You asked for tips on figuring it out. All I meant was that you should forget anything relating to corporate structure or the annuity business. That's boring stuff. My understanding is that you're writing a feature story about G&S."

We nodded, and she continued. "Your readers will hate you forever if you give them corporate gobbly-gook. There's no story in that."

"What should we write about?"

"The employees, and their lives outside of this place."

She'd skillfully maneuvered us away from business-related questions. It would be tough at this point to press her about the clientele purchasing annuities, or anything about it.

Zellie seemed undeterred. "Fair enough," she said. "Tell us all about yourself and your life outside of this place."

If Zellie's acceptance of her invitation disconcerted Ms. Newton, she gave no visible sign. She paused, however, to take a sip of water from the bottle in front of her.

"If you think it's interesting enough for your article, which I understand is about G&S, okay. I'll tell you the tale of Newton." She waited for an affirmation that we thought her early life was pertinent to our story.

Zellie appeared to enjoy the game Ms. Newton intended to play, and to my eye wanted to call Ms. Newton's bluff about having a better story to tell, and nodded encouragement.

"Go ahead," I agreed. "It's a great idea. The fascinating personal histories of the people who are the building blocks of the G&S mystique."

I couldn't believe my babble, but Ms. Newton seemed to buy it.

"I was born on a ranch in West Texas," she started. "My daddy was a ranch hand, and so were my two older brothers. My mother worked in the kitchen. I'm the first in my family to graduate from college, and the first to have what you folks would call a white- collar job.

"Not that there's anything at all wrong with working on a ranch. You work outdoors, and enjoy the fresh air, and even the smell of cow manure. It's good, honest work." She glared at us for a moment, as if daring us to question her characterization.

"Of course it is," Zellie said, and I nodded.

Appearing mollified, she continued.

"I wandered from job to job after I graduated from college, and was just about to head back to Texas to work on the ranch, when I met Morris Goldback."

"I say I met him, but that's fudging the truth. I served him a martini at The Louvre," she said, naming a ritzy local restaurant. I was a cocktail waitress, and he was sitting alone at a table in the bar. I had no idea who he was. I exchanged a few polite words with him, and he looked me over in a terribly impolite way, I recall. But his words were anything but rude. Gentler than I expected. You get a lot of leering drunks in restaurant bars, and I was prepared for that. But I didn't expect him to ask me to sit down.

"I told him management prohibited sitting with customers, and he made a gesture toward the front of the restaurant. The owner hurried over and asked what he could do for Mr. Goldback. That was the first time I heard his name, and it still meant nothing to me, but I figured he was someone important. The owner told me to sit down, and I did, even though I didn't like where this was going. I was a pretty, young thing back then, and unsophisticated, but I suspected this Mr. Goldback was hitting on me."

She paused. I knew that Ms. Newcastle was beautiful back then. She was very good looking now, and with the grace and quiet beauty that only comes with age. There was no doubt in my mind that the old coot was trying to get into her pants. But I was wrong.

"He was a perfect gentleman," she continued. "And for some strange reason, after a nice conversation with him, he offered me a job in the securities business he owned.

"I couldn't believe it. I was a business major in college, had good grades, and I knew my way around finance, but only from books. I couldn't even get an internship. I started here as a twenty-five-year-old clerk-typist and worked my way up the ranks. And it wouldn't have happened without Morris Goldback, a wonderful man."

"That's a great story," I said, "I'm sure we can use it in our feature."

"Rags to Riches, right? You journalists love a story like that."

"We do," Zellie intoned. "Is it true?"

Ms. Newton laughed. "Sharp, aren't you? Most of it is true. I came from West Texas, but my father was a country doctor, and my mom was a nurse. My two brothers are in fact ranch hands. I grew up in a middle-class family, and not only went to college, but have an MBA from the University of Texas. I started as a clerk-typist at G&S, and none other than Morris Goldback discovered me. No question, he was my mentor, and is still my friend."

"Thanks for telling us the truth," Zellie said.

"Oh, you would have figured it out anyway, and it was a fun story to tell. I promised you something interesting, didn't I?"

"And you delivered," I said. "You have a high opinion of Morris Goldback. What do you think of his partner?"

Ms. Newton tried to keep a straight face, but I'd scored a hit. She made a quick recovery.

"He took over when Morris retired and has built a huge conglomerate."

"Do you like him?" Zellie asked.

"I'm not as close to him as I was to Morris, but he's okay."

A tepid response, but Zellie let it go. She turned to me. "Do you have any more questions?"

I read Zellie's expression. We were done here. We'd get other information elsewhere.

"No," I said, rising and extending my hand. "Thank you for your time, Ms. Newton."

****

"I'm not sure I see any value in that interview," I said as we walked to the car.

"Not much," Zellie admitted. "If I were to sum it up, I say tight-lipped about the business. Goldback good, Sterling, not so much."

"She tried to hide it, but she doesn't like Sterling at all," I affirmed.

"I don't think we'll figure this thing out just by doing interviews."

"No. They're helpful, but even if they tell the truth, no one is going to just fall on their sword and admit that they're part of a massive fraud. We need something else. And I have a germ of an idea that might move things along."

"What is it?" Zellie asked.

"Let's let it percolate a while."

"Do you think Ms.Newton was wise to our true purpose?"

"Hard to say. But it sure looked like it. She shut down business questions right away and even reminded us of the more benign nature of our article. Either someone prepped her on what to say, or she's remarkably savvy."

"I'd choose savvy," I said.

"I agree. She likes the verbal sparring, for sure."

I gave Zellie a light punch on her arm. "So do you."

"Guilty as charged," Zellie said, with a laugh.

"Where to?"

"The office, I think. We need to prepare for our next interviews."

"Who's up next?" I asked as I drove.

Zellie looked thoughtful. Let's talk to the head of security," she said.

Her choice surprised me, and I said so.

"We need to talk to someone with a different perspective. If we talk to senior management, we'll just get the same tired blather. We'll interview them anyway, but the security chief will know where all the bodies are buried."

"But he won't tell us anything, either. And for the record, let's not talk about bodies."

"Fair enough," Zellie said with a laugh. "No bodies. And I think you're right that…," she looked at a name in her folder…, "Kyle Fortz, will be tight-lipped. But his reactions to direct questions might give us some clues regarding the threats he perceives."

"Worth a shot," I said, although I doubted we'd get anything from a guy named Fortz. I suspected he'd already set up defensive positions to guard against attacks by land or sea, or nosy reporters.

We returned to the office, newly outfitted with a secure wi-fi network. Ignoring our separate offices, which had already become a habit, we sat down at the conference table. Zellie called to set up the afternoon interview with Kyle Fortz, and we mapped out a line of attack, so to speak.

"How do we breach this guy's defenses," I mused.

I know Zellie would have hit me on the arm if we'd been sitting next to each other, but I was safely ensconced across from her, so she satisfied herself with a grimace.

"We aren't creating a battle plan here, General Patton. We'll ask some questions and see how he responds. I think we should be very direct. Military people like that."

"Now you're treating this like a military campaign," I accused.

"Well, his bio says he's a former U.S. Marine," she admitted, "so maybe this is battle plan-ish."

"Plan-ish?"

"You know what I mean."

I did. And I knew better than to congratulate myself verbally for being right in the first place.

CHAPTER FOURTEEN

Kyle Fortz looked like one. He stood a ramrod straight six feet six inches, had a buzz cut dome, steely eyes and an iron grip handshake. I think my grip met his standards, because he didn't seem to treat me like an out of shape couch potato. Still, my hand hurt, but I tried not to show it.

Zellie got away with a milder handshake, but from the way she acted, I think her hand smarted a little, too. Fortz' demeanor was all business, and the way he glanced at the chronograph watch on his wrist, he had little patience for our questions. I ignored his impatience and charged ahead.

"State your name," I said, brusquely. His reaction was priceless.

"Master Sergeant Kyle Wilmer Fortz, sir, Serial Number... huh, wait a minute. You just asked my name, which you knew already. It's Kyle Fortz, Chief of Security, Goldback and Sterling.

"Just the formal first question, Mr. Fortz, or should I say Master Sergeant Fortz? When did you leave the Marine Corps?"

"Two years ago, sir. And it's Mr. Fortz now."

"As the head of security, you must know most of the people working here, is that right?"

"Yes, sir. It's a requirement of the job."

"That includes management?" Zellie asked.

"Yes, ma'am. I know all the senior staff."

"What can you tell us about them?"

Fortz shifted in his chair. "I was told to cooperate, but I have limits. I won't jeopardize operational security."

I assumed this was just military talk. Still, it suggested something other than making sure no one blew up the place. It did not represent a defensive approach at all, rather it it heralded an aggressive offense of some sort. That may just be Fortz' manner of protecting the place, as in "the best defense is a good offense," but somehow I didn't think so. Fortz didn't seem like a guy who'd be a passive mall cop type. He'd chafe under what amounted to a desk job. When he referred to operational security, it activated my internal radar. I had to pursue it, but gently. He'd clam up in an instant if either of us deviated from questions related to the nice, touchy-feely feature article we promised to write.

"We don't expect it," I said. "That's your job. Security. So I guess you mostly sit at a security station watching video feeds of people coming and going from this place?"

I might as well have placed a stick of dynamite under his butt. Suggesting this guy was passive was like telling a sniper he was good at watching people.

Fortz flashed what must be a prodigious temper. "I don't sit at a desk looking at monitors. I have people who do that. I'm the head of security for a major financial firm."

"Understood," Zellie said in a placating voice. Her silk to my denim, I suppose. "My partner didn't mean to suggest otherwise. We're just trying to figure out what your duties are, and to get some insight regarding the people here, employees whom you know better than anyone. Mr. Fischer asked inartfully, that's all." She cast a fake chastising look at me for emphasis.

Fortz seemed mollified, but offered little more. "We have a director of employee relations, who can describe everyone's duties. He deals directly with all of us."

He gave a slight wave of his hand. "I'm just a retired military guy," he said in mock self-deprecation.

Just a simple retired Marine sergeant in a second career my ass, I thought, but tried to keep my posture and face neutral. Zellie and I would have to talk about this later. This guy warranted a serious background check.

Zellie held her pen poised. "What's his name?"

"Quentin Stanhope."

Fortz stood, signifying that the interview was over. I hadn't completed my questioning, but Zellie stood, so I rose and extended my hand.

"Thank you, Mr. Fortz."

***

"He wouldn't have told us anything more." Zellie said. "Amazing he even spoke to us."

"I know. He's a G. Gordon Liddy type."

"Liddy refused to testify at all, as I recall."

"Watergate was loads of fun," I said only half facetiously. "But what do we do with this guy?"

"Check his background with a fine-toothed comb. A guy like him isn't sitting at a desk."

We returned to the office and checked into Master Sergeant Fortz' military and civilian records. The first was harder than the last. Military records aren't available to the public, but Zellie is resourceful. I suggested calling Ted, who has his mysterious ways of obtaining information, but Zellie shrugged me off.

"I can handle this one," she said.

And she could. It didn't take her long, either.

"Look at this," she said about a half-hour later. She twirled her laptop around.

I pushed aside the important papers in front of me. Okay, the local newspaper.

"Looks like Sergeant Fortz had an impeccable, even distinguished, military record. Even decorated for bravery in Afghanistan."

"Yes, yes," Zellie said impatiently, "It looks like that. But check this out." Zellie scrolled down and pointed.

"Whoa. Not so impeccable."

"No."

Although Sergeant Fortz retired from the Marine Corps with an honorable discharge, his departure occurred just a few months after an event described only in cloudy terms as financial improprieties. The record didn't use those exact terms, but it sure seemed to mean that.

"I wonder what happened?" I mused after a brief silence.

"I don't know, but the result was Sergeant Fortz leaving the service after an otherwise unblemished military career."

"I guess we should look into it, but I'm not sure how it connects to the case. I'd hate to waste time and energy running down one employee's mistake. Especially one that didn't result in a prosecution of any kind."

"It might show that Goldback and Sterling have a propensity to hire people with shady financial histories to make it easier to recruit them for their current scheme."

"If there is one. It's an important position, too. But I agree, we should wait," Zellie added. "We should file it away for now and follow up on it later if needed."

"What about his post-military background. Anything interesting after he left the Marine Corps?"

"Nothing."

"Nothing interesting?"

"I mean nothing. The guy is a ghost. Well, maybe not a ghost. He was born in Norfolk, Virginia, the only child of a factory worker and a seamstress, attended public school in Norfolk, then college at William & Mary on a scholarship. He joined the Marine Corps right out of college, and worked his way up from enlisted man to Master Sergeant. That alone is impressive. But I told you already about his military record. It is his life after the military that is cloudy. No job that I could find prior to Goldback and Sterling. A gap of over two years."

"He told us that," I pointed out.

"He told us he left the Marine Corps two years ago," Zellie said, after scrolling back to her interview notes.

"So? His statement checks out."

"Yes, but what did he do for the two years after the military discharged him? There's no mention of it anywhere. No other job, no internet presence of any kind."

"It's only two years. You can't track everyone for that short a period. I doubt you could track my last two years with any kind of ease."

Zellie sighed, entered a few keystrokes, and turned her laptop around again.

I looked at a long list of things about me, including my name, address, phone number, job history, the A to Z Agency, and things I didn't even remember about myself. And I'm not on Facebook, Instagram, Twitter or any other social media platform.

"Okay, you made your point. So the same search shows nothing about Kyle Fortz?"

"There are a few things up to joining the military, but he's been completely off the grid since his discharge."

"We need to find out what he did for those two years. I suppose he could have just lived quietly off his military pension," I speculated.

"Maybe. It could be something innocent. But does he strike you as a guy who does that?"

"No. Maybe he was sick."

"I guess that's possible. He sure looks the picture of health. But there's plenty of invisible illness in this world."

"True enough. Let's see what we can find out."

"Shall we start in on the executive staff?" I asked.

Zellie looked down at the employee list. "That would be Justin McCoy, a senior vice president, with the company for fifteen years; Chief Financial Officer Tucker Ford, sixteen years; and Bertrand Sterling, the great man himself. All men in the most senior positions."

"Not a single woman in the group?" I asked, with a fair measure of incredulity.

"Well, there are three, but I wouldn't call them positions of power, except maybe one."

"Which one?"

"Executive Administrative Assistant Lois Carver, twenty years."

I nodded. "I bet she knows everything about G&S, and rules the executive suite with an iron fist."

I knew people like Lois at my prior employer and had befriended all of them. Woe to those who failed to give them proper deference.

"Who are the other two?"

Zellie looked at the list. "Cindy Diamond, senior financial analyst, whose picture you drooled on, with the company for a month; and Ruby Love, junior financial analyst, with the company for less than a week."

I rubbed my chin, leaned forward to look at imaginary notes in front of me, and steepled my fingers, as if deep in thought.

Zellie watched my performance with amusement. "You're having a tough time figuring out who to interview next, aren't you? I'll help you out. It's between a stodgy old man, and a woman who looks like Miss America."

"When you put it that way, I guess..."

Zellie interrupted. "You'll get your chance, don't worry. But shouldn't we talk to this guy next?" She pointed to a name on the list, and I leaned over to look.

"Harry Nickles? Who's he?"

"The chief custodian," Zellie said.

"What's your theory?"

"No one has their ear to the ground like a custodian. He's no doubt visited every corner of the place, and everyone ignores him. But he sees and hears everything."

"Like the proverbial fly on the wall. A gold mine of nosiness."

"Yes."

"Set it up. The pretty accountant can wait. Duty calls."

Zellie gave me an indulgent smile and picked up her phone.

CHAPTER FIFTEEN

Zellie put the phone down. "It's all set. We'll interview Mr. Nickles in two hours."

I looked at my watch. "Why so late?"

"He wanted to make sure the building was in order before he thought he'd have enough time to talk to us."

"Dedicated," I observed.

"Yes, I suppose so. And did it occur to you that his name is yet another name with a financial connotation?"

"Never crossed my mind. That's just small change. These people are after the big score."

"Still, he could be in on it, whatever 'it' is," Zellie used the universal hand signal for quotes.

"The custodian?" I asked. "Next it will be the butler."

Zellie laughed. "You just can't trust anyone these days."

***

"What are your responsibilities here, Mr. Nickles?" I asked, giving Zellie a chance to observe him.

Harry Nickles looked to be in his forties, and had close-cropped hair and a chunky physique. His muscles bulged through a button-down blue shirt, which neither fit him nor suited his demeanor. The blue tie he wore looked like it was strangling him. They must have told him to look presentable, but he appeared uncomfortable in business attire.

"I'm chief of custodial operations, which is a fancy name for being the senior janitor. And please call me Harry. Mr. Nickles was my dad."

"Sure. Harry, I'll hazard a guess and say that you're not wearing your usual clothes."

"Nailed it, Mr. Fischer. Cleaning offices in a dress shirt and khakis would be the next thing to stupid."

"Call me Arnie. And this is Zellie," I said, gesturing to my left. "How many other custodians are there?"

"One other man, Otis Livingston. We work in eight-hour shifts. He works from six to two, and I take the two to ten." He paused, and added "I don't like getting up early, and it's nice and quiet after five or six o'clock."

Bells rang in my head. This guy is often around after most people have left. Plenty of opportunities to snoop. Better take our time approaching the issue.

"Do you clean while people are around, or after they've left?" Zellie asked.

"Both, I guess. I mean, you do the quiet stuff when people are working, and the vacuuming when they're gone."

"How do you go about it?"

"Well, you know, I empty wastebaskets, dust, pick up the messes the workers cause — and there are plenty of them, believe you me. I clean the bathrooms, wash the windows - inside only. Um, stuff like that. Cleaning. Nothing fancy."

"Do you dust the desks?"

Uh oh, Zellie's moving in for the kill.

"Yes."

"Are there ever papers on the desks?"

Nickles fidgeted, "Sometimes."

"Do you dust around the papers, or do you have to move them?"

"We're not supposed to touch any papers."

"But you hate to do a shoddy job, don't you?"

"I take pride in my work. Otis does, too."

"So, purely to do a good job, you might have accidentally touched some papers on workers' desks, is that right?"

"Yes. Just to do a good job."

"Tough not to take a glance at the papers when you move them. Did you look at any of them?"

"Maybe a glance. You won't tell anyone, will you?"

"Depends. Tell us what you saw."

***

Jennifer fingered the file in her hand and sighed. At another time, she might have acted on the information, and pulled a disappearing act. But she was in this one to the end, do or die. She hoped it was the former. The information she held was valuable, for someone without scruples. She was that kind of person once upon a time, hell, she hadn't changed at all. But this was a bigger score, one with non-monetary stakes far greater than some insider trading scam she could pull.

She sat upright and closed the folder. She had work to do. Arnie and Zellie were interviewing staff members, and it was only a matter of time before they got to her. No way they could resist an employee with such a bogus financial analyst name as Ruby Love. And she wanted to prepare to give the performance of her life.

***

Nickles fidgeted, vainly trying to ease his mental discomfort by adjusting his position on the chair.

He cleared his throat, twice. He began speaking, then stopped. Zellie and I watched his performance without comment, patiently awaiting Nickles' revelation, which I think it fair to say we both knew already. But Nickles surprised us.

"I saw a letter on Mr. Sterling's desk, and I read it," he blurted out.

"What was in it?" Zellie asked, lowering her voice to a whisper.

"It was in an envelope marked 'Hand Deliver.' It was from Mrs. Sterling. And she told him she was sick and tired of his dishonesty and cheating." Nickles scratched his head for a moment. "I think she said philandering. And she said to expect divorce papers from her lawyer."

"Was there anything else?" Zellie asked.

"There might have been a few curse words. And I might not have told you the exact words, but that was pretty much it."

"Did it say who Mrs. Sterling thought Mr. Sterling was cheating with?"

"No, it didn't say that. But everyone around here knows Mr. Sterling is a skirt-chaser."

I moved on. "Did you read any other papers?"

"On his desk? No, but um...."

"Out with it," I said.

"He keeps a bottle of Scotch in his bottom desk drawer."

"And you might have taken a swig or two, am I right?"

Nickles dropped his head and stared at the table.

"Yes."

"Does anyone know about that?"

"Otis does. He's the one who told me about it."

"Did you read anyone else's papers?"

"No." Emphatic this time.

"Because no one left them lying around, or because they didn't interest you?"

"The second one. Lots of charts and graphs and numbers. I don't like that stuff."

"You told us everyone knew about Sterling's philandering," Zellie said, reading from her notes. "Are there any other things about the office or staff that are common knowledge?"

"Um, I guess so, but I don't understand the question. Do you have something in mind?"

I took a chance. "Who's honest, who's not, who's a straight shooter, and who'd think nothing of cheating an old lady? That kind of thing."

"Oh. Um, sort of. But it's only rumor."

"What's the rumor?"

"Mr. Ford is out to get Mr. Sterling's job. And, um, other things."

"Not surprising that a Chief Financial Officer wants the big chair. Happens in almost every company," I said.

"What are the other things Mr. Ford wants from Mr. Sterling?" Zellie asked.

"His wife," Nickles said. "Word is they've been sleeping together for months."

***

"Lots to think about after that interview," I remarked as we walked hand-in-hand to the car.

"No kidding," Zellie said. "And we have a few research projects."

"Family Court records," I assume.

"Yes, for one. Let's find out if Mrs. Sterling filed for divorce."

"What's the second one?"

"I think we need a clearer picture of the Sterlings' finances."

"Isn't Sterling filthy rich?"

"We assumed so, but let's find out for sure. And let's find out if Mrs. Sterling is independently wealthy, or if she's looking for a sizable chunk of her husband's wealth."

"Good questions," I said. "I have a better one."

Zellie pulled out her omnipresent notebook. "Okay, shoot."

"Good. You're ready. Write this down."

"What should we do for dinner?"

She punched me on the arm, eliciting an "ow," and then laughter.

"How about Baskerville's," I offered.

"No, not tonight. I'm too tired to listen to waiters in deerstalker hats referring to appetizers as 'elementary' choices, and entrees as 'the game is afoot.'"

"We have some leftover pasta and garlic bread at home," she said. "The research can wait until tomorrow."

***

The next morning, back at the office, Zellie clicked a few times on her laptop, closed it and sighed.

"What's up?"

"Finding divorce records in New Jersey requires a trip to the courthouse."

"Oh. Bummer." Zellie hated visiting the Monmouth County courthouse because, well, someone kidnapped her there once.

"I'll go," I said. "You find Mrs. Sterling's financial information, and I'll check some dockets."

"Thank you, but that's not all of it."

I waited.

"Finding individual financial information online is next to impossible."

"They do it all the time in the movies."

"I'm not a hacker, Arnie. Just an honest researcher."

"I know, and I love you for that. Among other things," I added, leaning over to kiss her.

"Any ideas?" she asked.

"I have one," I said, after thinking a moment.

"Fire away."

"She may be a large shareholder of Goldback & Sterling. Over 10% ownership requires disclosure. We can check EDGAR again. That won't give us everything, but it will show her ownership share and acquisition date, and that of Bertrand Sterling. It might be useful information. Also, the SEC requires, and EDGAR will have, the G&S financial statements and will disclose corporate officers' salaries."

"Okay, you go to the courthouse, and I'll revisit EDGAR, with a different focus."

I kissed her and headed out.

***

Arriving at the now familiar parking lot in front of the combination police station and county courthouse, I parked and went through security. I'd left my gun at home, so I breezed right through. I walked to the clerk's office and sat down at the computer terminals next to the bullet-proof glass window, where the court employees sat at their desks.

I located the electronic case file, and muttered about why I had to drive to the courthouse to look at a computer screen, instead of accessing it at home. Getting over my indignation, I viewed the pending case of Sterling v. Sterling, which contained the usual stuff of judge assignment, scheduling order, and the like. Then I clicked on the entry for Complaint, which laid out Mrs. Clarabelle Danko Sterling's allegations to support her request for the great State of New Jersey to grant her a divorce from the lying, cheating, dishonest scoundrel Bertrand Sterling. The document gave a long list of women, first names only, with whom the "perpetrator" had engaged in "dalliances." Further detail included allegations of "pathological" dishonesty in all things in which he became involved, and Mrs. Sterling's severe emotional distress.

The Complaint sought a huge settlement, and alimony in an amount that exceeded the gross national product of many nations. Okay, I'm kidding about that, but the number was huge.

It looked like Sterling would lose at least half his assets and have a monthly payment obligation that could put him in serious financial jeopardy.

There was some good news for our quest for information. A docket entry reflected Judge Minder's order to both sides to submit sworn financial statements, so the Court could assess Mrs. Sterling's need for alimony, and the manner in which to divide the assets. The order required filing the statements on a day which turned out to be tomorrow. It would require another trip to the courthouse, but it would be worth it.

***

Zellie scrolled through volumes of information, including what she muttered was "numbers out the wazoo." Every company had a financial statement, and many had slimmed down versions of various funders' and venture capitalist personal financial statements. This was Arnie's world, not hers, and she rued not taking the trip to the courthouse in their latest division of labor.

She sighed, and vowed to soldier on, continuing to look at the multiplicity of Goldback & Sterling subsidiaries and affiliated companies.

She read the prospectus for GS ASAP, and it contained no sign of the individual funders of the enterprise, but referenced what appeared to be a venture capital firm, Vulture Investments, LLC. From what she'd learned from Arnie, companies were sometimes funded by what people colloquially called vulture funds, but this one didn't cloak itself in a fancy sounding name. It went all out and called itself what it undoubtedly was — a lender that invested in distressed or dying companies. That was interesting, given that G&S was aggressively pushing clients to invest their retirement savings into the business in the expectation of receiving back a lifetime annuity. The seed money for the enterprise came from Vulture Investments, which would want a significant return on its infusion of cash.

"What would happen to the cash being put into the business by the retirees? G&S would need much of it to repay Vulture. Zellie supposed that in theory, there would be a sufficient infusion of cash from the retirees to pay out annuities, and repay the lender. Zellie was no financial whiz like Arnie, but she seriously doubted it. She had no proof, but she guessed that Bertrand Sterling intended to scoop up a boatload of cash. This looked more and more like a Ponzi scheme. She couldn't wait for Arnie to come back to the office.

***

I printed out the case for docket and Judge Minder's order and headed back to the office. I knew I was better suited to reviewing the financial information in EDGAR, but Zellie was a fast learner. She'd figure it out.

I returned to the smell of something tasty baking in the oven. Zellie was busily inaugurating the kitchen with something that smelled like cinnamon. Stronger than the usual aroma pervading our office from its prior occupant.

Zellie smiled at me as I entered, and in response to my unspoken question, said "Cinnamon cookies."

"What motivated that? A fervent dislike of looking at boring spread-sheets?"

"There is that," she allowed. "But I was so excited by what I found, and you weren't back yet, I had to occupy myself somehow, and I've been meaning to try out the kitchen."

She proffered a cookie, which was soft and warm. And good. Very good.

She left the cookies to cool off on a rack, and we carried a few of the delectable morsels to the conference room.

"What did you find?"

In my experience, EDGAR provided lots of useful information, but rarely generated excitement. I had to agree with Zellie, though, when she told me. It was the first whisper of circumstantial evidence we'd found so far that Sterling was a crook. We agreed it proved nothing, but it surely was smoke. And where there's smoke....

We kicked the issue around for a while, figured out next steps, including looking further into Vulture and the individuals who controlled the firm.

I told Zellie about what the court records yielded, and we agreed to a follow-up visit.

We decided it was time to interview the senior financial analyst, and Zellie set up the appointment.

CHAPTER SIXTEEN

We had already positioned ourselves at the conference table when Cindy Diamond entered the room. She carried herself well, with an erect posture and small, purposeful steps. She was about five foot two, and had soft, blond shoulder length hair which seemed to fall magically into place. Clad in a gray skirt and white blouse–standard business attire, she sat down demurely, with a slight pivot into the chair opposite us.

"Ms. Diamond, please tell us your background," Zellie started off.

"Born in Toms River, New Jersey. Graduated from Toms River High School, B.A. from Yale University, and MBA from Wharton School of Business. Worked at various Wall Street jobs after graduation from Wharton and took a job at Goldback & Sterling about a month ago."

Her clipped tone was interesting. Almost, but not quite, rehearsed. No doubt she was accustomed to telling it that way. But still, it made me a little uneasy.

"Why did you change jobs so much?"

"Oh, everyone in this business does that. Finding the best fit. In my case, I could work closer to home with this job. So I think I'll stay for a while."

"Other than its location, what do you like about the job? And I'll add the corollary question, what do you dislike?"

"They gave me a big promotion right off the bat. Own office and everything. I was a little surprised that with my educational background, my prior employers all put me into a cubicle. I felt like I'd worked too hard to start out there."

I recoiled at that answer. Another highly educated, but inexperienced kid wanting to start at the top, before knowing anything practical. My prejudice on this point stemmed from starting in a cubicle myself with hundreds of other newbies, before rising through the ranks through hard work and perseverance.

I knew Zellie was aware of my instinctive reaction to Ms. Diamond's statement, but she gave me a telepathic warning to stay silent.

"Office aside, how is your work different at Goldback & Sterling than your previous jobs?"

"I report directly to the CEO. Bertrand Sterling," she added.

"Do you like him?" I asked.

"Um, well, he's the boss, and I report directly to him."

I'd caught her off guard, and the confident facade seemed to crumble. At least momentarily.

"You said that already. What do you think of him as a person?"

"He's brilliant, and very personable. A great salesman, and outstanding business acumen."

"But..." Zellie pressed.

"He's a little... okay... a lot too forward. Creepy even, in his interactions with the women in the office."

"Including you?"

Cindy cast a brief glance down at her torso, as if saying "look at me, what do you think?"

"Yes, including me. Not sexual assault or anything like that," she added. "But he looks me up and down, and stares unpleasantly. Very uncomfortable, but it looks like that's the price I have to pay to get ahead. Who knows, maybe I'll have his job someday."

That last bravado seemed forced. In fact, everything she'd said so far seemed part true, but contrived, except the initial reaction to whether she liked Bertrand Sterling. No question, she hated the guy. We'd have to check out her background to see how much of that was true, but I had one more question before we delved into the degree of her involvement in the annuity business.

"Have you ever used any other name?"

"Cindy Bonkowicz," she said without a flicker of hesitation.

"Maiden name?"

"Bad financial advisor name. At least I thought so. Changed it to Diamond right after getting my MBA. Sterling knows," she added. "I told him during my interview."

"What do you know about annuities?" I asked.

"A lot. Do you have a specific question?"

"It's the newest business at Goldback & Sterling, isn't it?"

"Yes, but aren't you writing a puff piece for the newspaper?"

"We call it a feature piece, but I guess people have used your term," Zellie said. "And we think our readers will want to know about the latest and greatest product from this fine company."

"Um, I guess so." She paused and took a breath, as if deciding something. "But I don't know if it's such a great product," she added. "I shouldn't tell anyone this, much less two reporters, but if it's off the record, I might have an interesting tidbit for you. But you will have to find it out for yourself. I can send you in the right direction, but I can't be the source of this."

"Our lips are sealed." I said.

"Strictly on background," Zellie added.

"Okay, good. The math doesn't add up."

"Come again?"

"I ran the numbers. Twice. Actually, three times. The math doesn't add up. By that I mean that the income projections are okay, but the annuity payment forecasts bear little resemblance to a projected reality. In short, plenty of money coming in to GS ASAP, very little going out to the annuitants."

"That's a bombshell," I said. "Is there any chance that that you saw initial projections, and the company has revised them?"

"Maybe," she conceded. "Sterling asked me to review them, and I gave him a detailed report. So, he knows what you know. But he never got back to me on it, so maybe he gave it to someone else."

"Who might he give it to?"

"The new analyst, I suppose. Ruby Love."

***

"Time to talk to Ruby Love," Zellie said, when we'd left the building.

"Yup."

"I wonder why the website had no photo of her," Zellie mused.

"Maybe she's ugly."

Zellie gave me a look of disdain. "From what we know so far about Sterling, I doubt it. I guess it's just because she's new."

***

We walked into the conference room at Goldback & Sterling, and took our places sitting next to each other on one side of the long, polished wood table. A vague smell of lemon permeated the room, due no doubt to the spray wax used to dust the furniture. Ruby Love had not yet appeared. If she intended to at all.

I had a bad feeling about Ms. Love. No picture, a too obvious fake name and now, late for our interview. Not a good start.

At that moment, a dark-haired beauty with impeccable posture walked imperiously into the room. Ruby Love. Or Jennifer Marquette. Or what the heck was her actual identity? As soon as she entered, Jennifer placed a single finger over her lips. Zellie and I got the message, and I extended my hand.

"Thank you for meeting with us, Ms. Love," I said, as we all sat down.

"I bet you say that to everyone who comes in here," she responded. "You know we have no choice."

"I know," I said. "But I believe in being courteous."

"Sure you do," she said, an edge to her voice. "Just looking at the two of you, anyone can see that you're nice, decent, polite folks."

"Just doing our job, ma'am. No need to get prickly."

"I'm in here, talking to you, when I could be upstairs, making money. Whatever makes you think I'd be sweet and dainty?"

I ignored her tone. "Making money? I thought you were an analyst on a salary, not a trader."

"Bonuses. Enormous, very green. Bonuses. I love money, the more the better."

"You're in the right business for that," Zellie chipped in dryly. "What can an analyst do to earn a large bonus?"

"Find facts that support a good investment."

"How is your bonus calculated?"

"Who knows? Some lame bean counter in the business office probably has a spreadsheet he pores over every minute, then throws it all out the minute a pretty girl takes the time to talk to him."

"You're saying the firm doesn't determine bonuses wholly on merit?"

"Absolutely. On how meritorious an acting job a pretty woman can pull off sucking up to a dweeb in the accounting department." She paused, adjusted her glasses, and sat up primly. "Plus finding a good investment."

This tack Jennifer was taking was interesting. First, more or less telling us that our conversations were being monitored, then overtly pointing to impropriety. She wanted Sterling, or whoever else was listening, to hear it.

"How much can an analyst earn in bonuses?" Zellie asked.

"I have no idea," Jennifer said. "I'm new. But trust me, I'll do anything to maximize the size of my bonus." She paused and looked me straight in the eyes. "Anything. Including convincing an honest nerd that I'm in love with him."

I could feel Zellie's concerned eyes upon me, but I remained unfazed. I'd been down this road with Jennifer so many times, I felt immune. Mostly.

Zellie jumped in. "Very interesting, Ms. Love. What are your limits? You'd con a lovesick accounting guy. Would you embezzle? Rob a bank? Would you kill for money?"

Jennifer showed no reaction. "Just a little harmless hyperbole, Ms. Morgan. I was stating the ordinary ambition of someone in the finance business. As journalists," she added slyly, "you must have seen this before."

"Kind of like being mad at someone and saying 'I could kill you?'" Zellie asked.

"That's pretty much it," Jennifer allowed.

"So there are limits to what you'd do to get a bigger bonus. Are there limits to what you'd do or tolerate in a business you worked for?" I asked.

Jennifer paused, adjusted her glasses again, and crossed and uncrossed her legs, changing her position in her chair.

"I have never encountered a situation that required a choice that I couldn't live with."

Whoa, I thought. I wonder whether she's talking about ever, or just at Goldback & Sterling. Because she'd done some despicable things in her life. I caught myself before I said anything. Jennifer was playing a role for an unseen audience. Heck, she was always acting. At this point I couldn't tell who was the genuine Jennifer. I doubt she knew herself.

I glanced over at Zellie, who nodded. It was time to ask about the annuity business and explore whether Ruby Love had a different story to tell than Cindy Diamond. Or put differently, did we value diamonds over rubies?
"What can you tell us about the new annuity business?" I asked.

"That's GS ASAP. I work in Global."

"You know nothing about it?"

"I didn't say that. I know a lot about it."

"What can you tell us?"

"It's a terrific new product that ensures a steady stream of income for one's entire life, after payment of an initial premium."

"Is it directed at a particular group of people?"

"It is. Retired people, or those ready to retire."

"How long has this product existed?"

"Oh, this product has existed for decades. Our company's involvement in the business is recent."

"Less than a year?"

"That's a fair statement."

"How viable a product is it?"

"What do you mean? It's been around for decades. You're reporters, check out the history."

"I meant the GS ASAP version."

"You should review the prospectus, which lays out the specifics of our product in exquisite detail. If I said anything else, the lawyers would be all over me."

"You're a financial analyst. Have you reviewed the financials of the annuity business?"

"Yes."

"Do you have an opinion on the viability of the GS ASAP product?"

"Yes."

"What is that opinion?"

Jennifer took a breath, then a sip from the bottle of water in front of her. "I can't say."

"Why not?"

"Look — I've been told you're doing a feature article on Goldback & Sterling. Why all the questions about the annuity business and its viability?"

"Isn't it the current hot new product for the business being advertised everywhere?" Zellie asked, using our time-tested answer to that question.

"Sure, but it's only one of dozens of subsidiaries for G&S. Why not ask about those? As an employee of the parent company, G&S, I have much more familiarity with the larger picture than a small offshoot company."

"You just said that you have an opinion. What's the harm in explaining?"

"I shouldn't have said that. I already told you, it's all in the prospectus, all the financials and everything."

I feigned indifference, even though I was certain Jennifer wouldn't say a thing she didn't intend to say.

"Okay, we don't want to get you into trouble. We'll look again at the prospectus. Does it contain your analysis, or perhaps that of Ms. Diamond, who we already interviewed?"

"Not mine. Maybe Cindy, maybe someone else. I don't know who authored it."

"Can we get a copy of your analysis?" Zellie asked.

"Haven't you been listening? No."

***

Sterling tossed aside the transcripts he just read from those two reporters' interviews. The reporters seemed a little too nosy about things that had little to do with writing a puff piece about the company. They'd shown real interest in his employees' backgrounds, particularly that lady in sales, Ms. Newton. He made a mental note to commend her for her performance in there. She'd done a good job of keeping the focus on human interest. And Ruby Love. She interested him, and not just because she was hot. That statement about willing to do anything for money and never encountering a choice she couldn't live with. She seemed like a perfect participant in what he had in mind. He wouldn't tell her everything. Just enough to whet that voracious appetite for money. He'd let her think she'd get a piece of the action if she took part.

Cindy Diamond. What to do with her? Not trust her, that was certain. Fire her? No, that would be counterproductive. She'd turn into a whistleblower or something like that. She really didn't know much. And even acknowledged to the reporters that the company may have revised the figures. No, just leave her exactly where she is, and don't let her get access to anything related to GS ASAP. He'd keep her close, where he could monitor her actions. And enjoy the view.

The snooping custodian, Nickles. He'd fire that guy's ass as soon as the whole feature article thing was over. He would accept, for now, that the reporters designed their questions to learn about the much ballyhooed new annuity product as part of a favorable article about the benevolent Bertrand Sterling trying to help retired people. It might even boost sales. That was the point of him requesting their involvement. But it better be a puff piece, or those reporters would face severe consequences. He vowed swift and furious revenge if they went negative.

CHAPTER SEVENTEEN

"Maybe we should interview that CFO guy next, Tucker Ford. The custodian told us he had designs on Sterling's wife. And he'd be in the best position to tell us about the annuity business. Do you think we're ready to confront senior management?"

I looked up from the newspaper.

"Maybe, but it won't be him. Look here." I handed Zellie the paper.

"Omigosh. It's him."

"Yes. Our dead body. The police identified him as Tucker Ford, age 61, a native of Long Branch, New Jersey. Died of gunshot wound to his head. Divorced, survived by two adult children."

"Wow. Do you think it's related to our investigation?"

"I'd bet on it. We've seen enough smoke to know there are a ton of secrets in that business."

Zellie nodded. "We have a murder to investigate."

"We do. We can't just leave it alone. And we need to ratchet up our inquiries. And not limit the process to reporter interviews at G&S."

"Do you have something in mind?"

"I do. Time to bring in the big guns."

"What do you mean?"

"A certain little old lady and her devoted nephew."

Zellie started laughing. "You're not serious."

"I am. They can freely ask questions we can't. And they're smart and intuitive."

"She's not little, or particularly good at looking the part of an old woman."

"Somehow I suspect that she'd be good at pretty much anything she set her mind to."

"You have that right. Okay, no harm in asking. Make the call."

I called to set up the meeting. "We can head right over," I said after completing the call.

* * *

"Don't expect them to give us anything other than what's in the prospectus," Mrs. Minniefield warned. "You said they are militant about that."

"They are, but Roger Danish told us they work on commission. No sale, no money," I said.

"That creates an enormous incentive to give the client what he or she wants. Not deviating from the script, but maybe providing additional tidbits they think they can get away with to get clients to agree," Zellie added.

"And somehow, I think the two of you are resourceful enough to push the envelope with one of the sales staff."

"I'm not so sure about that," Mrs. M replied, "but I'm willing to try." She cut her eyes to Ted. "How about you?"

Ted paused. "What the heck," he answered, after a moment of thought. "It will be a nice change of pace, you playing the doddering elderly aunt, while I assume the role of a brilliant, incisive, handsome nephew. Hmm. No need to act at all."

We all just looked at him, and he burst out laughing. "I think we can do this. I'll just prepare a long list of questions. Pepper the salesperson with inquiries. He or she will have to answer at least some of them. Do you have thoughts on the questions to ask?"

"I do," I said, proffering a sheet of paper to each of them. "Lots of technical stuff," I cautioned, "so turn it into something a layperson would ask, albeit a brilliant, handsome one."

"Translate it into English, got it," he answered.

I looked over at Mrs. Minniefield. "Are you sure you're okay with this? Playing the part of an old lady?"

Mrs. Minniefield gave me one of those long, piercing stares. "With some makeup and study of old people's behavior, I'll pull it off."

I looked to see if she was joking, but what was I thinking? Mrs. M did not kid around. This was serious business, and she was telling me that, albeit with a touch of irony thrown in.

***

Jennifer thought the interview went well. She'd accomplished her two main purposes. One, to tell Arnie and Zellie that Sterling was monitoring their interviews. She didn't know that for sure, but she had little doubt. Sterling reached his exalted status by having the right information at the right time. That's what the securities business was all about. No way he'd let two strangers interview his staff without knowing what they said. And it was very important for her plan she was right, because the second, and more important purpose of her performance was to tell Sterling that she'd be willing to do anything for money. That was an easy sell to Arnie and Zellie. She'd shown that in her dealings with them. She had a slight touch of regret for that, but shrugged it off. Maudlin sentimentality was not her strong suit. Maybe it was just playing a role when she became involved with those mobsters, but ripping Arnie off the first time? That was pure theft and greed. At this point in her life, she did not understand her true character. A criminal, for sure. A force for good? Maybe sometimes. Maybe even this time.

***

Operation Befuddled Elderly Aunt set in motion, we left Mrs. Minniefield's home, and walked down the street to my house, where we took Lazlow for a walk, fed him and gave him fresh water. That done, we sat down in my living room to talk about the case.

"It's a bizarre one, for sure." I said.

"Not like our two previous cases." Zellie agreed.

"I guess the dead CFO is more like the others."

"True. We know how to deal with that. It's our skill set. And I can't believe I'm saying that. We never intended our little business to involve dead bodies."

"No, but we've become good at finding the murderers, and I think it would behoove us to find this one."

"You like the word 'behoove,' don't you?"

"I think it's classy."

Zellie gave a faint smile. "If you say so."

"Anyway, this murder has become part of our case, and we can't just let the police investigate it without at least monitoring their progress. The newspaper article I read gave little information other than the usual obituary stuff about surviving children, et cetera."

"I'll see if there's more online," Zellie said, heading for the old desktop computer. She'd left her laptop at the office.

"Great," I said. "But we can ask about it in our next interview. Inquiring about a dead CFO falls into the human-interest realm feature reporters would want to know about. In fact, it would be weird if we didn't."

"Okay. We'll ask. But what else can we do to investigate the CFO's death?"

"Maybe we should just ask the police," Zellie said.

"I don't follow."

"We're not dealing with the same bozo cops we dealt with before. Those two officers who came to Poricy Park seemed reasonable."

"That doesn't mean they'll talk to civilians," I cautioned.

"No, it doesn't. But it doesn't hurt to ask. Anyway, I have a better idea."

"Find someone who can get us a copy of the police report and officer notes?"

Zellie laughed. "I don't think Josh will know a police lieutenant down here."

Zellie was referring to our last case, in which a new lawyer friend I'd just met obtained a police report from an old police buddy.

"I doubt it," I acknowledged. "And I shouldn't ask. Should I?" I said it, but I didn't mean it. I'd already pushed the envelope on our friendship.

"No. Definitely not," Zellie said, to my relief. "I meant calling the Middletown Police press office. They have one. I checked."

I'm sure I looked doubtful, because Zellie hastened to add, "I mean it. I don't expect them to give every detail, but they'll be proud to extol the virtues of their crack investigative team, and tell us what they've done so far. In a publicity spin way. But I'm sure I can cut through that and get us at least some information on their progress. It might be helpful."

"Anything at all is more than we have now," I said. "Go ahead. Call them."

***

Sterling rubbed his hands together, and fidgeted in his chair. He rose, headed out the door, wordlessly passed Lois, and walked down the hall to the office of none other than Ruby Love.

He entered through her open door, slammed it shut, and sat down on one of the two chairs facing her desk.

Ruby said nothing, and with studied patience, awaited Sterling's pitch. For that was surely the reason for him entering that way, and ensuring privacy. Ruby did not miss the fact that Sterling had said nothing on his way to her office, not even a word to Lois. Ruby listened to everything going on outside, and she hadn't missed that. Lois ruled the office like a lioness tending her cubs. Nothing happened without her knowledge. Except, perhaps, whatever Sterling was about to tell her.

"I have a proposition for you," Sterling said.

"Why Mr. Sterling, right here in my office?"

"No, that's not what I mean...well, would a different place work...no, no, I mean something else."

Ruby observed Sterling's stuttering with amusement. She'd scored big on the who controls the narrative war. Time to press the advantage.

"I hope it's something just as exciting," she said.

"Yes, well, maybe not. It involves making a lot of money."

"I love money. I'd do anything to get lots of it. Anything," she emphasized. "Give me the details."

"It might be close to legal lines," Sterling warned. "We won't go over the line, I promise."

"My legal line is very, very fuzzy, I assure you. As long as it's worth it."

"Some nice people might could get hurt," Sterling added.

"Too bad."

Sterling seemed satisfied. "Okay, here's your part in this."

Ruby listened, nodded once or twice, and said, "This is no problem, but I need to know the whole plan to execute my part properly."

"In time," Sterling responded. "Better that you not know the full details yet."

Ruby didn't press the issue. She thought she knew the plan anyway, but she figured not asking would be suspicious.

***

"Yes ma'am. Providing information to the public is my job. Give me a moment, and I'll check the packet for that case."

Zellie looked at me and nodded. She put her phone on speaker, so I could also hear the Middletown Police Public Relations representative.

"Let me see," the representative said. "Okay, yes, Detective Johnson and Officer Yang responded to the call, and did the initial intake. Detective Johnson is one of the department's finest investigators, and Officer Yang is, um, a recent transfer here, but I'm sure she's a fine officer if she's Detective Johnson's partner."

"Are there any suspects?" Zellie asked.

"Oh, we don't disclose that information to the public. But I can assure you, Detective Johnson is capably investigating."

"I'm sure," Zellie responded. "Have they interviewed any witnesses?"

"Again, we do not share the details of the investigation with the public."

"Sure you do," Zellie said. "Sometimes you even release a photograph of a suspect, so the public can help locate the criminal."

"Alleged criminal," the voice corrected. "But we have no such plans in this case."

"Can I assume that means you have no suspects?"

"We do not release such information to the public." Her tone never changed. No exasperation, no impatience, nothing. She maintained a perky, helpful sounding tone.

"Should the public be afraid that a dangerous criminal is on the loose?" Zellie asked, winking at me.

"No. As I stated, the public should rest assured that the investigation is in the accomplished hands of one of our finest detectives, who will leave no stone unturned in his quest to bring the perpetrator or perpetrators to justice."

Zellie looked at me, shrugged, thanked the woman, and hung up.

"Frickin' PR people," she blurted.

"At least we know the investigation is in fine hands. And that not everyone in the Middletown Police Department hates us. She didn't hang up on you after hearing your name. And you were once a PR person."

"And just as good at saying nothing, while extolling the virtues of the client. Don't assume the Middletown Police Department no longer hates us from that performance. That lady doesn't work for the police. She's from a PR firm. Could even be my former company, except we didn't represent government. At least not when I was there."

"So why did you call if you knew she'd tell you nothing?"

"They have to give at least some information. Here, we learned that Detective Johnson will continue as lead investigator, and that they have no suspects either in custody, or at large."

"She refused to tell you details. I get the Detective Johnson information, but how do you figure the rest? And are police detectives usually the first responders to a 911 call?"

"I don't know. Maybe they were nearby. Anyway, the reason I know they have no suspect in custody is that they would extol their investigative skills as much as possible. That's what PR firms do. Let the public know they are safe because of their great skill. And if they'd identified a particular suspect with sufficient evidence to bring him or her in, they'd already have done so. If such a suspect was at large, they often ask the public's help in locating them. Thousands of people looking, instead of just a few police officers."

"So that wasn't a waste?"

"Nope."

"Did you disclose that much information when you did PR?"

"I'd never even acknowledge the client's name. I might agree that the sky was blue, and that it was sunny outside."

"Oy." I said.

"Another day in the life of a PR person." Zellie chuckled.

CHAPTER EIGHTEEN

"What's next? Do we pester Detective Johnson to find out more about the crime?"

Zellie pondered that for a while. "No, not yet. But we should do that. Funny he never interviewed us. We found the body."

"Maybe we're his chief suspects, and he's just waiting to lower the boom."

"I suppose that's possible. More likely, he considered that and concluded otherwise. We had no car to transport the body, nor any cart to haul the guy to the inside of the park, and we have a sterling reputation, did I just say sterling?"

I laughed. "Yup."

"Well, we have one. And we already gave our statements, even went down to the station later to sign them. No, they don't think we're the main suspects. Maybe secondary ones, but if Detective Johnson is as good as that PR person says, he already knows we didn't do it."

"So why not track him down and get more information?"

"We need to keep interviewing, at a minimum to not arouse suspicion about our true goal."

"Makes sense. Who's next?"

"Why not that director of employee relations guy?"

"Quentin Stanhope? Why him?"

"He deals with everyone who works there, and G&S has some peculiar employees. And maybe he can shed some light on our good Master Sergeant's missing two years."

"Maybe. Or he'll filibuster the question."

***

But he didn't. We didn't even need to ask the question. He offered the information up in the course of a conversation about the head of security.

"Sergeant Fortz is a fine man. Received an honorable discharge from the U.S. Marines after a distinguished career, which included being decorated for bravery in combat. Spent two years getting a masters' degree in finance and digital security at Rutgers University. He joined us after completing his studies. We're very fortunate to have him."

We received similar answers to questions about Sterling and the other officers, and Ms. Love and Ms. Diamond. The firm required outstanding academic credentials and work experience, and each one of the named people came from the finest undergraduate and graduate schools in the country. The guy was a walking crapola artist. Because no way Ruby Love had that background. So, the rest was pure nonsense.

We asked him about his education and employment verification procedures, and received a similar response that he and his staff rigorously checked school transcripts and references, and that not a soul could slip through the impenetrable screening process.

***

"Wow," is all I could say when we left.

"Double wow," Zellie agreed. "That guy just made everything up. He didn't bother to make it sound plausible."

"Is that what you did?" I teased.

"Not even close. I told the truth, albeit in a roundabout way. That guy couldn't be bothered with the truth, although I suppose he might have included a real fact. But I'll be darned if I can put my finger on a single one."

"What do you think it means?"

"We have to check out a few backgrounds. We can ignore Ruby Love."

"Thank goodness."

"Before we do, I think we should talk to Lois Carver."

***

After Sterling left, Ruby examined the file he'd given her.

It contained a spreadsheet with some very familiar numbers, ones reflecting an extraordinarily optimistic projection of future income for the fund that existed to pay annuities over the owners' lifetimes. Ruby cut through the significant financial obfuscation. She saw that GS ASAP expressed a belief that the fund could earn as much as 30% per year. Not new deposits, earnings. Like a savings account earning 30% per year. Not a chance.

Ruby filed that piece of information away. She already knew the annuity business was a fraud. And she had just received a snippet of Sterling's end game. His objective stared her right in the face. The fund itself. The money in an account ostensibly set up for payment of annuities. And it contained over nine hundred million dollars, which was being added to daily by new investors. Sterling hadn't told her he intended to raid that fund, but his vague overtures hadn't fooled her. She knew she had to find out as much as she could about how someone could access that fund for a purpose other than payment of annuities.

***

Lois Carver was a mid-sized white woman with iron grey hair, wire-rimmed glasses and an angular face that exuded competence. She reminded me of a smaller version of Mrs. Minniefield and appeared every bit as capable. She looked at us with piercing eyes, as if daring us to ask a dumb question. I let Zellie do the honors of initiating the interview.

"We know your name and title as Mr. Sterling's executive assistant, Ms. Carver, but please describe your duties."

"That's my job title, Ms. Morgan, but my duties far exceed that of an assistant to Mr. Sterling. I held an assistant title when I first started working for Morris Goldback some twenty years ago. It was not Goldback & Sterling then, just Morris and me and two accountants. Goldback & Sterling came much later.

"But to answer your question, my duties comprise supervising the financial staff in the executive wing of Goldback & Sterling, and all other personnel working there. Everyone from the typists and clerks and copy room staff to the financial analysts. Mr. Sterling knows I also supervise him to an extent. A sensible voice to keep his more, shall we say, volatile instincts in check. He knows I do that, and he wouldn't be mad to hear me say it. Oh, he might shout at me for it, but he knows my value."

"Are you an expert in finance?" I asked.

Ms. Carver eyed me with suspicion. "Are you suggesting something with that question, Mr. Fischer?"

"Not a bit," I said. "It's a simple question, no guile intended."

"I'm not an accountant, nor do I have an MBA. I have good instincts and am very good with numbers. I possess extensive familiarity with financial jargon, and can read a spreadsheet. I need all those skills to exercise my supervisory duties."

"Mr. Fischer intended no disrespect, Ms. Carver," Zellie said smoothly. "We need to know what direction to take in our conversation with you, and would steer clear of finance if that was not your area of expertise."

"Isn't this a feature article you're writing?"

"It sure is," I said. "About a financial powerhouse. And I'd love to avoid questions about the boring world of buying stocks and bonds, but if I did that, I'd just do a feature article on something else, something more interesting. But I will say this— interviewing someone who started at the beginning, and worked up through the ranks to become an integral part of the senior staff at a global financial company, that might pique my readers' interest."

Ms. Carver looked at me for a long moment and cracked a smile.

"Okay, fire away. I've been here since the beginning, and I'd love to tell you all about babysitting financial whizzes. First off," she continued, "I want to tell you both that Bertrand Sterling is a wonderful person and extraordinary financial talent. His consummate skill..."

For the second time, an interviewee placed a single finger to her lips while she spoke. She reached under the conference table and retrieved a tiny object. A microphone. She retrieved a small vial from her purse and pulled out what looked like putty of some sort. She carefully wrapped the putty around the tiny bug and attached it back under the table.

We looked at her in amazement, and she chuckled.

"I'm very prepared. Always have been. I thought it possible that sharing some real information with the two of you might prove useful. Because no way you two are doing a feature story. Are you gunning for my cretin of a boss?"

How to play this, I wondered. Come clean? I didn't think so. But we wanted her information and had only a moment to decide.

"We'll write a feature if that's all we have," Zellie said, "But if a juicy story presents itself, and it looks like it may, we'd be delighted to write that."

Lois considered that for a moment, gave an almost imperceptible nod, more to herself that to us.

"Okay," she said. "Morris Goldback is a wonderful person and financial genius. He engendered great loyalty by everyone who came in contact with the man. He liked to identify good character people a little down on their luck, take them under his wing and provide opportunities not otherwise available to them. I'm a good example of that. So is Ms. Newton, our sales chief. And his business grew exponentially from its modest roots."

"But the growth of the business came with it a need to bring in partners, and that's how Bertrand Sterling came into the picture. He had the privileged background and educational pedigree that Morris often eschewed in the past, but Sterling had money. To be exact, his wife did. Sterling became Morris' partner, and when Morris retired, became the CEO."

She paused, cleared her throat, and looked pensive.

"I'd do anything to get Morris back."

We listened without interrupting her. I sensed that she was about to lower the boom on Sterling, and I was right.

"Sterling botched almost every decision. In the beginning, I tried to give him good advice, which Morris always welcomed. But Sterling is an arrogant ass. He ignored my sensible suggestions, and frankly those of our late CFO, Tucker Ford. Tucker was one of Morris' guys, as Sterling put it. He rejected everything Tucker said. Our executive VP, Justin Mc-Coy, is a Sterling hire. And sycophant. He'd rubber stamp any Sterling decision. Unlike the hires Morris made, Sterling based his upon his assessment of their perceived loyalty and use to him personally. Also, he likes women. Beautiful women. You've interviewed Cindy Diamond and Ruby Love?"

We nodded.

"Both good examples. Pretty, yes. But their backgrounds and even their names are a load of hooey. But you knew that already."

Again, we nodded.

"He's up to something," she said. "He's always up to something, but this feels different. And not just loading up on a fake financial staff. He's testing those two, for sure. My guess is that he's seeing whether one or both of them will help him with whatever financial scheme he has in mind. And I'd bet on that bogus Ruby Love."

"A dishonest scheme?" Zellie asked.

"I have little doubt. He knows a lot about his business, and is capable of respectable transactions, but he's never been shy about ignoring business norms, and straying into illegal territory if it suited him. Morris never did that, but Bert... he's a loose cannon. And the way he treats women... ugh."

"Do you have any specifics?" I asked.

"About a financial scheme, or how he treats women?"

"Both. We're reporters. Both are juicy material."

Lois studied the two of us for a long moment. "You're not that different from Cindy and Ruby."

I had a bad feeling about that statement and saw Zellie fidgeting.

"How so?" I managed.

"You're not reporters. And you're not writing a puff piece for the Clarion."

Zellie and I remained impassive, waiting for Lois' next statement.

"You're gunning for him," Lois said. "Everything I've seen and heard supports that. And you're new to journalism. You don't have the first idea on how to act like reporters. They have a certain demeanor, honed after years of covering high school football games and birthday parties for people turning 100. You have none of that, because you are private detectives."

***

Cindy spotted Lois leaving her desk to attend her interview by those two reporters. Sterling had left earlier, to go to a meeting, she thought he'd said. And she didn't see Ruby Love around. A narrow opportunity existed to do some snooping. And she knew what to look for. She left her office, and hurried past Lois' empty desk. Her eyes briefly cut to the security camera, but she knew the guys watching the monitors wouldn't give a second thought to a frequent visitor to Sterling's office.

When she opened the door, it creaked, and she gave a furtive glance over her shoulder. Seeing no one, she entered the office, and closed the door behind her.

She knew if Sterling or Lois returned, she'd have no escape. Only one way in and one way out. So she had to work fast. She rifled through the files in the cabinet against the wall, but found only routine matters. Nothing related to the annuity business. And nothing that fit the piece of the puzzle she sought.

Sterling had whetted her appetite for information relating to the annuity business by giving her that spreadsheet. And she knew he'd purposely omitted the most important parts. She wondered why he'd given it to her. He had to know she'd figure out it didn't add up. He'd shown no interest in her analysis. Because he knew it already. Was it a test of some sort? To gauge her honesty? Or... to gauge her dishonesty?

She had to move fast. Sterling's meeting wouldn't last forever, and Lois could return any minute. She eyed Sterling's desk and hurried over. Pulling at the bottom drawer, she found ... a bottle of Scotch. She tried the top drawer. Locked. She muttered an epithet. Except for the delay, the lock wasn't a problem. She removed a set of picks from her pocket, selected one, and had to work hard before the drawer popped open. And presto! Just what she was looking for. She scanned the sheaf of documents with skilled precision and returned them to the drawer, which she re-locked with the pick. She turned to leave. Before she made it to the door, she heard a noise outside.

What to do now? There was nowhere to go but back through the door, and discovery by whoever was out there. And if it was Sterling or

Lois, headed directly at her. Cindy eyed the window. They were on the third floor, so exiting out that way was impossible. She thought about how the building looked from the outside and made a quick decision. Rushing over to the window, she opened it, and crawled gingerly onto the ledge running around the building. Terrified that she'd fall, she balanced on one hand, and reached back to close the window.

She looked down. Bad idea. She was at real peril here, not just of the possibility of falling to her death. That was bad enough, but also people could see her. How would it look if they saw a senior financial analyst crawling around on a ledge around the building? She chuckled wryly. Clients wouldn't invest, thinking she had lost everything in the stock market. She knew that wasn't the only risk. The other risk was that Sterling or someone else would spot her, and she would lose her job, and so much more. Her other employer would not be happy.

Her predicament just emphasized the inadvisability of scrambling onto the ledge. But she had no choice, and she held some very useful information in her smartphone. But how to get it to the right place? She looked ahead. And saw it. A drain pipe running down the building. She crawled the short distance and examined it. It felt sturdy. She hoped so. It was a long way down. Cindy eyed her nice business attire and sighed. She grabbed hold of the drainpipe, which thankfully held firm, and pulled herself forward, and looked down again. She didn't want to, but she needed to make sure no one was around. The coast was clear. Exercising extreme care, she stood on the narrow ledge, and grasped the pipe.

"Here goes," she muttered, and holding the pipe firmly in both hands, she stepped off the ledge.

* * *

I flinched, I admit it. I felt my body quiver. Zellie remained impassive.

"We don't have detective licenses. Never have. We've stumbled into some situations about which we showed a talent for asking questions and looking into things. The precise skills that appealed to the editor of the Clarion. They don't just hand out press credentials, you know."

Lois smiled. "No, they don't." She winked. "I understand. You're reporters. And anything you do to take that SOB Bertrand Sterling down is okay with me. Doesn't matter to me if you do it as detectives or reporters... or owners of a cinnamon bun shop."

That brought a smile to Zellie's lips. Lois Carver was a smart cookie, and had checked us out.

"They're delicious," Zellie said. "And the smell is divine."

It was Lois' turn to smile. "I'll tell you everything I know about this company, but most of my knowledge is about its people. I don't have a head for finance."

"Or you'd be running the company now, I'm guessing," I said.

"No question," she laughed. "And why I've stayed with that cretin is beyond me."

"Are you paid well?"

"Yes. Very well. The money is no doubt intended as an incentive to keep my mouth shut."

"But you're not."

"I am a rock of silence for our clients. I would never tell you a word about their finances. That's sacred. But Bert? I'm a geyser of talkativeness."

So she told us all about Bertrand Sterling. His family life, his troubled marriage, his ogling and harassment of the women in the office, and his keen desire for more and more money.

"Isn't making money the whole point of this business?"

Lois studied me for a moment. "When you worked in this business, would you have done anything, and I mean anything, to make as much money as you could?"

I thought about that. And that she knew I'd been in the business.

"Not anything," I said. "I had a burning desire to make money for our clients. That's what they paid our firm for."

"I mean personally," Lois said. "How far would you go to line your own pockets?"

"Not very far," I admitted.

"Bert is not like you. Morris was, mostly. But Bert is cut from a different cloth. He makes money for Bertrand Sterling. If our clients make money, too, he's okay with that, because they continue to hire the firm, and he makes more money."

"If everyone is making money, what's the problem?"

"Bert cuts corners. He fudges numbers, he lies, he cheats, he doesn't give a hoot about the securities laws."

"Can you prove that?" Zellie asked.

"Not a bit," she said. "Maybe you two can. But I know it for sure."

CHAPTER NINETEEN

"We have a lot of things to do," I remarked, as we settled back at the conference table in our office.

"Where should we start?"

"Let's consider the possibilities. We should reach out to Detective Johnson about his murder investigation. We should look deeper into Sergeant Fortz' background. And we should prepare for our final interviews."

"Justin McCoy, the executive vice president, and the man himself, Bertrand Sterling."

"Yes. I think we need to speak to McCoy. He's mysterious, in a way. No one seems to talk about him. What does he do? How does he fit into G&S?"

"What role did the executive vice president have at Mort?" Zellie asked.

"Not much. Played a lot of golf, as I remember it. He was an officer of the company, but a mostly absentee one."

And just like Justin McCoy. We confirmed this with just a few clicks on the computer, and two strategic phone calls. We found that he'd attended no board of directors' meetings, and was a charter member, along with Sterling, at a local golf club. We decided not to interview him.

"That leaves Sterling on the G&S interview list," Zellie observed.

"Yes. And I think if we want to talk to him, we'd better do it in a hurry."

"Why?"

"Everyone else seems suspicious of us," I said. "And we now know for certain that Sterling was listening to all our interviews."

"So, he's suspicious, too."

"Yes, ma'am."

"Should we even bother? It almost seems like a waste of time. What's he going to tell us, anyway? The company line?"

"Maybe a lot, if we press him. And we don't need him to allow us access to the staff at this point. We've talked to everyone on our list. We can pin him to the wall now."

"Back to being detectives?"

"That's the idea. Unlicensed ones."

"But no need for our usual disclaimer, because we have press credentials."

"Beautiful setup, isn't it?"

"But before we do that, let's talk to Detective Johnson. He might give us information that will be useful in our Sterling interview."

***

Grasping the drain pipe, Cindy slid down, her business suit scraping against the dirty tube, fraying her clothes and scratching her hands. Worse, her progress toward the ground seemed too fast, and she worried about injuring herself on the ground. She grasped the pipe tighter and made things worse. She stopped her progress completely, and for a moment, was hanging on to the pipe as her only defense against plummeting the remaining two stories.

Almost crying in fear, she loosened her grip a bit, which rewarded her with continued movement at a slower, more manageable pace. She breathed a sigh of relief, but she knew she was not yet out of the woods, as she slid the remaining distance to the ground. Approaching the end of her unceremonious journey, she released her grip to land with some grace on her feet, but her momentum carried her face first onto to muddy ground behind the building. Unhurt, except for some scrapes on her hands, she struggled to her feet and looked down at herself in dismay. She couldn't go back into the building looking like this. She had to get home, fast. Fortunately, her phone was intact, containing the precious pictures of the documents in Sterling's desk drawer. But she needed it for a more conventional reason — to call Lois to tell her she had an emergency and had to go home unexpectedly, but that she hoped to be back later.

Reaching Lois' voice mail, she left the message and hurried to her car. Only to run into none other than Bertrand Sterling. Eyeing her mud-covered body, he paused, and inquired whether she'd just had a quickie, and that, while the firm frowned upon sex outdoors on the company grounds, he'd always make an exception for her, if she cared to repeat the experience. But he'd prefer to first change out of his business suit.

Cindy responded with a mumbled explanation of tripping a falling as she hurried out to a family emergency and declined his offer of a romp outside. Sterling just laughed as he continued on his way back to the office. A chastened Cindy watched his back for a moment. And muttered under her breath.

"I'd kill that SOB if I could get away with it."

She unlocked her car, got in and drove away.

***

Detective Johnson was a stocky man, with a weathered oval shaped brown face, and intense dark brown eyes. He pointed to two chairs in front of a cluttered desk. Included among various framed items on his wall was a plaque evidencing his receipt of a Bronze Star for bravery in combat. An impressive man.

"What can I do for you two famed detectives?"

Zellie answered for both of us. "We're not licensed to do that." She proffered her press credential.

"Members of the fourth estate, are you?" He picked up his desk phone, punched two numbers, and said into the receiver, "Diane, I have two reporters here. Could you give them the usual non-answers and send them on their way? Okay, thanks anyway. I'll deal with them myself."

This wasn't going well, I thought. He was about to usher us right out. But I looked at Zellie, then at Detective Johnson, and they seemed to share a private joke.

"She's a little more perceptive than you," Detective Johnson said, with a slight chuckle.

My eyes cut to Zellie, and she explained.

"He didn't call the press office. He hit only two digits on the phone, and the list of intercom numbers, which I read upside down, all have three digits. Also, Detective Johnson told the alleged press person to give us the usual non-answers. He wouldn't say that. He'd refer us to the press office and kick us right out of here. If he said anything to the press office, he'd say something like 'please help these nice folks, or 'you can answer their questions better than I can.'" She looked at Detective Johnson, who nodded.

"My favorite is 'please give them as much information as possible. They should get absolutely everything we can give them.'"

He looked at Zellie. "But I'm impressed. The upside-down reading ability is common, but putting two and two together like that, not so much. I take it you want to know the status of the investigation of the murder. Natural, since you found the body. Okay, I will give you as much information as possible. Oops, sorry, force of habit."

He looked at us for a moment. "I rarely interview suspects in my private office," he said. "And as discoverers of the body, well, you get the idea."

We both nodded.

"I don't think you did it. You would have had no reason to call us, and we might never have discovered the body but for your romp in the park. Why were you there, anyway?" His voice remained casual, but even I noticed that this had become an interview of suspects. We might have made a mistake in coming here. Detective Johnson did not intend to miss the opportunity to get us to answer questions with his disarming charm.

"Oddly enough," I said, "we were looking for a quiet day away from the noise of daily life. We grew up here, and Fossil Creek in Poricy Park was both a local curiosity and a scientific marvel. We hadn't been there in years and thought it a good place to get away from it all."

"Uh huh, uh huh," Detective Johnson wrote something in a notebook on his desk, and made a point of not allowing Zellie to read it upside down again. "Go on."

"Go on how? That's it."

Voice still casual, Detective Johnson showed incredulity.

"You found a dead body, buried under some leaves deep into a local park, and it was just a coincidence?"

I saw what he meant, but I didn't like where he was going with this. "Coincidence or not, that's what happened. I can't change the truth just to make something seem different."

"No, you can't, and shouldn't," he said. "And I might leave it at that, but the two of you have been spending an awful lot of time at the office, I should say former office, of the dead man. Is that another coincidence?"

Zellie jumped in. "We're doing a story on Bertrand Sterling and Goldback and Sterling. We had no idea when we found the body that the dead man had any connection to G&S. We discovered that by reading the newspaper."

"So you say, so you say. Okay then, what have you discovered in your foray into journalism?"

Zellie and I looked at each other for a moment, a fact not missed by Detective Johnson.

"Wondering how to keep your stories straight?" he inquired in that infuriatingly pleasant voice. "Should I conduct separate interviews?"

"This is not an interview," Zellie said. "We sought you out, which is a sensible thing for journalists to do when the original story veers into police territory. We have no desire to keep anything from the police, and are prepared to tell you everything we've learned. We do have obligations and rights as journalists, which we will not waive, but that obligatory statement aside, here's who we've interviewed. She ticked off a list of people by name and position at G&S. They all stuck to the corporate script, but sometimes veered off into veiled criticisms of the company. We're still following up on those. Our original feature seems to have turned into an investigative piece, particularly because of a murdered senior official. We'd wanted to talk to him, and only afterwards learned he was the body we found."

"An odd coincidence," Detective Johnson said again.

"I guess so," Zellie said. "I just don't see how it connects with us. We didn't tell anyone we intended to go to the park that day. It was a spur-of-the-moment thing."

Detective Johnson looked at us for a long moment. Apparently satisfied with something, he said, "I know you are law-abiding citizens, and while I hate coincidences, I believe your description of the events leading up to your discovery of the body. I can't see even the slightest motive for you killing the guy, or any evidence at all that you even knew him." He looked at us again. "And I've looked hard. People who discover bodies are natural suspects. But discovering dead bodies is not new to you. You have quite a track record of finding, running into, tripping over corpses, and even having them fall on you. So, finding this one is just another in a long line. Annoying to the police, for sure, but hardly suspicious. I'm prepared to make a deal with you. I'll give you as much information as I can, and you do the same."

As much as we each could left a wide swath of information that both sides could withhold. Zellie looked at me, and I nodded.

Zellie gave Detective Johnson a summary of our interviews, leaving out our suspicions about the fake names, how we got the assignment in the first place, or that we started out with suspicions about the business. Detective Johnson told us what was in the autopsy report, none of which was surprising. I guess what we agreed to with Detective Johnson was that we'd both keep close to the vest. But we had the spirit of cooperation, right?

We shook hands with him and left the building. After we exited, I asked Zellie what she thought of our cooperation agreement.

"We cooperated. He didn't."

"He gave us the information in the autopsy report."

"Which contained nothing of value. No, Detective Johnson is a charmer. He won't give us anything. But I'm glad about one thing."

"What's that?"

"I think he's the real deal. After our experiences with Officers Dumb and Dumber, it's nice to know someone with a brain is on the job this time. It's a murder case. Let's leave the murder to him, and we'll investigate the potential bilking of little old ladies."

"Works for me. I'd be happy never to see another dead body."

CHAPTER TWENTY

T ed and Mrs. Minniefield looked for a moment at the imposing Goldback & Sterling building, before proceeding to the front entrance for their appointment with the annuity sales staff. As Arnie & Zellie suggested, they'd made an appointment with Roger Danish, saying, without mentioning a name, that he'd come highly recommended for his thorough and kind demeanor.

Roger stood when they approached the meeting room, showing particular solicitude to Mrs. Minniefield. He extended his hand, and Mrs. M looked at Ted first, as if asking him if it was okay to shake Roger's hand. Ted gave a slight nod, and Mrs. M extended a few flaccid fingers in his direction, which Roger took and raised them to his lips for a soft kiss. Ted showed no evidence of gagging on the spot, and Mrs. M murmured "thank you, young man."

After they all sat down, Roger went into full sales pitch, extolling the virtues of not just annuities, but the specific product offered by GS ASAP, almost without taking a breath, and leaving no chance for interruption. Not that Mrs. M or Ted wanted to interrupt. Arnie had suggested in his notes that they let Roger talk himself out, even if it took a while, because Roger had a mandate to stick to the script, which they knew already. That didn't stop them from doing a little play-acting, with Mrs. M playing the part of a of a doddering, clueless old woman, which was the way it seemed Roger perceived all his potential clients. Mrs. M mumbled a few words having nothing to do with the subject, like "cheese, I like cheese." Roger paused only a nanosecond before continuing his canned sales pitch, while Ted resisted the urge to break into hysterics.

Roger concluded his presentation, and proffered a copy of the prospectus to Mrs. Minniefield, who looked at Ted. Ted took the folder from Roger, promising to review it with Mrs. Minniefield, and said that they had a few questions.

"Anything you need. I'm here. He looked at his watch. But I'm late for my next appointment."

Ted got up, and helped Mrs. Minniefield to her feet.

"No problem, Roger. My aunt will just take her eight million dollars to your competitor, who does have time to answer questions. Come along, Aunt Mabel. This was a waste of our time."

"Wait. Please." Roger motioned to the chairs, which Ted eyed for a long moment, then gave an enormous sigh, and helped Mrs. M to sit down again.

Ted looked at Mrs. M, who gave the outward appearance of abject confusion, and touched her hand.

"We took the time to come here, so we might as well see whether Roger can give us more information. And I promise, we'll go for ice cream after."

"I like ice cream," Mrs. Minniefield said.

"So do I," Roger said. "Now what questions do you have?"

"May I ask Roger our questions, Aunt Mabel?"

"What flavor?"

"Butterscotch."

Mrs. Minniefield muttered something that sound like satisfaction, and Ted proceeded with his questions. Arnie had warned them that Roger would try not to answer anything, but would instead follow up with a phone call directly to Mrs. Minniefield, bypassing Ted.

Roger parried three initial general questions, answering in terms that sounded like a parroting of the prospectus which both Ted and Mrs. M had studied. But Ted kept at it, finally getting to what they really wanted to know, the size and health of the fund created to pay the annuitants.

Roger again referred to the prospectus, and the financials contained therein, but Ted, silently thanking Arnie, pointed out that the financials were characterized as "pro forma." So they were not, by definition, audited financials, and the company had based them on assumptions rather than actual operating information. And more to the point, the prospectus omitted the total amount in the fund created to pay the annuitants, or a history of timely payments to other annuitants.

To his credit, Roger did not get flustered. He smoothly stated that "inclusion of pro forma" financials was necessary because it was a new fund, but one backed by the "gold standard, or should I say silver," he laughed at his little joke, "in the industry, Goldback & Sterling."

"How much is in the fund now, Roger? Give me an answer, or we walk out."

"Please don't do that. I'm not supposed to tell you anything not in the prospectus. I could get fired."

"The only people who will know are right here in this room."

"No, I'm sorry, I just can't."

"Let's go, Aunt Mabel. We'll make another appointment." Ted named a major investment house.

"Are they the ones who gave me cookies?"

"That's them."

"And I'm getting ice cream?"

"Butterscotch, as promised."

They got up to leave.

"One point two billion," Roger said as they headed for the door.

Ted looked back at Roger, smiled, and said, "Thank you, Roger. We'll be in touch."

As soon as they exited the building, Ted turned to Mrs. Minniefield.

"Tired of acting like a child?"

"Very. That guy ate it up. I think he's stupid enough to believe all people over 70 are doddering idiots."

"We got the information, though."

"Yes. Well played, nephew."

"Thank you, Aunt Mrs. Minniefield."

***

I disconnected and turned to Zellie, who raised an eyebrow.

"Ted. He and Mrs. Minniefield met with our good friend Roger Danish."

"How did it go?"

"Predictable, I'd say. Ted says that Roger behaved like we expected. Stuck to the prospectus until visions of his commission on Mrs. Minniefield's imaginary eight million dollars took over his brain. Danish said the fund set up to pay annuities contains one point two billion dollars."

Zellie whistled. "A lot of temptation if the aim is to bilk the clients."

"Or maybe an adequate amount to pay the annuities. We could read it either way."

"I suppose so." Zellie looked at me. "What's bothering you?"

I paused for a moment, thinking something through. "I don't think we even know whether that money is in a separate account, or whether Sterling has any access to it. And how does a lowly salesman like Roger Danish have that information? And we don't even know whether he's telling the truth. He could have just made it up."

"How do we find out?"

"Two ways come to mind," I said.

Zellie waited.

"Bart Singletary, for one. Bart can do the financial analysis of the prospectus and the information we obtained from EDGAR and Hoovers, that I don't have the skills to do."

"Will he do it?"

"I think so."

"Okay, call him. And what's the other idea?"

"Roger will call Mrs. Minniefield directly. I guarantee it."

Zellie broke out into a broad smile. "And he'll think he's dealing with a dim-witted old lady, who's helpless without her devoted nephew."

"That's the idea. She's expecting the call and has some surprises in store for our dear little morning pastry."

"Does he know enough to give any valuable information?"

"I think he knows more than he lets on."

***

"Sure, I can do that. A change of pace from the exciting world of insurance. Just get me the prospectus... oh wait a sec... I have it already. And I think I already made some back-of-the-envelope notes... now where did I put them? Anyway, I knew you'd be back, so I took the time... but promptly lost it, but I'll find it."

"Um, okay, Bart. Thanks."

"It will cost you," he warned.

"The agency is broke. No paying clients."

"You should get into the insurance business. Lots of money in insurance. If you can stand mind-numbing boredom. I don't want your money. I want a date with Zellie."

"Not happening."

"A kind word?"

"Maybe an e-mailed thank you from both of us. But her printed name will appear on the email."

Bart laughed. "You know I wasn't serious. I'd never charge you anything."

"I know. Just that irrepressible sense of humor."

"You got it. And you'll get my analysis. Just as soon as I find it."

"Thanks."

I disconnected.

"What was that all about?"

"He'll get us the analysis, which he says he's already done."

"Do you think he really has done it?"

"Bart's something of a demented genius. After he talked to us, I'm sure he did it just for the fun of it. And he wanted a date with you in payment."

"He what?"

"You heard me right. He wasn't serious. Just Bart being Bart. No date. No charge."

Zellie pretended to pout. "I'm a little disappointed. Bart looked cute in that leisure suit. We would have cut a fine figure together out on the town."

"Sure. Beauty and the buffoon."

Zellie laughed, but turned serious. "Even if we know the funding requirements for the annuities, and the total amount in the fund, what can we do to stop Sterling from raiding the fund.? He could have done it already."

I gave that some thought. She was right. All we could do was find limited information. We could write an exposé, which would please Pradeep, and fulfill our duty to him. But stopping the fraud before it happened, that was another matter altogether.

"I wonder what internal controls are in place to protect against embezzlement?" I mused.

"What do you mean?"

"There must be a mechanism. External audits, multiple sign-off on disbursements, that kind of thing."

"How do we find that? And more to the point, if there are protections in place, will they stop the fraud from happening? So we wouldn't need to worry?"

"I don't know the answer to the first question. Yet. As to your second question, I doubt any procedures could stop a determined criminal, especially the CEO of the company."

My phone exuded its familiar sound. It was Felicity Amour, inquiring about whether we'd thought more about the details of the wedding we wanted.

"To tell the truth, Felicity..." I caught Zellie's eye. "We've been so busy, we haven't discussed it much." I listened to Felicity's reassurances that

that she was just checking in, that we should take our time, give it some real thought, no pressure, et cetera, et cetera.

I hung up and looked at Zellie. "Any more thought on that front?"

"Let's stick to the original plan. No big wedding. We're too old for that. And who would we invite to a big wedding? My rude cousin Benny from Long Island? Your creepy uncle Ernie from Weehawken? Not a chance. Let's stay with the original idea of keeping it small — our parents, Ted and Marla, Rupe and Sarah, and Mrs. M. That's it."

"Works for me. Any ideas on location?"

Zellie thought about that for a few moments. "Here, I guess. Our friends wouldn't need to travel."

"Our parents would," I pointed out.

"Should we get married in Florida?"

"We don't need to decide that yet, but maybe it's a good idea. Our parents aren't getting any younger, and travel might be hard for them."

"True. But it's our wedding. We pick the place."

Her firmness on that point might have surprised some people, but I knew Zellie. She rarely let other people tell her what to do, including her parents. Although I suspected she thought my parents were more the issue than hers.

I was glad Zellie remained firm in not wanting a big wedding. If that's what she wanted, it was okay with me, but I preferred to spend the money on a wedding gift for her. I'd given her a diamond engagement ring, covering the romantic part, but I wanted to give her a more practical gift as a wedding present. And I had just the thing in mind. She'd been driving her reliable Honda for about ten years. It had well over 100,000 miles on it, maybe closer to 200,000. It still ran beautifully, but it was time for a new car. I'd seen her admiring a Honda CR-V, and would love to buy the small SUV for her, but might not have the money if we spent a fortune on a big wedding. I still didn't have access to my full severance package from Mort, and the trustee handling the liquidation controlled all funds. They'd released some money to me, but not even close to the full amount. I still had my 401K, thank goodness. I also had enough savings to buy Zellie a new Honda, and the way was now clear to do so.

***

Bart e-mailed me his analysis the next morning. The subject line read "NOT A CHANCE IN HECK." I guess that covered his conclusions pretty well. Bart had somehow tracked down the amount of money lent to the business by Vulture Capital, which he claimed was a public record, had calculated the number of annuitants necessary to achieve a break-even point, considering the need to pay both the annuitants and Vulture, and reasonable operating expenses, and had concluded it was impossible. Someone had set it up to fail, either from negligence or fraud. Bart declined to offer an opinion on which. Um, unless you could consider his last words - "scam, scam, scam!!!" to mean anything.

I printed out the spreadsheet he'd attached, and his executive summary, and showed it to Zellie.

"Whoa. He's sure."

"Yes. I'll call him."

Bart answered right away. "I'm guessing you received my e-mail," he said.

"Yes, and thank you. Since you seemed unsure of your conclusions...."

Bart guffawed. "Unsure, I'm not. Seriously, Arnie, real people could get hurt by that scum."

"I know. And we're committed to stopping it, if we can. Any ideas on how?"

"I think you have to involve the Feds. This is right up their alley."

"Why do you think they haven't acted already?"

"I don't know. Bring them some hard evidence and let them do the rest. A lot of money is involved, and it could get dangerous. Wasn't the CFO over there murdered?"

"Yes."

"It's related to this nasty business. You can be sure of that."

CHAPTER TWENTY-ONE

Marilyn Magnuson was the only agent I knew at the FBI, and the person who vouched for Jennifer's scheme, so I called the number she'd given me. She answered right away.

"Special Agent Magnuson. What's up Arnie?"

"We have lots of suspicions, and no hard evidence, but something's crooked at Goldback & Sterling."

"We know. That's why we approved the operation."

"Do you have any guidance on how we should proceed from here?"

"You're doing just fine. So you're newspaper reporters now. Are you giving up the detective business? I promised to help you get a license, but if you're no longer interested…."

"We're interested. But a little flummoxed on how to move the investigation forward. Or more to the point, what's our goal here?"

"Keep looking for evidence of the fraud. We'll do the rest."

"May I ask who the FBI team members are on this investigation? It can't be only you and Jennifer. Do you have an informant inside G&S?"

Marilyn paused. But only for a nanosecond, and she ignored my informant question. "I can't tell you the team members. Operational security. You have my number. Call me anytime. And be ready for Jennifer to give you further instructions."

"She hasn't said a thing to us. We interviewed her, and she gave us nothing."

"It wasn't the right time or place. Be patient. She'll let you know when she's ready to move."

I was a little put off by Marilyn's attitude, but kept my mouth shut. Until I hung up and groused to Zellie.

"She didn't tell me anything. It sounds like Jennifer is running the show. She told me to be prepared for Jennifer to give us the word when she's ready to move."

"Move how?"

"She didn't say. Nor did she identify any FBI agent or informant involved in the case."

"Strange," Zellie said. "I understand not naming an informant, but the operation involves no other FBI agents? Just her and Jennifer?"

"A lot of things are odd about this case. If it wasn't for those poor people being cheated, I'd say we just move on."

"I agree. But we have to stick with it."

"I know one thing. We need a break," I said.

"Can't argue with you there. I'm exhausted. What do you have in mind?"

"Takeout from either Chow Chow Ming's or Build Your Own Falafel, and a movie."

"Let's go with the falafel. We had Chinese last week."

"Middle Eastern it is. Any idea on a movie?"

"How about Caddyshack? It's a classic."

"Works for me. Can't go wrong with silly humor."

See, that's Zellie. Not a chick flick girl by any stretch of the imagination. She can watch that stuff, and so can I, movie buffs that we are, but sometimes you just want to sit back and laugh. And being barred from all local theaters for talking too much left us with my extensive DVD collection and Netflix. And we could talk as much as we wanted at home.

So, we ate our falafels and settled down on the couch to watch Caddyshack. For about the tenth time. As we knew most of the lines by heart, we shouted them out before Bill Murray, Chevy Chase, Rodney Dangerfield and Ted Knight could do so. It was that kind of talking that endeared us to theater audiences in Middletown. Not.

I suppose being blackballed from theaters was mildly embarrassing, although the worst part was being escorted out of one theater by Godzilla. Well, maybe not him. That might have been the movie we were at, although I don't remember. But the guy was big. Anyway, it turns out we prefer watching at home. It's more comfortable, and we highly regard behavior at home that people consider rude in a theater. And we have way cheaper popcorn. So, we forgot about the case for an evening, and had a nice time enjoying each other's company.

* * *

When the phone rang, Mrs. Minniefield studied the caller ID. Goldback & Sterling. As expected, Roger Danish was following up. Without her pesky, smart nephew around.

Mrs. M picked up the phone and answered in the most addled voice she could muster, then listened to a sales pitch. When she interjected that she couldn't decide anything, or sign any papers without her nephew's advice, Roger gave a smooth assurance that she could have the papers reviewed by her nephew, and recommended that she also get an attorney to look them over. If she'd just come to the office, he could give her the papers for her advisors to consider before she signed anything. Mrs. M told Roger that she knew he was a nice honorable young man, and just picking up some papers wouldn't do any harm, and it might even save her nephew the time to do so, as Ted was a very busy person, and she didn't like to trouble him.

"It would do him a favor," Roger put in, and Mrs. M murmured appreciation for Roger's thoughtfulness. She made an appointment to see Roger in an hour, then hung up and made a call.

When Mrs. M called, I advised her to keep the appointment, and to succumb to Roger's pressure, and sign the documents he proffered. I told her I expected that he'd describe the document he proffered as something other than an annuity agreement, maybe an acknowledgement of receipt of the agreement, or something benign like that. And I advised Mrs. M to sign with a very specific name. She laughed when I told her.

"What do you think it will accomplish?"

"I'm not sure. Rile someone up, I hope. I suppose it might put you and Ted in danger, although I doubt it."

Mrs. Minniefield gave an almost inaudible response. And I wasn't sure I heard it correctly. It sounded like she said, "It wouldn't be the first time." I told Zellie about my conversation with Mrs. M, and she and I agreed it was time to interview Sterling.

"No questions off-limits, except telling him our true mission. Although he must now know who we are, and what we do."

"He must. Other people in the office, including Lois, figured it out right away."

"So why let us keep at it? He could have shut down our access."

"Maybe he didn't figure it out until after our initial interviews, and by that time he preferred monitoring our interviews through that listening device under the conference table over shutting it down."

"Do you think he'll let us interview him?"

"Only one way to find out." Zellie picked up the phone, spoke to someone on the other end, disconnected and smiled. "It's all set. Interview today at 1:00 pm."

"Great. Who did you set it up with?"

"Lois Carver."

"He still might not show up. She has every interest in us continuing our inquiries, so she'd arrange it."

Zellie thought about that, rubbing her index finger along her temple. "I think he'll show up. I know his type. Arrogant, self-assured, positive he can win any meeting."

"Is winning a meeting a public relations thing?"

"Didn't you try in your business?"

I laughed. "Everything was a negotiation. Everything."

***

Mrs. Minniefield retrieved a cane from her car trunk. She considered bringing a walker, but decided that was over the top. She didn't need a cane herself. Nature had been kind to her. She had purchased it to use as a prop for today's meeting.

Mindful of the existence of cameras monitoring the parking lot, Mrs. M wobbled her way to the front entrance, gave her name to the man at the desk, and he ushered her to a conference room, where Roger Danish stood and extended his hand. With a great show of solicitude, he helped her into a chair.

He exchanged a few pleasantries, inquired after the well-being of her very nice nephew, cleared his throat a few times, and proffered a sheaf of papers.

Mrs. Minniefield gave them a cursory look, but her sharp eyes detected their contents in a glance. It was a technique developed over a long period in her former career.

"Just a few formalities before I can release the agreement," Roger intoned. Mrs. M only half-listened. Roger behaved as predicted. A kind of bait and switch. Get her to sign something for the ostensible purpose of acknowledging its receipt, but buried within was a legally binding agreement for a financial product.

Mrs. M dutifully signed where Roger indicated, expressing her gratitude for his kindness in saving her nephew a trip.

Roger gave every appearance of being pleased at how easily he'd obtained her agreement and never looked at the actual signature. He made a show of copying the documents for her to take home to review with her advisors. Mrs. M spotted Roger's surreptitious switch of one document, but said nothing. Roger helped her out of the chair, and handed her the cane. She murmured her thanks and wobbled out the door.

***

If we had any doubt that Sterling knew our true motive, he put that notion to rest forthwith.

"I know who you are, and what you're doing," he said after we sat down. He'd chosen his private office for the interview, probably thinking it gave him an advantage, with his high desk chair towering over the low guest chairs.

I started to respond, but Zellie's glance told me to stay silent. So we waited for Sterling to continue.

"The two of you are private detectives," he said, with some triumph in his voice.

"No, we're not. We're reporters doing a feature story. We have no license to be private detectives, but we have press credentials. And we have to make a living. Someday we hope to make money being detectives. But right now, we can't pay the bills that way. So reporting it is."

"I'm not buying that load of crap," Sterling said. "You're trying to dig up dirt on this place. Trying to bring down this fine institution that I built with my own two hands."

"Didn't Morris Goldback build this business?" I asked. It was time to poke him a little and see how he responded.

"Morris is a dope. He spent more time looking after charity cases than growing the business. I turned this place into a world-class operation. I did it. Morris would have been content to be a small, locally based company."

"Mr. Sterling," Zellie started, "If you're so sure we're detectives trying to find dirt on the company, why on Earth are you meeting with us today?"

"To make sure you have all the facts. I've dealt with people like you before. And it didn't go well. For them."

"Is that a threat?" I asked without emotion.

"Call it a promise."

Zellie scribbled something in her notebook.

"What are you writing?" Sterling said, trying to read upside down without success.

"I just wanted to get your exact words for our article. Not a threat, a promise. Is that right?"

"You can't write that. It was off the record. This whole interview is off the record."

"We never agreed to that, nor would we ever do so." I produced a small recorder. "I'm certain you agreed to the taping of our interviews. Ms. Morgan's notes are just a supplement." I played Sterling's words back to him.

"I agreed to taped interviews for my employees, not for me," he said. "Give me that recorder."

"No sir. I'm keeping it."

"Oh, never mind. Tape the interview. I'm only concerned with how it sounded. I wasn't threatening you or anyone else. It's just the hardball response you give in this business if you want to survive."

"So, the interview can continue?" I asked.

"Sure. I have nothing to hide. And I think you'll find that I'm a veritable fountain of information."

I peppered him with financial questions, which he seemed to enjoy answering, even complimenting me on my research into financial matters, noting that I'd grasped some things quickly in such a short time. He obviously didn't know my background.

I worked my way around to the new annuity business. Armed with Bart's analysis, I probed the financial stability of the business, asking him to confirm that the fund created to pay claims contained $1.2 billion at the present time.

Sterling stopped short.

"How do you know that?" he demanded. "Who told you that number? When I find out, they're fired!"

I feigned innocence and stared at my notes. "I thought it was common knowledge. Maybe I got it from EDGAR."

Sterling looked at me for a long moment. Then he laughed. "You're good at this newspaper game. Covering for your sources. No problem. I'll find the leak. And close it permanently." Sterling intentionally took the harshness off his voice, so the tape would show a benign need to close financial leaks. But his meaning was loud and clear to us.

"Anyway," he continued. "The number is wrong. And I don't think it would hurt to tell you the true amount." He made a show of consulting a sheet of paper. "As of yesterday, at 5:00 pm Eastern Standard Time, the fund contained $905 million." He chuckled. "I should have let you report that it was $1.2 billion. It might be good for business, having the public think the fund was much larger than it is. But we at Goldback & Sterling have a code of ethics. We never fudge numbers. Never."

"Or you'd go to jail," I said.

If my statement miffed Sterling, he didn't show it. "That too," he said with a smile.

My questions about the security of the fund yielded a less hostile response. Sterling seemed almost to brag about the protections he had put in place.

"The payments to the annuitants are one hundred percent automated. We prohibit access by any staff member. In fact, the system simultaneously records every distribution to an annuitant, with no human input at all. We'd fire and prosecute any staff member who tried to interfere."

"Could you change that?" I asked. "You are the CEO."

Sterling didn't bat an eye. In fact, he smiled. "Not a chance. I set up an automated system, to show that Goldback & Sterling is serious about the security of our clients."

"But even the best systems need maintenance or tweaking sometimes. Nothing is perfect," I persisted.

"Of course." Sterling gave a careless wave of his hand, as if brushing away a flying insect. "But I can't do it myself. If I authorize it, I need the entries of passcodes of the Executive Vice President, the Chief Financial Officer, the Chief of Security, and at least one non-management financial analyst before I can make any changes. As you can see, I set up the system so that even I can't change anything without four other people affirmatively consenting, including someone not even in the inner circle. I wanted both the appearance and actuality of absolute security for our clients' funds, so they can be sure GS ASAP will pay their annuities like clockwork." He gestured at Zellie. "You should write that down. It's a great quote for your article, if you intend fairness to Goldback & Sterling, and are not just trying to smear us."

I asked a few more questions about the viability of the annuity business, but Sterling just deflected all of them, and it was clear the interview was over.

He looked at his watch and pressed a button on his desk and spoke into the device. "Please escort my visitors out in the usual fashion."

He turned to us. "I'd love to continue this," he said, "but I have an appointment. Thank you for coming. I hope that you'll see that this is a good business, employs a lot of decent people, and does wonderful things for the community. Your article, if in fact you're writing one, should show that, if you're at all honest." He pointed at the door. "You can let yourselves out."

Sterling had meant that only figuratively. An armed security guard accosted us at the door and escorted us out of the building. Before he did so, he frisked me, removed the cassette, then dropped the microcassette recorder on the floor, where it shattered on impact.

"Oops. My bad."

Zellie was in good spirits after we left the building.

"Why the smile? The SOB took away my cassette recorder."

Zellie laughed. "That old thing? That was just a prop. I recorded the whole thing on this." She held up her phone.

"I had in right on the table in front of him, and he never noticed. I taped the whole interview."

I pulled out my phone and looked at it. "This thing can record?"

Zellie laughed. "Yes, old geezer. It can do that, and much more."

"Good to know," I said. "It's amazing. You learn new things every day."

"Yes, we do. And you did a great job in nailing Sterling down on the amount of money in the fund."

I thought about that. "You know, he might have lied about that. Without checking it out for ourselves, we won't know for sure. I think the security features he bragged about might even be more important."

"How so?"

"He was proud of them. That alone suggests he was telling the truth about it."

"Why is it significant?"

"Look at who he needs to break into the system."

Zellie considered that for a moment, then took a deep breath. "Sterling, his crony, the Executive VP, the Chief of Security, the Chief Financial Officer, and a non-management analyst. Cindy Diamond, or..."

"Ruby Love. Also known as the one and only Jennifer Marquette."

"Why did Sterling set that up? He could have just left himself with the authority. Why involve anyone else?"

"I'm guessing it was outside pressure. Or maybe his board of directors. CEOs can't just act on their own. Or a public relations move. It doesn't matter why. He set it up that way. He must have figured he could always count on the Executive VP and his loyal Chief of Security to rubber stamp anything he proposed. That leaves the Chief Financial Officer..."

Zellie shivered. "Who was murdered."

"Do you think Sterling hired Cindy and Jennifer hoping he could manipulate them into agreeing to help him steal from the annuitant fund?"

"I'm sure of it. And he found Jennifer. Or more to the point, Jennifer found him."

"I know who will win the battle of the manipulators," Zellie said.

"Me too. We can only hope that her intention is to stop the fraud, as she told us when we first met."

"I don't know about that. If I recall correctly, Jennifer gave us an explicit warning not to trust her. You told me Marilyn said the same thing."

"That's true," I admitted. "I wonder what scheme the two of them have cooked up?"

CHAPTER TWENTY-TWO

Sterling thought about the interview for a few moments. He might need to move up his timetable. The interview hadn't gone well. He'd thought he could just breeze through their questions and convince them that Goldback & Sterling was an upstanding organization. He'd also misjudged their reaction to his implicit threat, causing him to retreat.. He knew full well that those two so-called reporters were amateur private detectives. And he also knew that they had their sights set on him. It didn't take much to figure that out. But his calculation that he could bamboozle them had failed, and his attempt at intimidation had just seemed awkward. Far from backing down, they'd called him on the threat. And he'd just made things worse by having his security staff take away their recorder. No, words wouldn't work to get them to back off. Stronger stuff was called for. He picked up the phone and barked a few words into the receiver. He hung up, thought for a moment, exited his office and walked down the hall to the office of Ruby Love.

***

Gleeful at his coup in getting Mrs. Minniefield to sign the agreement without involving her pesky nephew, Roger submitted the paperwork to his supervisor, Barbara Newton, without noticing the name Mrs. M had used. He also bragged to her about how he'd aced out the nephew.

The fake signature was not, however, missed by his very thorough and precise boss, who berated him both for his ineptitude and his tactics. Roger had apologized for getting the wrong signature, but remained defiant about the manner in which he'd obtained it, telling her that the "big boss" Bertrand Sterling, in the video they all had been required to watch, had implied that they should get as many applicants as possible, in as short a time as they could. Roger had interpreted that as pushing the sales staff to not waste time in closing the deals.

After dismissing Roger, Ms. Newton picked up the phone and called Chief of Security Fortz to report the incident. Then she called Lois Carver to tell her. She and Lois were friends, both recruited by Morris Goldback. The signature on the paperwork had a decipherable name — Carla Sapphire.

***

"I'll need you tonight, after hours," Sterling told Ruby.

"Why, Mr. Sterling, that's mighty forward of you. But I suppose we can work something out."

Sterling was momentarily flustered, and he didn't know if she was serious. Ruby was hot. They could just lock the door, and... he caught himself. He had more important things to do right now.

"Um, that's not what I meant. Although I wouldn't rule it out."

Ruby remained impassive and acted as if the two of them were discussing the color of paint in the office.

"What I meant was that the time for that little project I discussed with you is fast approaching. You should be ready in a moment's notice. I will let you know the exact time soon. It might be in the middle of the night," he warned.

"I don't sleep much. Just call me or text, take your pick, and I'll do anything you say." She paused. "Anything."

Sterling's heart jumped at Ruby's last comment, but he said nothing more.

***

When he returned to his office, Sergeant Fortz was chatting with Lois, who seemed uninterested in Fortz' overtures.

The two men entered Sterling's office and closed the door.

Sterling gave Fortz an outline of the interview with the two reporters and told him they were detectives who "could mess up everything."

"What magnitude of response are you ordering, sir?"

"Proportionate, for now. Let's see where that leads."

"Done. Anything else?"

"Not at present."

"I have something for you, sir." Fortz advised Sterling about the fake name used by Mrs. Minniefield.

"Not the first time someone's done that. Why the special interest?"

"The name used on the application was Carla Sapphire."

Sterling raised his eyebrows. "Seriously?"

"Yes sir. Ms. Newton, our sales chief, reported it."

"I bet they're working with those reporters. Look into it. It might change the magnitude of our response."

"Yes, sir."

* * *

After Sterling left her office, Jennifer made plans. She figured she had Sterling off balance, and that was a good thing. Something had caused Sterling to move up his timetable, and she guessed that his interview had spooked him somehow. The reason didn't matter. Sterling was skittish. That was enough. Nervous thieves make mistakes, and Sterling would make one, too. And she'd jump whenever the time came. She hoped it was soon. She was tired of being Ruby Love. She just wanted her life back, and Sterling was her ticket to freedom.

* * *

"Do we have any further steps we can take?"

"Nothing urgent."

"Good. I have a few errands to run."

"Okay. I've been putting off a few things myself. Meet for dinner?"

"Good idea. How about Garbanzo's?"

"Sure. See you at about 6:30?"

"Perfect."

I was glad Zellie had some errands to run, because I had a very particular errand that I needed to do solo. I'd take this time to visit our local

Honda dealer. I didn't know anyone at the Honda place. I'm sure Zellie did, as she had her venerable eleven-year-old Honda Accord serviced there, but I didn't want her along with me. I already had a good idea of what she wanted, because she'd ogled the Honda CR-V in the newspaper ads from this dealership.

So I walked in cold and a forty-something gentleman in a sport coat and tie immediately approached me. I explained my interest, and he showed me several models of their "pride and joy."

"She likes green? Look over here. Not a bright green, but a very classy Dark Olive Metallic. It's beautiful, right?"

"It is," I acknowledged. "Is that sticker price firm?" I asked, knowing full well it wasn't. But one has to play the game at a car dealership.

The salesman pretended to think about it, hemmed and hawed a little, then lowered his voice to a whisper. "Don't let the boss hear us, but I think I can get you a deal on this, for below cost."

"Thanks. Just out of curiosity, how can you make a profit selling something for less than you paid for it? Isn't that a bad business plan?"

"We make up for it on volume," he replied, still whispering.

"Kind of like selling five-dollar bills for four dollars."

"Exactly. Um, no. This is different. This is the car business."

"Ah. You have me there. How about I have the precise cost to the dealership on this paper I took off the internet?" I whispered. "Since you will give me the car at below cost, shall we say let's agree on I pay $500.00 less than this figure."

"I can't do that."

"No problem. I'm willing to negotiate. I understand that's part of the automobile business. How much below cost were you offering?"

"Your figures are for a stripped-down model. This one here is loaded, with every conceivable extra." He listed all the extras, and I waited patiently.

"You mean these?" I proffered the list of extras included in the price I'd obtained. We sparred a little, and agreed on a reasonable price for a Metallic Dark Olive Honda CR-V, fully loaded. I signed the applicable paperwork, and he gave me an estimated delivery date of one week.

***

I met Zellie at Garbanzo's for dinner. Neither of us said a word about our errands. We just talked and laughed and ate a good meal. It was nice to put the case aside for an evening.

After dinner, I took her hand, and we walked out on the pier overlooking the river situated right behind the restaurant. It was a clear night, and we just looked at the stars for a long time.

An embrace turned into a long kiss, which we held for a full minute. We disengaged and turned to look down at the water, which shimmered in the light cast by the full moon. Our reflections stared back at us like silent witnesses to our love. We continued to hold hands and look at the water, neither one of us wanting to interrupt the magical moment.

Zellie abruptly broke the silence. "We should get married. Soon."

"Agreed. The sooner the better."

"How about next Sunday?"

"Quick, but we decided on a small wedding, so I'm sure we can arrange it."

"So next Sunday is good for you?"

"Yup. We're getting married next week!"

After we hugged, I took Zellie's hand, and we ran together back to the car. Oops. We had two cars. Romantic ride home was a no go. I kissed her, and we drove to my place in separate cars.

I thought about that while I drove. We still had two houses, but no single home to call our own. It might be time to sell both our parents' old houses and get something that was ours together.

***

The next morning, I suggested we strategize our next steps at the office.

"We have a beautiful space, and we seem to prefer being home."

"Good point. Let's go."

Zellie grabbed her purse and laptop, and we were off. I drove us in my rental. I pulled out of my driveway and turned right to leave the neighborhood. As soon as I reached Dwight Road, I heard two loud sounds, and my rear windshield shattered. Unable to comprehend what was happening, I screeched to a halt, skidding to the side of the road. Zellie and I ducked down, fearing more gunfire, but it remained silent. I checked us both for injuries, found a few cuts, but nothing else. I took Zellie's hand, and felt her shivering. It had shaken me up, too, but I had the presence of mind to call 911.

CHAPTER TWENTY-THREE

To my surprise, Detective Johnson showed up in response to the 911 call, again accompanied by Officer Yang.

After dispensing with the preliminary questions about whether we needed medical attention, or wanted to go to the hospital to get checked out, and receiving negative responses, they surveyed the scene, and returned to us. Detective Johnson began asking questions.

"What happened? Can you identify the shooter? Did you see more than one? Did you see another car? Did you see anyone before or after the shooting? Did you see anything at all that you can remember?"

We tried to answer his questions, but they mostly boiled down to "we saw nothing." There were two shots, and the rear windshield shattered. I had just tried to keep the car from crashing into the trees on the side of the road, while avoiding shots from a direction or directions I couldn't see.

I glimpsed Officer Yang give a sharp look at her boss. If I'd blinked, I would have missed it, but it seemed almost reproachful. Her tone was kinder than his.

"Did you touch anything before we arrived?"

"Nothing. We know better than to disturb a crime scene. I was afraid even to look around for fear of disturbing footprints or other evidence."

She nodded. "Good."

I looked at the two officers. "Did you find anything?"

Officer Yang looked at Detective Johnson, who nodded.

"Two bullets in your car. Two shell casings found in the wooded area near the road. They look like they came from a rifle, manufacturer unknown. We'll need the ballistics people to know for sure. Also, we found distinct footprints where we located the shell casings."

I looked at Zellie, who hadn't said a word.

"Can we continue this later? We're standing on the side of the road, and I think we're both a little shaken up."

"Sure. I was about to suggest that we reconvene downtown. But it's always best to get what information you can from the witnesses at the time of the incident."

"Thank you. Why did you show up for this?"

"I heard your name and decided right away that my personal prophecy that you'd piss someone off had come true."

"Did you really forecast this?"

Detective Johnson just smiled. "I'll see you tomorrow morning in my office at 9:00 sharp."

I nodded. "We'll be there. And we'll have a tape recording that I know you'll be interested in."

It was my turn for a cryptic smile. I thanked him, and Zellie gave him a weak look.

I looked at the car. "Can we take this?"

Officer Yang nodded. "We've calculated the angle, removed the bullets, and cleaned up some glass. There's nothing more to examine here." We rested for a while, and Zellie gradually became more animated.

"Do you think one of Sterling's goons shot at us?"

"Who else could it be? It's not like we've aggravated anyone else."

"At least not this month," Zellie said. "We've caused some very dangerous people problems in the past."

"I can't believe it's related to a past case. No, we stirred Sterling up enough to shoot at us, or someone else at G&S."

"Was our attacker trying to kill us, or warn us?"

"The shooter aimed the bullets at the rear windshield, but hello, who was behind that windshield?"

Zellie's look of concern said it all.

"We weren't going very fast, but the crash still could have caused us grave injuries."

"We were lucky," Zellie agreed.

"Our unknown assailant knows where we live," I pointed out. "And he or she must have followed us and waited for our departure. There was no other way to locate a proper position to to take those shots."

"The shooter had an accomplice."
I nodded. "One to watch for us to leave, and the other to fire the shots."
"I'm glad it's Detective Johnson taking the lead on this, and not those dumb cops we've dealt with in the past."

"Me too. I wonder what he'll think about the taped interview?"

* * *

Angry, as it turned out.

"Someone threatened you in connection with an investigation into a potential fraud you knew I had an interest in and you told me nothing about it? What is the matter with you two? Do you want to get yourselves killed? You need to leave these matters to the police."

"We thought you'd tell us Sterling's comments, which he hastened to take back, we're too benign to take any action, and that we'd be wasting your time."

"You thought wrong," he said, then paused. "Okay, maybe you were right. At least about us taking action. No way to prosecute the guy on that." He pointed to Zellie's phone. "But it was important information to have."

"Is it enough to bring him in for questioning?" I asked.

"Fair question. In view of how I yelled at you for not disclosing it before. I might have been a trifle overzealous in my criticism of you. Because no, I don't think we have enough evidence to bring a guy like him in for questioning. He'd come with seven lawyers, four paralegals, and a stenographer, and I'd get no chance to ask a single question, much less prosecute him for shooting at you."

"What did the ballistics report show?" I asked.

Officer Yang answered. "Bullets and casings came from a Barrett M95 sniper rifle."

"Whoa. That's military grade."

Johnson nodded. "You know your guns. I thought I'd read that about you. We can't connect the bullets or casings to anyone in particular. No matches yet."

"You're checking legal sales?"

"Yes, but that takes time, and it's an unfortunate fact that criminals rarely purchase guns at Walmart."

"This is not your everyday hunting rifle either."

Johnson shook his head. "No, it's not."
"What will you do?" Zellie asked.

"What we can, which is trying to trace the purchase of the gun. I will warn you, though, this kind of thing is hard to track down. The shooter has all the look of a professional. He's thought this one out in advance, to situate himself in just the right spot. He must have arranged for someone else to let him know when you left your house. And his weapon, well, you already know."

"But he or she made a significant mistake," I said, making a point of including a woman as a suspect, even if Detective Johnson didn't.

"What's that?"

"Don't professional snipers usually pick up their shell casings after they shoot?"

Detective Johnson visibly bristled. "Don't you get it? Stop trying to figure this out! Leave it to us. And a better theory is that he didn't have time to pick them up."

Zellie's eyes narrowed. "They had plenty of time. We were careening off the road, while trying to duck from bullets coming at us from an unknown direction. Not only did he or she have time to pick up the shells, there was ample time to walk over and shoot us both."

"That didn't happen," I said, taking Zellie's hand, which was quivering.

"No, it didn't. Which suggests that they wanted to warn, not kill."

"That's some warning," I observed. "They could have killed us anyway."

"You lucked out," Detective Johnson said, "So heed the warning, and back off. You've ruffled some dangerous feathers."

"Are you going to haul Sterling's ass in here or not," Zellie demanded. "Or are you afraid of his lawyers?"

I held up my hand, trying to calm Zellie down, but Detective Johnson remained stoic. He'd likely seen outbursts like Zellie's before. His voice was less harsh. "You two have suffered a shock. The best thing you can do now is go home, forget about Bertrand Sterling, and let us do our jobs. That may or may not include hauling the SOB in here," he said with a smile. "But we will do that only if we believe it will be productive now. It doesn't preclude bringing him in for questioning later, if that's deemed advisable." He paused. "And I have never, ever been afraid of lawyers. In the absence of hard evidence, treating someone as a criminal is inappropriate, and unproductive. And a taped veiled threat, immediately recanted, does not qualify as hard evidence."

Zellie was still angry, I could tell. "So, the answer is no. I get it." She picked up her pocketbook and rose as if to leave.

"Zellie..." I said, but Detective Johnson gave a backward wave. "It's okay, you can go."

Officer Yang offered one more comment as we headed for the door.

"If Bertrand Sterling ordered the attack on you, we'll bring him to justice."

I nodded at her, and we left.

Zellie stormed out of the police station. I walked along, saying nothing. I knew from experience to let her blow off steam. I agreed with her to a point.Someone had shot at us and the police would not do much about it. I knew why they couldn't bring Sterling in for questioning. There was no physical evidence tying Sterling to the crime. Heck, there wasn't anything at all other than the veiled threat he'd made. But he had threatened us, no question about it.

We had arrived in Zellie's car. I had returned my rental earlier that morning. Fortunately, I'd paid for the collision damage waiver. I had to, as I had no car insurance of my own anymore. No car, no insurance. I had to do something about that, but hadn't gotten around to it. What I wanted was Matilda, but alas, she'd gone to car heaven.

Zellie got behind the wheel, and I manned the passenger seat. I thought about suggesting that Zellie not drive in anger, but decided against it. She looked more purposeful than mad at present, so I said nothing as we pulled out of the parking lot, and headed... I didn't know where. I hoped to a late breakfast at AB, but we passed it as we headed... oh no. A sudden realization hit me. She's not going....

But she was. I put my hand on her arm. "I don't think this is a good idea."

"The police won't do anything. I'm going to make it clear to Bertrand Sterling that he can't shoot at us and get away with it."

"He'll sue us for slander," I said. "We have no proof that it was him."

"I know it was him. Don't you think so?"

"I do. But going to his office and threatening him strikes me as...."

"Poking a tiger with a stick?"

"Um, yes."

"It will shake him up. Maybe he'll make a mistake that the police can do something about."

"Setting ourselves up as bait hasn't worked that well for us," I pointed out.

"Oh, he won't do anything in his own building."

"It's not there that I'm worried about. Zellie, sweetheart, this is a bad idea."

We pulled into the parking lot for Goldback & Sterling. Zellie parked and turned to me. "We have to do something. This investigation is going nowhere."

"It might be further along than you think. Why shoot at us if we haven't touched a nerve?"

"I doubt they'll let us in to see Sterling anyway," she said.

"Probably not."

"Let's try, anyway."

I gave up. If she was this angry and determined, I wouldn't stand in her way. Assuming I could stop her even if I wanted to.

"Okay, nothing ventured, nothing gained. Let's go."

We were right. They didn't let us see Sterling. And someone, maybe Sterling himself, had barred us from the building. Two burly security guards escorted us to the exit and shoved us out the door. But not before Zellie shouted that Sterling couldn't intimidate us and get away with it.

"Well, that went well. Not." Zellie said.

"Feel better for trying?"

"I do. Thanks for supporting me."

"I've got your back."

"And I have yours."

We walked hand in hand to the car and headed to AB for a late breakfast.

***

Having been burned by Delilah the last time we went into AB, I resolved to not even look at her when she came up to our table. I'd ask without looking. That would work. I knew it.

Putting my plan into action, I looked the other way. Zellie greeted her, and I did as well, with my head turned.

"What's with the cold shoulder, Arnie?"

"Are you wearing a T-shirt?"

"Of course I am. Do you expect me to go topless? It's not that kind of place."

Zellie cracked up, and I smiled in spite of myself. Delilah was quick on the uptake, that's for sure. She got me again. I turned and viewed her shirt. Emblazoned across her chest were the words "Check Them Out."

"Okay, you got me already. Let's see the other side."

She twirled around to show the words "Our Wonderful Bagels."

We ordered our meals, and I turned to Zellie. "What's bothering you? You're not usually prone to outbursts like that."

"Those shots scared me."

"Well sure. They scared me, too. That's natural."

"I know. But maybe I was more scared because we're getting married, and I couldn't bear the thought of losing you, losing us, and I guess my fear turned into anger at anyone who might interfere with that. I just wanted to do something, anything to get this resolved so we can get married and have a long life together."

I thought about that. While I might not have used those words or actions, I understood the sentiment. We had something precious worth fighting for.

While we always had been part of each other's lives, this was different, and I knew it. I took Zellie's hand and covered it with mine. I looked into her eyes, which glistened with faint teardrops.

"I understand. I feel that way, too. And we will never, ever lose each other. Let's kick the stuffing out of anyone who gets in our way. We won't back down. Period."

Zellie nodded and placed her hand on top of mine, making a sandwich. As we disengaged, Delilah appeared with our meals, which we ate with gusto.

We left a tip and paid the check on our way out of the restaurant. As we strolled hand-in-hand to Zellie's car, a loud explosion rocked us.

CHAPTER TWENTY-FOUR

The tremendous force of the blast knocked us both to the ground. I rose to a kneeling position, gingerly touching my face and elbows. They hurt, but I felt no blood. I looked at Zellie, who'd managed a sitting posture. I saw no blood on her and was gratified that we'd been some distance away when the explosion occurred.

"Are you okay?" I ventured, and she gave a slight nod, with her head still down.

I looked over at Zellie's Honda. It was a smoking wreck. The windows had all blown out, and the roof bore a nasty-looking hole in it. The car was unsalvageable, but I knew Zellie wouldn't be without a car long. At least that had been taken care of, although I hadn't planned on anything like this happening. I'd hoped Zellie's Honda could serve as an extra car for us, maybe to use as an unobtrusive vehicle for stakeouts, or to follow suspects, neither of which we were in a habit of doing. Or maybe I could use it until I found a suitable replacement vehicle for myself.

I thought this would make Zellie angry again, but I was wrong. She had her head in her hands, and she was crying. I moved over and put my arm around her.

"It's only a car. At least we're not hurt."

She looked up at me with red eyes.

"I know, and it was old and had a lot of miles on it. It was time to get a new one, anyway. I'm upset for another reason."

"About what we talked about a little while ago?"

"Yes, but something else, too."

"What is it? Please tell me."

"Was this detective stuff a big mistake? We keep putting ourselves in danger. It's almost like we are looking for trouble."

"We can do something else."

"That's just it. I like being a detective. And we're good at it. But are we just kidding ourselves? We wanted to start a nice little 'find stuff' business. It's turned us into hard-boiled private eyes. That's not us."

"We're not kidding ourselves. We're good at this, and we've helped put murderers in jail. We didn't choose dangerous cases, they both kind of fell on us. We can and should pick less hazardous cases. But we have this case now, whether we like it or not, so let's..."

"Beat the stuffing out of the bad guys."

"I might have used a more colorful word this time, but that's the gist of it."

I helped Zellie to her feet and called Detective Johnson.

He arrived a short time later, with the omnipresent Officer Yang. He asked us whether anyone was hurt, and we assured him we only sustained a few bruises. Turning to Officer Yang, he said, "What do you think?"

She surveyed the wreckage. "Can't say for certain until we get this back to the lab, but it looks professional. She pointed to the angle of the blast, and the manner in which the debris scattered. Somehow that meant to her it was a particular type of explosive.

"Maybe a small amount of C-4, but I can't be sure."

"That's a military explosive, isn't it?" I asked.

"It is," she agreed. "But sadly, not limited to the military. We've seen it used by other groups, too."

I started to ask whether they would bring Sterling in for questioning, but before I could finish my sentence, Detective Johnson interrupted. "Not here," he cautioned, gesturing at the gathering crowd. He barked orders to the two other police officers who'd arrived while we were talking. "Secure the area and make sure no one touches a thing. Did you touch anything?" he asked us and we assured him we had not. "Okay," he said to the officers, "Let CSI do their job, and arrange to tow this wreck when they're done."

He turned to us. "You'll need a lift. We can talk in the car on the way. Do you want to go home, or to a car rental place?"

I looked at Zellie, and we made a silent agreement to go home. We could go to the car rental place later, or even tomorrow. Or we'd request that they deliver a car to us.

"Home please," I said, and gave Zellie's address. My dog walker Betsy would look after Lazlow and bring him over later. I texted her and got an immediate reply of "Will do."

Detective Johnson turned around in the front passenger seat to face us. "I know what you will ask," he said. "And the best answer I can give you is that we will conduct a thorough police investigation into the two incidents, including whether they are related." He held up his hand before one of us jumped on his words. "And I'm 99 percent sure that they are." His palm still facing us, he added, "And our investigation may or may not include bringing Bertrand Sterling in for questioning. Irrespective of that decision, we will find who did this, you can be sure of that."

Zellie shook her head, disgust registering on her face, but said nothing.

I didn't think continuing to fight with Detective Johnson served our interests, but I needed to express my opinion, anyway.

"I'm very disappointed that bringing in the main suspect to at least ask him some questions is not at the top of your list of things to do in your 'full' investigation." I didn't use the visual finger quotes, but he got the idea from my tone.

"I know you are," he responded. "But let me be clear, we're professionals, and we're very good at solving crimes. I understand that you have a view of how I should conduct a criminal investigation, but respectfully, you know squat about how to do it."

"We know enough to identify someone who threatened us as a prime suspect," I rejoined. "And you haven't even offered us any protection. But I get it, you're the boss, and we're just the people being attacked. We have no right to say anything."

Detective Johnson softened. "Okay, point taken. But we're short staffed as it is, and assigning an officer to babysit you would be a waste of resources, at least at present. It seems like these are not so much attacks as warnings. Maybe you should heed the warnings and leave it to us. Look, I get many people telling me how to do my job, and most of them are not as smart as you are. We're not ruling out bringing Sterling in. We just want to make sure it counts when we do, because we'll only get one shot at him before his lawyers tell him to clam up. They might do that anyway. Okay, we're here. Please stay out of this and let us do our jobs. Please."

***

As neither of us now had transportation, we arranged for the rental agency to deliver two cars. We rested for the remainder of the day, but I watched the clock. I had something I'd made up my mind to do at around five-thirty. I told Zellie nothing about my plan, probably because I thought she might talk me out of it. Or worse, want to join me. No, this was something I needed to do alone.

At the appointed hour, I announced to Zellie that I had something I needed to do. Zellie just nodded, and asked no questions, for which I was grateful. I was a little worried about her, though. She seemed subdued, that fire from earlier in the day fading. I figured she needed a rest after our big day. Rest might have benefitted me, too, but I had important business to attend to. Or more precisely, a score to settle. I tapped my gun, secure in its shoulder holster. It was a precaution only. I had zero intention of using it.

***

Bertrand Sterling gathered up his papers, shoved the eyes-only ones into his secure top drawer, and closed and locked it. He rose from behind the enormous oak desk and headed for the door. It was five o'clock. He ordinarily worked late, but sometimes went out for a few beers before coming back to the office. Sometimes, if he got lucky, he didn't come back at all.

He needed a few drinks today. It had been a long morning, culminated by the report of two angry people being escorted from the premises after demanding to see him. He hadn't done so, but he knew who they were, and they sure weren't newspaper reporters writing a puff piece about him.

"Just escort them out. And not gently," he'd barked into the phone when one of the guards manning the security desk called.

Anyway, he needed a drink. And some female company. Hopefully, a beautiful woman who liked the fact that he was rich. He sighed. If only that were still true.

Arriving at the bar, he engaged in some small talk with a pretty redhead, and was soon deep in conversation when a man entered and accosted him. After a heated discussion, with a few shoves thrown in, the man stormed out.

Only to be replaced shortly after by another angry man.

***

I entered the bar and spotted Sterling at once. My guess was right. He was talking to the bartender. He turned, a drink in hand, and spotted me.

"You. Stay away from me. I have nothing to say."

"I have something to say to you. You're going to jail. It's only a matter of time."

Sterling looked around. Oddly, no one was watching or listening to us. They all seemed engaged in conversation with their friends. No one was interested in two old coots arguing.

"That's slander," he said. "You'll hear from my attorneys." He named a well-known large New York international law firm.

"Truth is an absolute defense," I said, quoting Marla.

"Get away from me." He shoved me, and I shoved him back. Hard. Sterling attempted to punch me, and I blocked the blow with ease. I had the benefit of my Dad teaching me how to box when I was a teenager. Mom taught me how to dance, Dad how to fight, or at least how to defend myself. Both valuable lessons.

I returned Sterling's punch with a right cross that decked him. People stopped talking and gaped at the prone figure on the floor, and at me standing over him, shouting "Stop harassing us, or else."

I had just finished my sentence when two bouncers took one arm each and escorted me to the door where, for the second time today, someone shoved me out the door. I walked around back to where I'd parked my car, but didn't get in. I was fuming and needed the night air to settle down. But I couldn't calm myself. I wanted to go back into the bar and hit Sterling a few more times, but I knew that was futile.

I noticed the back door. Maybe I could get in that way. But no, They'd just throw me out again. Get a grip, I told myself, as I eyed the back door.

***

Sterling picked himself off the floor. He ignored the drink he'd dropped and headed for the exit. As he'd parked in back, he headed out the back door. He rubbed his jaw. That guy Fischer had given him a wallop, and it hurt like hell.

He reached for his car keys while trying to remember where he parked. He didn't notice the man in the shadows until it was too late.

"You again!" He gasped the words, just as the man fired at close range. Bertrand Sterling fell in a heap.

CHAPTER TWENTY-FIVE

I returned home, where Zellie raised an eyebrow, which was her version of "what have you been up to?"

I told her what happened, and she shook her head.

"What were you thinking? Getting into a bar fight?"

"I didn't start it," I protested. "The guy shoved me, I shoved him back, and he took a swing at me."

Zellie gave me a once-over. "He didn't connect."

"Nope."

"But you did."

"Knocked him on his ass."

"Dad's boxing lessons, I presume?"

"Pretty much. But the guy has a glass jaw."

"You shouldn't have gone there."

"I know that now. It seemed like a good idea at the time. I thought I could tell him firmly to stop his goons from trying to kill us. As if he'd listen to reason. The guy's a menace."

"Well, I'd be harder on you if I hadn't gone off the deep end myself. We need to do something about that, but taking a swing at Sterling in a bar wasn't the wisest move. His henchmen have taken shots at us and blown up my car. What's next, firebombing our houses?"

"Kinehora!" I said, reaching over to cover her mouth. "And did you use the term 'henchmen?'"

Zellie brushed my hand away and chuckled.

"Yes, I did. And you're still involuntarily trying to stop a bad event by saying 'kinehora' and covering the speaker's mouth."

"I do, don't I? I've been doing it my whole life. Or at least since my grandmother taught it to me. She was a big one on superstition. And we don't want a firebombing, right? So you can't be too careful."

"If you say so." Zellie looked absently out the window. "But what can we do to stop the next attack?"

"I don't know," I admitted. "I might have been wrong to approach Sterling in the bar, but I wanted to do something, anything to keep us safe."

Zellie patted my hand. "I know, and it's water under the bridge now. But it probably just aggravated him, so we'd better be extra careful."

"Agreed. And maybe the police will stop Sterling."

"Maybe." Zellie sounded doubtful. I shared her sentiment, but said nothing.

***

The next morning, I received a phone call from Officer Yang, who requested I come down to the station. She declined to give me any details, but said it was urgent. I asked whether Zellie's presence was requested, and she replied that they only needed me. I hung up, mystified.

"It was my car that was blown up," Zellie said when I told her. "Why would they need just you?"

"Maybe Sterling filed a complaint about our fight," I speculated. "I did punch him."

"It was self-defense. Didn't he throw the first punch?"

"He did, although I blocked it easily. And who knows what he told the police?"

"Should you ask Marla to come with you?"

"To answer for two punches thrown in a bar? I'll just find out what they want first. Maybe it has nothing to do with the fight."

"I suppose that's possible. But at the first sign…"

"I know her advice well. If the police ever interrogate you for anything, tell them you want your attorney present. Cooperation is one thing. Being a suspect is quite another."

***

I parked in front of the police station and walked through a metal detector at the entrance. I left my gun at home. After giving my name at the front desk, a policeman escorted me to a windowless room with a table and three chairs. Figuring they wanted me to sit in the single chair, I plopped down and took a sip from the bottle of water my escort had given me.

Then I waited. For more than a half hour. At long last, Officer Yang and Detective Johnson entered the room and sat down facing me. They said nothing at first, while Detective Johnson studied a file. I decided not to break the silence.

"How are you today, Mr. Fischer?" Detective Johnson's voice was pleasant, as if chatting with an old friend.

"I'm okay, I guess, if sitting in a windowless room at the police station is your cup of tea. The last time I was here, we sat in your office. May I ask what's changed?"

"I think we'd better ask the questions, Mr. Fischer. You just concentrate on giving answers."

"Where were you last night?"

"Wait a minute. Did Sterling file a complaint? That weasel threw the first punch. Which I blocked and responded with a single punch of my own. That's it. And now he's filing a complaint? Unbelievable."

Detective Johnson and Officer Yang exchanged a quick look.

"What did you do after the um, altercation?"

"I went straight home."

"Did you stop anywhere?"

"I don't think so. Wait. I stopped to get gas. What's this all about?"

"We found Bertrand Sterling dead outside the very bar at which you had the fight. And we're not saying you did it, but as a formality, we better read you your rights before you say anything else."

Officer Yang pulled out a card and read me the familiar refrain, ending with my right to have an attorney present during any questioning. Mindful of Marla's advice, I immediately invoked my right to counsel.

"If you think you need an attorney, fine," Detective Johnson said. "This is just preliminary. But no problem, we'll wait for your attorney to arrive. Who's your lawyer?"

"Marla Perez."

The two of them exchanged another look.

"Marla Perez is your attorney? Impressive, but very expensive choice. Very interesting." He made a note in his file.

"It's not interesting at all. She's a close friend."

Officer Yang handed me a phone, and the two of them left the room. I called Marla's direct line. She answered on the first ring, and I gave her the lowdown.

"I'm on my way. Zellie filled me in about the fight already, but the murder changes everything. Don't say a word until I get there."

"I already told them where I was and that there was a single punch on both sides."

"That's not a problem. They knew that already. Facts are fine, just don't editorialize. Your opinions are not facts. Anyway, say nothing more until we confer."

"Yes, ma'am."

I pressed the call button, and Officer Yang appeared at the door.

"Ms. Perez is on her way here. She should be here in fifteen minutes."

"Quick response. She must be a good friend."

I nodded, and Officer Yang closed the door.

Marla arrived, and they gave us a room to confer.

"I think this room is safe," she said. "Monitoring an attorney-client conference is a big no-no. They could be hauled up on criminal charges if they do so."

"Good. But I did nothing to the guy, except what I told you and the police. He shoved me, I shoved him back. He threw a punch, and I blocked it and punched him a single time. Admittedly, my punch knocked him on his butt, but he started it."

"There must be more to it than that. Why were you in the bar in the first place? You're not a drinker, and you hardly went there to pick up a woman. It's a notorious pick up bar."

"No, I didn't go there for that. I went there to find Sterling and talk to him."

Marla just looked at me.

"Okay, I went there to tell him off, and to demand he stop his goons from harassing us. But I didn't go there to punch him."

Again, the look.

"It might have crossed my mind. But I didn't do it until he started it. That's the whole truth. I told him to stop harassing us, or else."

"Or else? What did you mean by that?"

"Oh. I shouldn't have said that, huh?"

"Nope. And the police know you said it, count on it."

"But I didn't follow up on it. Someone else did it, not me."

"I know. The trick is getting the police to understand that. I need to ask this, did you bring your gun with you to the bar?"

"Was Sterling shot?"

"I don't know how he died, but I like to be prepared. Did you?"

"Yes. I thought I might need protection. He had people shoot at us and blew up Zellie's car. I had reason to believe he was dangerous."

Marla sighed. "I agree with you. But the police will say you carried a weapon to a bar to see someone you were angry with."

"Oy."

"Well put. When did you last discharge your firearm?"

"I haven't fired it since last week at the shooting range."

"You're sure of that?"

"Positive."

"Okay, good. What did you do after you left the bar?"

"I walked around back to where I parked my car, and stood there for a while, calming down."

"For how long?"

"I don't know, maybe five minutes. Then I went home."

"Directly home?"

"Yes. No, I stopped for gas."

"Did you see anyone?"

"No. I pumped my gas, using a credit card."

Marla smiled and touched my arm. "Thank goodness for credit cards."

"What? Why?"

"It will give an exact time stamp of when you were at the gas station, which hopefully will give you an airtight alibi for when Sterling died. Assuming that the coroner can determine the time of death with some precision. Okay, let's go. We will be cooperative. Just the facts, not opinions, and no editorializing. Specific answers to specific questions. Just tell the truth. But wait for me to give the go-ahead, and if I hold up my hand, stop, even if it's in the middle of a sentence. Are we clear?"

"As a bell. Thanks, Marla."

"Don't thank me yet. Wait until you're in the clear."

I nodded, and Marla pushed the button to call for my inquisitors.

***

"I assume that you have advised your client not to say anything, is that right?"

Marla smiled. "To the contrary, Detective, my client is well-known for not only cooperating with law enforcement, but helping them put some very dangerous criminals in jail. But before he responds to questions, we have a reasonable request."

Detective Johnson's eyes narrowed. "And what might that be? Your client is a suspect in a homicide. He's not in a position to make requests."

Marla smiled again. "The only request we have is to be told how Mr. Sterling died. You've answered that by telling us it was a homicide, and further that my client, who came down here voluntarily to cooperate with you, is a suspect in that crime. My client is eager to tell you everything you want to know, but I can't advise him to do so if you've already jumped to conclusions."

Detective Johnson gave Marla a long, hard look. If he thought it would intimidate her, he was mistaken. Marla had ice-water in her veins. A sweetheart of a friend, but woe to her adversaries. She calmly returned his stare until Detective Johnson broke it off.

"Okay, counsellor. Someone shot Bertrand Sterling three times in the head. He probably died from the first shot, so maybe that tells you something about how angry someone was with him."

"You can't think Mr. Fischer did that. He's a law-abiding citizen. He tries to catch criminals. He's hardly a cold-blooded killer."

"Look counsellor, let me put my cards on the table. We have witnesses that saw Mr. Fischer arguing with Sterling in a bar, they saw him punching him, and they heard him threaten Sterling. They also saw the outline of a gun under his windbreaker. Does that sound law-abiding to you?"

Marla nodded at me. "Time to tell Detective Johnson what happened last night."

"I went to the bar last night to ask, okay, demand, that he stop harassing us. As you know, someone shot at us, and later blew up Zellie's car in a parking lot." I looked at Marla, and she nodded. "We had reason to believe Sterling was behind the attacks on us. I know I'm supposed to stick to the facts, but as I've already expressed that opinion to you before...."

Detective Johnson nodded. "Go on."

"I told him he was going to jail, it was only a matter of time. He accused me of slander and threatened to sue me. I said that 'truth is an absolute defense to slander.'" A faint smile appeared on Marla's lips. "He shoved me, I shoved him back. He threw a punch, I blocked it and punched him back. Once. Then I told him to stop harassing us, or else. At that point, two bouncers escorted me out of the building."

"What did you mean by 'or else'?"

"It was dumb of me to say that."

Marla held up a hand. "Just the facts."

"Did you intend to kill him if you kept being harassed?"

"No! Absolutely not!"

"Were you going to beat him up?"

"No."

"What then?"

"He's already answered you, Detective. It was a dumb thing to say. He's acknowledged that. We'll stipulate that even going to the bar was a dumb thing to do. But two grown men arguing like schoolboys in a bar hardly constitutes cause to suspect someone of murder."

"What did you do after you left the bar?"

"I walked around back to where I parked my car, and stood there for a while calming down in the night air."

"For how long?"

"Five minutes at most."

"And that's when Sterling came out of the bar through the back exit, and you shot him."

"No! I got into my car and headed home. I never saw Sterling after our altercation."

"Did you head straight home?"

"I stopped for gas."

"Where?"

I told him.

"Did you see anyone?"

"Not that I remember. I paid at the pump with a credit card and pumped my gas without going into the mini-mart."

Detective Johnson looked at Officer Yang.

"I'll check it out," she said.

"Where's your gun?"

"At home, in my gun safe."

"When's the last time you took it out?"

I looked at Marla, and she nodded.

"Before I went to the bar. I thought I should have protection, since I believed he had attacked my fiancée and me."

"When's the last time you discharged your weapon?"

"Last week, at the shooting range."

Detective Johnson looked at Marla. "We'll need to take possession of the gun to do a ballistics check."

"Of course. Do you want me to deliver it?"

"No, I think we should take possession ourselves."

"I have a suggestion. We'll go together to Mr. Fischer's house to retrieve it, so it can be properly marked and accounted for."

Detective Johnson paused, then nodded. "Okay, we'll do it your way."

He looked at me. "Don't even think about leaving town, Mr. Fischer."

"Middletown?"

Marla took my arm. "He means don't go far away. I don't think he'd arrest you if you went to Red Bank."

Detective Johnson's lip quivered, but he said nothing.

So we proceeded in a convoy to my house, where Zellie had waited anxiously for my return. She watched me go to my safe and enter the combination, then step aside while Officer Yang retrieved my Sig Sauer. She carried it to my kitchen table, where she and Marla exchanged receipts and Officer Yang marked the gun to Marla's satisfaction. After Officer Yang departed with the gun, Marla, Zellie and I sat down at the table, and we told Zellie what had transpired. Marla declined an offer to stay for lunch. Zellie and I both hugged her, and I expressed my fervent thanks for her help.

"It isn't over yet. And I'll expect you to pay me." She paused. "My fee is one bagel infusion, my choice, at AB. It's non-negotiable. Don't even try."

"I won't. I promise. Thank you."

She stopped at the door and turned toward us. "Don't worry. You're innocent. And I believe Detective Johnson knows it."

"Why do you think that? He practically accused me."

"It's just his technique. His body language was all wrong. He gave us information. He'd never do that if he really thought you did it. Also, he invited you downtown for a talk. He didn't send officers to arrest you and give you a perp walk. No, he doesn't think you did it. But he has to cover all bases, and he's doing that. Don't worry." She looked at Zellie. "Don't you worry, either."

CHAPTER TWENTY-SIX

"Who do you think killed him?" Zellie asked after Marla left.

"Well, I sure didn't."

"I know." Zellie had a twinkle in her eyes. "You wouldn't do such a thing. Beat him up, yes. Kill him, no."

"Um, thanks for the vote of confidence. I think."

"You're very welcome."

"That guy must have had a zillion people who wanted him dead."

"I'm sure. Can we narrow it down?"

"I don't know. Quite a few of the people we've met could have done it. And there's a universe of others we don't even know. I wonder who takes over now that he's dead?"

"The Executive VP? The Chief Financial Officer is dead, and now the CEO is, too. The dominoes are falling in his favor."

"What about Sterling's wife?"

"She'll be a large shareholder now. Maybe she'll want to take over. Anyway, she won't have to settle for one-half of his property. Now she'll get it all."

"We might have to watch what unfolds in the next few days."

*　*　*

We got our answer sooner than we thought. It was all over the news. Morris Goldback was back at the reins of the company he founded. Lured out of retirement by the company's board at an emergency meeting.

The company's press release said that while Mr. Goldback had enjoyed his retirement, he'd reluctantly agreed to assume the joint roles of CEO and Chairman of the Board of a "great company." While he mourned the loss of that "truly fine financial mind and consummate leader, Bertrand Sterling, he hoped that his presence would provide a measure of stability in this time of great loss."

I read the passage to Zellie, who laughed out loud.

"What a load of crapola."

"You would have written it better?"

"Maybe not. It's good crapola."

I shrugged. "PR people. You all know how to sling it."

Zellie just smiled. "Okay, so we know who's taking over the business. Does that tell us anything about who killed Sterling?"

"It might," Zellie said, half out loud.

"Do you think Morris Goldback did it?"

"It hardly seems likely. The man didn't have to retire. He could have stayed right where he was and never let Sterling take over."

"We don't know that. Maybe Sterling executed a hostile takeover."

"How can we find out?"

"Public companies must fully disclose many of their activities online. I don't know if that one is. A tender offer, which is an offering by one entity, whether it be a person or a company, for the shares of a company, is public. A board vote to oust a CEO is also public. So we check to see if that happened. It's possible that a backroom deal resulted in Goldback resigning. I don't think the company would disclose that online, just the fact of the resignation."

"What should we do?"

"Two choices. One, pore over the online records until we find the information we need, or find that it doesn't exist."

"What's the other choice?"

"Call Bart. He lives for that kind of gossip."

"I choose that."

I picked up my phone and called him.

"Sure, I know what happened. But it will cost you this time. Too many calls for help, not enough love for Bart."

"What do you have in mind for payment?"

"Two hours of your and Zellie's time."

"For what, may I ask?"

"The two of you are going to listen to an insurance presentation."

"Oh, dear Lord, not that."

"Yes, that. You two need insurance."

"You take two hours to sell someone insurance?"

"Nah, I can do it in fifteen minutes."

"Then why....?"

"Because I'm messing with you. They forced him out. Sterling pulled some shenanigans with a shill doctor to say Goldback was no longer fit to run a company of that size. Rather than have it presented to the board, and have it spread out over the news media, he resigned."

"How do you know that...? Never mind, I don't want to know."

"Aw, and it's a great story, too." Bart laughed uproariously and rang off.

I told Zellie what Bart said, and she looked at me in disbelief.

"How can he know that? And is his information legit?"

"Sure. Um, I don't know. But he knows stuff. He always has."

"If he's right, Goldback had a great motive to kill Sterling."

"Other people did, too," I said. "Remember all those Morris Goldback people? All hired by Goldback, and fiercely loyal to him?"

"Lois Carver and Barbara Newton, for two."

"Yup. Both hired by Morris Goldback with few educational credentials and both rose quickly through the ranks. Lois Carver to the role of executive assistant to the CEO, and Barbara Newton to sales director."

"Was their loyalty to Goldback enough reason to kill to get him reinstated?"

"I don't know. And how would they know that the board of directors would rehire Goldback as the CEO?"

"Good question. One good thing," she said. "The threats against us will stop."

"That's good. I have little doubt my confrontation with Sterling would have increased them. And one of them might have been fatal."

"But...."

"What is it?"

"What if Sterling wasn't behind the attacks?"

"It had to be him. They started right after that tough interview."

"True enough. It was him."

"How should we look into Sterling's murder? We have multiple suspects."

"Let's do it the way we always do," Zellie responded.

"I wait for you to find things on the internet?"

Zellie smiled. "Sure, let's do that. I'll just search 'who did it?' and magical, mystical Dr. Google will identify the murderer."

"Um, I guess that means no."

"Let's try analyzing the data we have, try to fill in the missing information through interviews and research, and find out who killed Bertrand Sterling."

"Okay, let's do that."

"Yes, and why don't we go to the office. We wanted one, and we don't use it much."

"No, but we don't have clients waiting for our stellar services, either."

"Maybe after we get our license, it will be more normal."

"One can only hope. Okay, let's go."

"We're still driving a rental car. We must do something about getting cars now for both of us," Zellie said.

I knew I'd taken care of that problem for Zellie, so I delayed.

"Yes, we'll go look for a car for you soon. I'll wait a little while to buy one. I made a mistake buying a big SUV when Matilda was under the weather. Now that she's no longer with us, I want to think a little more about a suitable replacement."

"Okay, let's finish breakfast, and we'll leave in, say, a half hour."

We dawdled over coffee for a while, then Zellie grabbed her pocketbook, and we walked out to the car.

"Okay, let's go."

We drove out of the neighborhood, and onto Dwight Road, then turned left onto Middletown-Lincroft Road to head to the office. We went past the train station, and proceeded all the way to Kings Highway, and turned right, heading toward Route 35. We weren't speeding, but I was going at a healthy clip, when I saw an enormous tree branch on our side of the road. I hit the brakes, and... they didn't respond. At all. A car heading in our direction on the opposite side was perilously close. I had no choice.

"Brace yourself," I yelled, as we plowed into the tree limb. The wheels thumped over the bough, and the car came to a stop. The impact smashed the front end of the car, but the airbags had deployed, and our seatbelts held firm. I glanced at Zellie. She looked as shook up as I felt, but seemed unharmed.

The driver of the other car stopped and ran over to our vehicle. He asked us whether we were okay, and we both nodded.

"What were you thinking? I saw the branch on your side of the road, but you should have just stopped. Why on Earth did you keep going?"

"Brakes didn't work," I managed.

"Oh man, it could have killed you. We'd better call a tow truck. And hey, you two don't look so good. I think you're in shock." He took out his phone. "I'll call. Do you have someone who can pick you up and get you to a doctor to check you out?"

I assured him we did, and I took out my phone and called Ted. I turned to Zellie. "It's his turn. Marla came to my rescue already this week."

Zellie managed a weak smile.

Ted showed up in under ten minutes. Worry lines creased his forehead, and he had an out-of-breath look on his face.

"Are you guys okay? Do you need an ambulance? A doctor? Chicken soup?"

"I think the last one will do," I said. "We're okay. Please, just take Zellie home. We're more shook up than injured. This nice gentleman already called a tow truck. I'll wait here with him."

Ted looked at the guy standing with us, and nodded.

"Were you in the accident with them?" he asked, an edge in his voice.

"He was, but not the way you think, Ted. Our brakes failed, and we couldn't veer into his lane because we'd have had a head-on collision. He stopped and got out to help."

"Oh, good. Um, thanks, Mr....?"

"Marino. Giuseppe Marino. Most people call me Joe."

Ted put out his hand, and they shook.

"Thanks for helping my friends, Joe."

"I'm happy to help." He looked at me. "I can give you a ride home after the tow truck arrives."

Zellie spoke up. "There's no need for that. I'm fine. The three of us will wait together."

"Okay, I'll get going then." He headed for his car, turned and gave a slight wave, and left.

"Nice fellow," I remarked.

"Yes... he seemed like one. But wasn't he a little too prepared to stop? And who offers to wait a long time for a tow truck to arrive and then give a stranger a ride home?"

"I don't know. Maybe he's a good samaritan. Why are you so suspicious?"

"I guess I'm just being overcautious. Too many things like this are happening to us. I don't trust any stranger, and I'm glad you didn't accept his offer of a ride. Who knows? Maybe he'd pull a gun on you once you were in his car."

I doubted it, but I kept my mouth shut. I thought he was just a nice guy. He gave us his name and everything. Um, I only knew his name because he introduced himself. Better check him out when we get back home. Because no way we were going to the office. And I wanted to call the mechanic at the place I'll tell them to tow it to. I raised my hand to hit my forehead in an expression meaning "silly me." Come to think of it, they need to tow it to the rental car agency. I'd rented the car. Geez Louise, I needed to get a car. I couldn't keep getting rentals. This one was sure as heck unreliable. but I wondered. Why would the brakes fail on a rental car? The cars were new. This Chevy Malibu was a current year model. It shouldn't have brakes that fail. Someone messed with them. We were still being attacked. But by whom? I told Ted and Zellie my thinking, and Ted gave a low whistle.

"Cutting someone's brake line, that's serious. It could have killed you."

"Do you really think someone cut the line?" Zellie asked, with a wrinkled forehead and a pained look. "You thought I was being paranoid about Joe Marino."

"Maybe we're both just spooked. We'll know soon enough."

The tow truck arrived and took my rental car, and Ted dropped us off at my house. We walked Lazlow and gave him a biscuit, which he chomped down noisily. When he settled down for a nap after that exhausting experience, I called the service department at the rental agency and posed my question.

"No question, someone cut the brake line. I can send you a picture, but it's a rental car. No reason for you to approve the repair. And I inspect the cars myself before they're rented out. It had to happen after it left our agency. Did you park it out of your sight at any time after you received it? If so, that's when someone cut the line. Who'd do such a thing? Were you on Route 35?"

"No, thank goodness. We hadn't made it there yet."

"Lucky."

"Yes. Thanks for taking my call."

"No problem. And I'll send over a replacement vehicle. Tough to do, but try not to leave that one out of your sight."

I hung up and reported the news to Zellie.

"Omigod, you were right. What now?"

"Time to act like detectives, not reporters, and find out who killed Tucker Ford and Bertrand Sterling, and who is trying to kill us. And why do they care about us, anyway?"

"We're getting close to something the killer is trying to protect. But what?"

"Follow the money."

"Okay, where do we start?"

"Mrs. Sterling seems like a good beginning point. It's pretty clear she'll benefit financially. The other suspects on our list are more tenuous."

"Tenuous, maybe. But they're all looking for something. Maybe money, maybe power. Or both," Zellie said. "But we have to start somewhere, so Mrs. Sterling seems like a good choice."

"I'll check with the court, but I doubt anyone will file financial statements in the divorce proceeding, so we're out of luck there."

I called, and received the expected news that a death put the case, and the judge's order to disclose the parties' finances, on hold pending the dismissal of the case. I told Zellie.

"Okay, we have to do without it. I'll start with a general background check, find all of her connections, and work from there," Zellie said.

"I'll call my sources in the financial industry to see if she's a player in those circles."

"Good idea." Zellie turned to the computer screen and typed away, while I wandered into the living room to make some calls. We worked so well at home, I wondered why we had an office at all. I decided that paying clients, if we ever got them, wouldn't be comfortable coming to my house or Zellie's for a consultation. And neither would we. So we needed an office. Just not at present. Fortunately, the rent was cheap, um, nonexistent.

I made a few calls, left a few messages, and made some notes. This much was clear — she wasn't a financial whiz, or even actively involved in the finance industry. She was a socialite, for sure, but I had no information that she was a player in what used to be my world.

Maybe Zellie had something. I wandered back into the den and saw her idly playing with her hair while she viewed something on the screen. She turned and smiled and pointed at the computer.

"Look at this."

I leaned over her shoulder, inhaling a faint scent of perfume. Zellie didn't use it much, but it was a nice fragrance and I told her so.

I looked at the monitor and read a brief biography of Clarabelle Sterling. Born in Peoria, Illinois, a graduate of a prestigious prep school in Massachusetts, and of Bryn Mawr, with honors. Married right out of college to Miles Danko, who died after twenty-two years of marriage. They had one child, a son. She inherited her husband's controlling interest in ten banks in Pennsylvania, which she sold that same year. Met her current husband, Bertrand Sterling, through the investment banking firm she hired to help her market and sell her late husband's interests. Stayed married to Sterling until his recent death. A fixture in the Junior League and the Daughters of the American Revolution, and serves as a director on the boards of several charitable foundations.

I looked at Zellie. "That was easy. Why is there a biography on her?"

"She's a rich socialite, active on the charity circuit, and her husband just died under mysterious circumstances. Need I say more?"

"No. I guess it's to be expected. So she's rich, and not just from inheriting from Sterling."

"It would seem so."

"I guess money wouldn't be a motive for her killing Sterling."

"Maybe not, although sometimes even wealthy people want more."

"I guess so. So we can't rule her out as a suspect just on that."

Zellie's lips curled and her merry eyes suggested something that she hadn't yet revealed. She was hiding something.

"Okay, out with it."

Zellie scrolled up on the page, revealing the name and age of Clarabelle Sterling's son with her first husband.

CHAPTER TWENTY-SEVEN

Jennifer knew she needed to act fast. As far as she knew, she was the only one other than Sterling, Senior VP Justin McCoy and Kyle Fortz, the chief of security, who knew about the entry of the codes into a laptop which sat tantalizingly locked inside the desk in Sterling's office. And she wasn't even sure McCoy had full awareness of why he'd entered his code. The man was not dumb, but he'd long since given up paying attention to details. He left his dear friend Bertrand Sterling to take care of that stuff. She'd never met the man, but she always had her ear to the ground, and didn't miss much. She didn't eavesdrop.... okay, yes, she did. All the time. Fortz was another matter. He was sharp, and very dangerous.

Anyway, she needed to get into the office. Right away, before Morris Goldback moved in. And he was nobody's fool, from what she'd heard. He'd figure it out in a nanosecond, and the plan would fall apart.

***

Clarabelle Sterling's son was Roger Danish. Born Roger Danko, but changed his name to Danish. Aged 31, an employee in the sales department of Goldback & Sterling.

"Must be how he got his job," I speculated.

"Makes sense."

"We need to find out more about him," I said.

"I'm on it."

"I wonder why Roger changed his name? And why to Danish of all things?"

"Good questions," Zellie said over her shoulder. "And I have the answer to first one, I think. We may never know answer the second one, unless we ask Roger."

"Okay, I'll bite. Why did he change his name?"

"I'm guessing because he didn't like his mom much."

"His mother?"

"Judge for yourself." She pointed at the screen.

"He sued his mother? For what?"

"Looks like he was none too happy she inherited all of his father's assets."

"His father cut him out of his will?"

"It doesn't say that here. I just have what looks like a news article. I'll try to get access to the Lehigh County, Pennsylvania court records."

"How do you know it was Lehigh County?"

"It says it right here. Allentown, Pennsylvania, third largest city in the state, in Lehigh County. Hopefully, the records are online. Let me see, okay, they have a website." She drummed her fingers, mumbled a few things, then said, "Aha."

"You found something?"

"The Registrar of Wills."

"Great. Did you find Roger's father's will?"

"Um, no. They're not online. I'll try to get the docket from the lawsuit. Maybe that's online. Let me see... nope. But you can get records by mail."

"We don't have the time for that, but give me the number. I'll call and see if I can make the request on the phone."

Zellie read me the number, and I called. A pleasant-sounding woman answered and identified herself as a clerk. I made my request, and she demurred at first, saying that people ordinarily made those requests in person, or by mail. I didn't feel right about saying it, but I told her we were reporters trying to get our facts right for a story about the late Bertrand Sterling, and she seemed even more tight-lipped. Served me right, lying to her like that. So I told the truth. We were unlicensed private detectives, and that I had no right to ask questions of any kind, much less request records from a government entity.

A long silence ensued. I'd just about lost hope, and wondered if she'd called the police, or was arranging for a phone trace. But she just laughed.

"In my thirty years here, I've never heard that one. Are you pulling my leg?"

"Nope. That's the whole truth."

"Give me the case number, and I'll pull it up. If you want copies, I can quote you an exorbitant fee, and mail the documents to you. Or I can just do you a favor and read something to you."

"Um, I choose that."

"I thought you might."

"Won't you get in trouble?"

"For helping a respectful out-of-state customer? Nope. We in Lehigh County put people first. What do you want to know?"

I told her, and she read me some portions of the complaint Roger filed in his lawsuit. I thanked her profusely and hung up.

Zellie looked at me with a single raised eyebrow.

"His father cut Roger entirely out of his will. And he and his mother became estranged. It's in a bit of legalese, but the gist of it is that Roger hates his mother."

"Wow. There goes the theory that his mother got him the job with Goldback & Sterling. If we want to find out how Roger knows so much, we need to figure out how he got the job. He can't have just applied, can he?" Zellie asked.

"I don't know. Maybe. He's a salesman, not an executive vice president. It's not like he has a plum job."

"It's not entry level, though. He's on the front lines, selling their newest product, one that they've heavily advertised."

"You have a point. When I started out, I had no office, just a cubicle, and I didn't get to touch anything sexy until years later. Someone helped him. But who?"

"I don't know. But I know someone we can ask." She gave a name.

"Do you think she'll help?"

"We won't know unless we check. I'll call her now." Zellie picked up her phone and entered a number.

"Hi Lois. It's Zellie Morgan. Yes. Yes, I heard. May I offer condolences?" Zellie chuckled at the response, which I assumed was something like "condolences for the death of that creep?"

They had a brief conversation, then Zellie listened a little more, expressed her thanks and rang off.

"Bertrand Sterling got him the job."

"What? Why? Roger hated Sterling's wife. He sued her. And then Bert hires him?"

"That's what Lois said. And she knows it for a fact, because, as his executive assistant, she arranged it for Sterling."

"Does she know anything about Sterling's relationship with his wife?" I asked.

"Only that they're estranged. Not divorced, separated."

"That jives with what Mr. Nickles told us he saw in the letter, and what I viewed at the courthouse. That she served him with divorce papers."

"It looks like Roger allied himself with his step-father against his mother."

"More and more it seems like Mrs. Sterling had a huge motive for murdering her husband. She was divorcing him, and now she gets it all."

"Time to interview Mrs. Sterling. She has a huge motive."

"Maybe not so strong. It seems like she's independently wealthy."

"True. But maybe we've looked at this backwards. Maybe she worried that he would claim a share of her wealth, not the other way around."

"Wasn't he wealthy, too?"

"I wonder. Remember, he was in bed with some aggressive lenders. The vulture capitalists. That's why we thought he intended to steal from the annuitant fund."

"That sounds like more of a reason for Sterling to kill his wife, not the other way around. But it's a good point. Mrs. Sterling seems like the type to want to maximize her wealth. She took everything from her husband's estate, cutting out her son."

"Mr. Nickles told us she was sleeping with Tucker Ford. It's pure speculation, but maybe she took revenge because she thought Sterling killed her lover."

"I doubt it, but we can't rule anything out."

Zellie found Mrs. Sterling's phone number online, called, and left a message.

"Do you think she'll call back?"

"The man who answered was very nice. And no, I don't."

"What should we do instead?"

"I guess we should talk to Cindy, Jennifer and Sergeant Fortz again, considering what we've learned, but maybe not Cindy and Jennifer yet."

"You have something in mind. I know that look."

"We'll never get a thing of value from Master Sergeant Fortz in a straight interview setting. That guy gives new meaning to zipping his lips. We can't ask him if he's behind the attacks on us, even if at least the first two seem to have been done by people with military training."

"Before you continue, I have an observation based upon what you just said."

"What?"

"You referred to the first two attacks as involving military training and hardware."

"Don't you agree?"

"Of course. But what about the third one? Was that done by another person?"

Zellie rubbed her chin with two fingers. "Different method, for sure. So it's possible."

"And if so, that's two different people who hate us."

"I guess in a weird way, that means we're making progress. We've shaken everyone up."

"Seems like it. Anyway, I interrupted. What do you have in mind regardingSergeant Fortz?"

"I think we try to catch him in an unguarded moment."

"Not at his home, I hope.

Zellie shuddered. "No, we won't do that. I was thinking of catching him at the shooting range. The two of you can talk guns, and ammo, and stuff like that. Bond the way people who love weaponry do."

"And while he's holding a firearm, somehow I get around to asking him why he shot at us and blew up your car?"

"Well, you'll be holding a gun, too."

"I feel so much better knowing that."

"So it's settled. You'll run into him at the shooting range."

"One little problem, oh great planner of my risking my life."

Zellie smiled at me. "And what might that be?"

"How do I know when he'll be there?"

"I have an idea about that."

And she did. I've been going to that range for about thirty years. I knew the owner, and all the staff. I just had to give a description of Fortz. And they knew him right away. Some kind of war hero, they told me, and he showed up every Thursday at 11:00 am, like clockwork. I'd never seen him there, but I wasn't looking for him, either, so we might have crossed paths. We settled it. Guns on Thursday.

CHAPTER TWENTY-EIGHT

"We have a break in the action now. Why don't we plan our very small, very intimate wedding?" I suggested.

Zellie's eyes shone. "Yes, let's do that. Okay, I'll call my parents, and you call yours."

"Maybe you could call mine. I think they like you better than me."

"Nope. Not happening. And no they don't. They love you. They're just a little, um...."

"Cold?"

"I would say less demonstrative than my parents."

"That's for sure. Oh, I know they love me, and I'm pretty sure they're happy I'm marrying you."

"Pretty sure?"

"Not demonstrative, remember?"

Zellie laughed. "Call your Mom."

So I did. And it delighted her. I think. Okay, I'm not being fair. She was happy to get my call and accepted my invitation to come stay at my (their old) house. She muttered something about "kids these days doing everything last minute," but that was only after her immediate acceptance. The call was brief, but pleasant.

I told Zellie, and she tittered. "Kids," she said. "Fifty plus aged kids."

"Kids to her, I guess. She's in her eighties."

Zellie sobered. "I guess it is last minute. Maybe we should have given more notice."

"No way. We're getting hitched next week."

Zellie called her Mom, and I wandered off. Her call might last an hour or more. Zellie loves her mother, and so do I. Anna Morgan is a wonderful woman.

To my surprise, Zellie finished her call after only a few moments. To my unspoken inquiry, she said, "They'd love to come, they love us both, and they'll change their plans to come up next week. She had a lunch date, so she couldn't talk long." Zellie paused and absently looked out the window.

I knew that look. "Out with it. What else?"

"Mom didn't say so, but I think she was a little put off by the last-minute notice, too. She didn't say what they were, but they had plans that they have to change, because this is more important to them. Arnie, I think we made a mistake. We should call back and give them more notice. Ted and Marla, Mrs. Minniefield, and Rupe and Sarah, too."

I looked into a pair of very troubled eyes and nodded. Okay, I'll call my Mom back, and you call your Mom before she changes her plans."

"We'll let them know a future date, with lots more notice."

"Yup. We'll even send out a save the date notice, then an actual invitation."

"Good. But we're still keeping it small."

I picked up my phone and called my Mom back. I heard an audible sigh which I took as one of relief, and I was right. She thanked me for being so considerate, and said that "at her age, planning a long trip takes a while." She hadn't told my Dad yet, because he was out "somewhere, running an errand." She was more talkative than I had heard in years, so I was especially glad we'd come to our senses. If we wanted them there, and we both did, we needed to consider their logistics. Gong to a Justice of the Peace on your own is one thing. Involving others is another.

Zellie told me her conversation was much the same. Her Mom hadn't changed any plans, because her Dad was out "somewhere."

We put it off for a month. Zellie found some pretty note cards, and we sent them off to our parents, and our friends.

That done, I stood up, stretched, yawned, and sat back down.

"Exhausting work?"

"It would seem so."

At that moment, Zellie's phone chirped. She picked it up and listened to the caller for a few moments, then said, "Great, we'll be right over."

She disconnected and looked at me. "Believe it or not, that was the one and only Clarabelle Sterling, and she wants to see us."

"Why? I mean, great."

"Who knows? She said that there was a lot to do, given her husband's death, but talking to two friendly journalists was not something she wanted to pass up."

"Friendly journalists? We're neither friendly nor actual members of the press."

"From her tone, I think she knows that. But that begs the question. Why?"

"I guess we'll find out. Let's go."

***

Jennifer sat at her desk, considering her next move. She needed to get into Sterling's office, and fast. The whole thing was coming to a head, and she wanted to take care of her business before it happened. That was always her hallmark — being one step ahead of everyone else. She didn't consider herself to have a superior intellect, and didn't play chess, but she could plan several moves ahead like Bobby Fischer. She needed a diversion. A small fire in the office kitchen would do nicely. Nothing big, but it would create enough of a commotion for Lois to leave her desk to check it out. Lois would take charge, she knew that.

She padded out of her office, leaving her door a fraction ajar. Seeing no one, she walked the few steps into the small break room. As it was mid-morning, the room was empty. Quickly moving toward the garbage bin, she pulled the top off and viewed a pile of used paper goods, which would serve well as kindling. She removed the disposable lighter she'd bought from a convenience store on her way to work, and lit the paper, which erupted into flames. Jennifer replaced the lid and zipped back to her office, closing the door. When she heard the commotion outside, she waited a few moments, and headed directly to Sterling's office. As she surmised, Lois had left her station.

Jennifer knew she had to act fast and didn't hesitate. She ignored the fire alarm, which had sounded, and waved at the security camera, pantomiming her urgent need to retrieve a file. She opened the door, and made her way to Sterling's desk, made short work of the lock, and retrieved the laptop. Silently mouthing "don't be greedy," she entered a few keystrokes, and replaced the laptop. She grabbed a random file, and exited in a hurry. It didn't appear anyone had seen her enter, and she knew the bored security people would not question a quick entry and retreat, especially since she'd acted as if it was the most normal thing in the world.

She waited for the commotion to die down, then strolled over to Ms. Carver, and advised her she felt sick, and needed to go home. Lois agreed, telling her to get some rest, and wishing her a speedy recovery. Jennifer thanked her and exited the building, ambling toward her car. She'd have a speedy recovery, all right, but she wouldn't be returning to Goldback & Sterling. Ever.

***

We arrived in short order at the Sterling estate. For that's what it was — a fence encircled compound. We spoke our names and business into the speaker at the front gate, and the gate opened. We drove along a curling stone driveway, past a beautifully maintained lawn and gorgeous gardens, up to a mansion. We parked, and approached the front door, at which stood a tall, well-dressed, um, sentry, who politely requested we produce identification. He then examined each one under the electron microscope he had next to him. Well, no microscope, but he was thorough. He handed back our licenses and press credentials and opened the door to admit us.

I expected a series of butlers and footmen, and other assorted people serving as a gauntlet to prevent easy access to her ladyship, but it surprised me when a woman greeted us. She stood about four inches shorter than me and dressed casually in a simple sweater and designer jeans. She had stylishly coiffed blonde hair and a friendly smile. Extending her hand, she said.

"Hello, I'm Clarabelle Sterling. And I'm sure Carl here verified your identities as Mr. Fischer and Ms. Morgan." He nodded.

Zellie and I both shook hands and identified ourselves.

"Come with me to the living room, where it's more comfortable."

I looked around at the expansive home, and one thing about it struck me as very odd. The three of us were the only ones here. At least in this part of the mansion. Maybe there were hundreds of people elsewhere. The place was that big.

We sat together on a comfortable sofa, while Mrs. Sterling perched on the edge of an overstuffed chair. She looked at us expectantly.

"Thanks for agreeing to see us, Mrs. Sterling," Zellie said. "I know you must be beyond busy dealing with the aftermath of your husband's death. And may we express our condolences?"

Mrs. Sterling looked at both of us through intelligent blue eyes. "Please call me Belle, and may I call you Zellie and Arnie?"

We both expressed agreement.

"No condolences are needed. I came to dislike Bertrand Sterling, and I intended to divorce him. His dying just saved me some paperwork. And I'm sure the two of you know this already."

She didn't wait for an acknowledgement and went on. "I had the two of you checked out. You're not journalists, but other than that minor subterfuge, you are honest, resourceful and persistent, and have the moral compass so lacking in Bertrand Sterling." She paused. "You're wondering why I'm saying this. It's because I want to hire you. I know you requested this meeting, and I intended to decline, but I gave it some thought. I want your help."

I was momentarily speechless and turned to Zellie, who looked pensive.

"What do you have in mind, Mrs., um, Belle?"

"The two of you are detectives, or journalists, whatever cover you want. And there is something needing investigation by someone other than accountants and lawyers."

"If you had us checked out," I said, "you know we have no licenses as private detectives. We can't accept money for detective work. Perhaps you should hire a licensed private detective."

"See, that's what I mean. You're honest to a fault. Okay, how about I offer a reward?"

"For what?"

"Finding the truth. How about that?"

"Is there a specific truth you're looking for?"

She smiled. "That's good. A sense of humor, too. No, just the truth. I will lay my cards on the table. With my husband's death, I have a large interest in the firm of Goldback & Sterling. I know Bert was a conniving, womanizer and outright crook. He didn't really hide that fact. But the man who is taking over has this shining golden reputation. And maybe at one time he was a good-hearted soul in part of his life. He believed in recruiting non-financial people and found some good employees that way. But he isn't like that now, and he always was a fraud. Morris Goldback may not be what he seems. He could be a very dangerous man. I don't know for sure. I think if you look, you'll find that out. If he's a crook, I need to know. If not, that's fine, too. My share in the firm will be secure. What do you say?"

I looked at Zellie, and she nodded. We didn't need to confer.

"We can't take money for looking into this, even if it's styled as a reward. But thank you for your kind words about us."

"As you wish," she responded. "But please think about it."

I nodded, and so did Zellie.

"May we ask you some questions, Belle?" Zellie asked.

"If I want you to investigate, I can hardly refuse. Fire away."

"Why did your son sue you?"

Belle sighed. "You think it was about money. And in a way it was. But maybe not the way it appears. Roger has a gambling problem, which made me believe he could not manage a substantial inheritance. His father, my late husband Miles, knew it, and didn't include Roger in his will. His father and I tried mightily to get help for Roger, but it's a disease. Miles gave up. I guess I did, too. I could have shared the inheritance with my son, but I chose not to do it. I just didn't think he could handle it. He would have just gambled away anything he received. I'm not proud of my actions, but I didn't know what else to do."

"So he sued you."

"Yes. He alleged that I exercised undue influence on his father."

"But he lost the suit."

"He did. Winning that suit didn't feel good. Prevailing in a legal action brought by your own son."

"I'm sorry," Zellie said.

"Yeah, me too. But I can't do anything about it." She managed a weak smile. "Any other painful memories you want to dredge up?"

"It's regrettable," I said. "But we need to know the interactions of the various players in this case."

"You think Roger is a player? He's a sales associate."

"How did he get that job?"

"He applied. Oh. I didn't help him. How could I? He doesn't even talk to me."

"Roger seems to know a great deal about GS ASAP," I said. "Including some things it seems unlikely that one of many sales associates would know."

"Roger loved his stepfather. No doubt Bert got him the job. As Bert and I became more and more estranged, Roger and he became closer and closer. I think they saw their close relationship as a good way to torture me, the person who wronged both of them. But it didn't last."

"What do you mean?"

"They had a big falling out. At least that's what I heard. Bert and I had many mutual friends. You may not know this, but when couples split, their friends' loyalties often split. Some try to be friendly with both, but most just go with one. Let's just say I heard it from a spy in his camp."

"Was it violent?"

"Oh, I doubt it. Although I only know what I heard."

"Who told you?"

"I think I'll keep that to myself. I don't think you'll have trouble verifying it and getting details without me exposing my friend. But it's very sad. Now Roger has neither me nor his stepfather. I don't know where he'll turn. My door is always open, but only if he gets help for his problem. And I don't think he will. But I can't say I even know my son, or much about him anymore. Anything is possible."

"We expected to see a lot more people here, given the size of this place. But it seems like we're almost alone."

Belle looked around. "It's quiet, but there's a reason for that. I don't live here and haven't for some time. Bert stayed here, and I moved into a townhouse in Rumson."

"So why meet us here?"

"I have to close this place down. If you wait a little while, you'll see a steady stream of people helping me do that. In the meantime, it's just me and Carl."

"I hate to ask this, Belle, but..."

"Oh, go ahead. I've bared my soul to the two of you, what can you ask that will upset me more?"

"Was Bertrand Sterling covered by a life insurance policy?"

Belle laughed. "Okay, you have something more to upset me. But not the way you think. There's no insurance. My lawyers checked. He had a policy, what they call a key employee policy, but somehow Bert figured out a way to get its cash value. And I wasn't the beneficiary, anyway."

"Who was?"

"Who else? His business partner, Morris Goldback."

"Does Morris know the policy was valueless?"

"You'd have to ask him."

"Will you inherit a substantial estate from Bertrand Sterling?"

Another laugh. "I doubt it. Bert needed money. As far as G&S is concerned, I have my doubts about its solvency, in view of an unfavorable preliminary report provided to me by the firm's accountants. As a major shareholder now, I will get a full report when they complete the audit. But I already know Bert was starved for funds, because he tried on many occasions to get money from me. And that doesn't bode well for me to inherit anything from him.

"To be clear, I don't care a whit about that. I was the one in the family with the money. I invested my inheritance well, with reliable wealth managers, never with Goldback & Sterling. Bert signed a prenup. He would never get more than a pittance from me. And other than the established fact that I disliked Bert intensely, I had no reason to kill him."

"I hate to ask this, Belle, but..."

"Oh, go ahead. I have nothing to hide."

"Were you and Tucker Ford romantically involved?"

Belle gave a big sigh, and looked at me for a long moment. I expected her to tell me it was none of my business, but she didn't.

"Tuck and I were friends. We shared a mutual dislike of Bert, and maybe we used our trysts as a way to get back at him. But it was never serious for either one of us. His murder hit me hard. I lost a dear friend."

"I'm sorry. I shouldn't have asked."

"No, it's okay. But do you see why I so much want you to investigate this? It's not just financial, it's personal."

I looked at Zellie, and she shrugged. We were done here. We thanked Belle for her time and promised to think about her offer. She walked us to the front door, and we left.

* * *

"We've heard no character questions about Morris Goldback from anyone else," I mused once we were back in the car. "Do you think she's legit?"

"I don't know. But it seems like someone, maybe more than one person, is trying to stop us from investigating. She's encouraging it. Let's see if we can find anyone else to say a bad word about Morris. We've heard nothing but praise for the man, except that story Bart told us about how Sterling ousted Goldback and became the CEO. We assumed Sterling concocted it, but maybe it was true."

"Okay. We'll look into it. But not everyone is trying to stop us. Lois Carver, for one. Even Jennifer, although nothing is ever what it seems with her. And most people have seemed very cooperative, including Cindy Diamond."

"Well, someone is going to great lengths to scare us off."

"True. And we don't know who. It may even be one of the most cooperative people. You know, keep up appearances while secretly doing something else. Okay, I'm convinced. Trust no one."

Zellie didn't reply. She was looking at the rearview mirror as I drove toward the office.

I looked over. "What's up?"

"That white van has followed us since we left Mrs. Sterling's house."

"Are you sure?"

"Positive."

"It's a little silly. We're not hiding where we're going. We're going to the office. Let them find that out."

"Arnie, someone has already shot at us, cut our brake line, and blown up my car. Shouldn't we be just a tad nervous about a van following us? There's no one behind them, and the road gets narrow up ahead. If they want to do something, that's the place they'll do it."

"Good point." I stepped on the gas, and the van kept pace a short distance behind. I couldn't stop without them ramming me, and there was no place to pull over, if that was even advisable. I had my gun with me, but I couldn't drive and shoot at them at the same time. I sped up more, and the van matched our speed. Zellie kept watching the mirror.

"He has a gun!" she exclaimed.

This was not looking good. They intended to shoot at us, then bump us into the deep gully that ran parallel to us on the right side of the road. I had only one option. I waited until the last car on the other side of the road passed in the opposite direction, then swerved toward the other side of the road, trying to miss a head-on collision with the car barreling toward us from the other direction.

CHAPTER TWENTY-NINE

Missing a collision by what felt like inches, I pulled over into the breakdown lane on the other side of the road. Our car faced the wrong way, but was safely out of range of the van, which had to speed by to avoid colliding with oncoming cars. The van disappeared from sight.

"Are you okay?" I looked anxiously over at Zellie, who nodded and finished jotting something in her notebook.

To my look of inquiry, she said, "I got the license plate."

"Wow. Quick thinking."

"Not as quick as you. That was some gutsy maneuver. But very effective."

"It was the only option. I envisioned us tumbling down that gully." I pointed to the other side of the road.

We called 911, and Detective Johnson arrived a short time later with Officer Yang and several uniformed officers. Zellie gave him the license plate, and he motioned to one officer to run the plate. The man came back a few minutes later, and looked at Detective Johnson, who nodded.

"Stolen, sir. Reported missing this morning."

"Where from?" he inquired.

The officer named a local shopping center and was dismissed.

Detective Johnson gave us a long look, but neither of us budged. If he had something to say, I thought, he can say it. I'm not breaking the silence.

"You two are magnets for trouble," he finally said.

Zellie's eyes flared. "So somehow it's our fault you haven't stopped these attacks on us?"

Detective Johnson looked at me in a silent plea for help from Zellie's anger, but I shook my head.

"She's right," I said. "We're very upset about this, and we haven't seen evidence that you're doing anything about it. Maybe you are, but we're not seeing it."

Detective Johnson wagged an index finger in our faces. "Look, you two. I won't say this again. This is police business. Back off!"

Maybe because she saw us ready to further engage in an argument with her boss, and wished to diffuse it, Officer Yang spoke up.

"Should we assign an officer to protect them, sir?"

Detective Johnson glared at her, but relented.

"I'm assigning a uniformed officer to monitor your houses. We can at least cut off any home invasions. For the rest of the time, another officer will follow you. He'll be in a marked squad car, so you will know that he is not someone trying to kill you."

"Wouldn't it be better to have an unmarked car, to lure them in, so you can make an arrest?"

Detective Johnson's mouth opened, but for a moment, he was speechless. I watched, fascinated.

"Haven't you been listening?" he boomed. "You are not involved in catching bad guys. And we are not using you as bait. We would never do that."

"Okay, okay," I said. "Message received. Have they finished examining my car?" I asked. Upon his affirmative answer, we climbed in and drove off.

Zellie looked over at me. "They won't use us as bait? That's refreshing."

"I know, right? How many times in the past have law enforcement used us a bait, or we used ourselves as bait?"

Zellie's lips curled in a smile. "At least twice. One each in our last two cases."

We drove to the office, our squad car shadow in tow, and I took a seat in the conference room. The two big offices remained empty, with their doors closed. I expected they'd stay that way. Zellie brewed a pot of coffee in the kitchen.

"None for me, thanks," I called.

"Me neither," she replied. "This is for Don."

"Who's Don?"

"Officer Donald Gleason. Our bodyguard."

"Oh, right. Good idea. That's his name? Wait a minute, how could you possibly be on a first name basis already? We just met the guy."

"I stopped to say hello while you came in here, and he introduced himself and told me to call him Don."

"And the coffee is more public relations?"

Zellie laughed. "It's in my blood. But not this time. It just seemed like a nice thing to do. It can't be pleasant sitting out there."

"No, it can't."

Zellie brought the coffee out to Officer Don, and returned a few minutes later and sat down across from me.

"He's seen nothing yet," she advised.

"In ten minutes? I hope not."

"While we were in here, he did a brief reconnaissance. No one lurking, watching, or hanging out waiting to kill us."

"That's good."

"I'll see Fortz tomorrow at the shooting range. We should come up with some questions for me to ask. I'll play it mostly by ear, based upon his reactions, but it never hurts to prepare."

"Good idea. Let's brainstorm, and you can jot down some notes."

I looked down at the table. No pad. No pen. I stood up.

"I have both in my office cabinet. The office I never use. I should just bring some office supplies out here."

I walked over to the office door and turned the knob. The door was slightly ajar when Zellie called to me.

I turned to see what she wanted and pulled the door open as I did so. I heard a loud sound, like a huge spring uncoiling, and a thunk on the opposite wall. Zellie ran out of the conference room, and we both gaped at a large arrow embedded in the wall. Zellie shuddered, and I went weak-kneed. If Zellie hadn't called to me at that exact moment, I'd have the projectile buried in my chest.

"I'll go get Don," Zellie said, "You go sit down."

I gave a wordless nod, and plopped down on a chair in the conference room, my whole body wracked by uncontrollable shaking.

Officer Don came racing in with Zellie.

He bent over me. "Are you okay, sir?"

I nodded. "I'm o… o… kay, just can't stop quivering."

"You're in shock. Just stay put for now." He patted my shoulder, then glanced at the wall.

"That's some nasty-looking arrow. I will leave everything as is, so the CSI folks can examine it. Do you want to go to the hospital to get checked out?"

"No, I'm okay. No physical injury. But that was too close a call. If Zellie hadn't called to me at that moment, I'd be dead now."

I looked at Zellie. "What were you asking me, anyway?"

"To get me a staple remover."

"A staple remover saved my life?"

A faint smile came to Zellie's lips. "I never got the staple remover. Would you mind…"

"No. No way. I'm not going in there until all booby traps are removed."

Officer Don spoke up.

"I know you're kidding, and that's a good sign, but no one goes in there including me. We have professionals who know how to approach this. If there's anything else, they'll find and disarm it." He pointed to Zellie's office door, which remained closed. "And they should start right there."

"Do you think there's another one on that door?" Zellie asked, a brief quaver in her voice.

"I'd bet on it. So the door remains closed." He looked at both of us. "When the detectives get here, I'll run you on home. And don't worry, I'll check everything out before you enter, if the other officers watching your homes haven't done so already."

After thanking him, we sat down. We didn't have to wait long. The familiar faces of Johnson and Yang graced our presence again. Their demeanor was deadly serious. They asked Don a few questions and came over to us. They expressed concern, which I needed at that moment. I had no stomach for the police firing questions at me right now.

"Officer Gleason will take you home. I doubt there is anything more you can tell us, and you've had a rough day. If I think of anything to ask, I'll call you." I nodded my thanks, and he turned to implement his order.

Officer Yang lingered for a moment. "We'll get whoever did this. They've left a lot of evidence here. Traps like this one often have a signature and leave parts that we can track."

We thanked her and left, with Officer Gleason following close behind.

Our two houses were clear of any booby traps, Officer Gleason reported. But there had been one more, attached to Zellie's office door, that the police disarmed.

"I'm taking over the watch here," he said. "I'll be outside, so don't worry. Get some rest."

We thanked him and went inside my house, ate some hastily prepared sandwiches, and went to bed.

The next morning, we looked outside and Officer Gleason was still there. He'd spent the night watching my house. Zellie wandered outside with some coffee and to talk to him. When she returned, she told me that everything had been peaceful, but that Don had to leave to catch a few hours sleep before heading out to join fellow officers in a major police operation. He expected another officer to take his place, but not right away.

I was okay with that. A part of me chafed under the constant scrutiny, and I told Zellie so.

"Me too," she admitted. "But I could sleep last night. How about you?"

"Yes. I was dead. Oops, bad choice of words."

Zellie said nothing. She was engrossed in the morning paper.

"Look at this," she exclaimed.

I looked over to a banner headline in the local paper that read "$108 Million Missing from Investment Firm Accounts."

At that moment, my phone buzzed. It was Mrs. Sterling.

She wasted no time getting to the point.

"Did you see today's paper? I received the information last night. The auditors completed their review of the books and found a $108 million shortfall. I'm at a loss how the news media got a hold of the information already. Must be a leak somewhere, but no matter. Do you see why I want you to look into this?"

I assured her I understood, and expressed my dismay that the theft would hurt retired people, many of them elderly.

"Elderly? What? Oh, you're talking about the annuity business. No, that's intact. The theft was from the Global funds. The participants in those funds are wealthy investors. People like me," she added, with a touch of irony. "But I have my money elsewhere."

"I don't see how..." I started.

"I'm not asking you to recover money for a bunch of rich people. We can afford it. And it's a comparatively small amount of money, spread around among many investors. No, something is very fishy and I need to know if Morris Goldback is the right person to fix things. So please, you're in the middle of this anyway, please get to the bottom of it. I will make it worth your while. If you can't or won't accept money, I'll find another way. A big gift to charity, or something. Anyway, gotta run." She hung up.

I felt like a hit-and-run victim, this time being verbally run over by one Belle Sterling.

I reported the call to Zellie, who had finished the article and pushed the paper over to me. I read it, and it contained similar information as to what Belle told me.

I threw up my hands in despair.

"What can we do about this? There must be ten different police and securities fraud agencies looking into it. What can we possibly add? And why is Belle so fixated on us?"

"I don't know," Zellie said. "But we're not giving up. The police may not figure this thing out. They may even catch whoever is attacking us, but that's only a part of the story. I think you keep your meeting with Sergeant Fortz."

"It's not a meeting. He doesn't know I'll be there."

"He will soon enough."

I nodded. "I have a problem, though.

"What?"

"The police still have my Sig."

"Maybe you can retrieve it on your way."

"Maybe. But if not, I can borrow a firearm at the range. I'd rather use my own, though. I have to shoot well enough to catch his attention."

I was fortunate. When I called to inquire, I was told that I could pick it up that morning. I'd just need to sign for it. This accomplished, I headed over to the shooting range.

CHAPTER THIRTY

Fortz was already there when I arrived and, as pre-arranged, they assigned me to the same area as him. He spotted me right away. He hadn't started yet, and to my surprise, he extended his hand, and asked if I was a regular, as he'd never seen me.

I shook his hand and told him I'd been coming for years.

"Let's see what you've got," he said. "A friendly wager, say fifty bucks?"

"Make it a hundred," I replied gamely. I knew I was good, but this guy was a Master Sergeant. I had to establish a connection, so a hundred bucks seemed like a small price to pay to show cockiness.

"Done," he said. "FBI or Marines?" He was referring to the two different pistol qualification courses, which were a perfect way of gauging our relative skill levels. If he expected to flummox me, he was sadly disappointed.

I didn't hesitate. "Let's go with USMC. I did FBI last time." I gestured toward the range. You go first."

Fortz blew through the forty shots in the course, and scored an impressive 385, well within the range of Expert.

"Your turn," he said, with a grin.

"Tough score to beat," I said.

"Do you want to concede?"

"No, I might as well try."

I dispatched the three stages and forty shorts in short order. My score of 392 out of 400 wasn't even my best, but I didn't tell him that.

His look was priceless as he handed over a crisp $100 bill. I waved it away. "How about you buy me coffee instead?" I pointed to the lounge.

"No, take it. That's some good shooting. But sure, let's sit down and have a cup."

We sat down with our coffees and talked about guns, and I eventually guided the conversation to his current job as head of security at Goldback & Sterling.

He gave me a brief glare, then laughed. "A journalist to the core, huh? Okay, I'll bite, what do you want to know?"

His congenial attitude astonished me. It bore a striking contrast to the tough tone he'd taken in our interview. So I asked him about his time after he'd left the service, and to my surprise, he told me the whole story about being accused of embezzlement, which he denied, and his agreement to leave his career position in the U.S. Marine Corps with an honorable discharge, and knocking around, drinking too much, until Bertrand Sterling approached him about a position with the company.

"I didn't do it," he said, referring to the embezzlement. "And Mr. Sterling didn't hold it against me."

"So, you were loyal to him," I said.

"Yes. It's a big loss. If I get my hands on his killer, I'll..."

"Shoot him," I offered.

"Have him arrested," he said. But not convincingly.

"Why are you telling me this?" I asked. "You more or less stonewalled us when we interviewed you."

"I don't know. Maybe because you have kind eyes." He laughed. "No, that's not it. More like you could knock a raisin off a pig's ass at twenty-five yards without killing the pig."

It was my turn to laugh. "They don't teach that in journalism school," I said. "Another method for gathering information."

I turned serious. "Look, I have to ask," I started.

"Fire away. With words, not your firearm."

"Did you fire shots at us in the car?"

He gave a look of surprise. Maybe contrived, I couldn't tell.

"What? Why? No way." He paused. "As you saw today, if I had, I wouldn't have missed, and you wouldn't be here today. And I'd have saved $100. What happened, and when?"

I told him, and he whistled. "Close call. Even if it was a warning, too many things can go wrong. We both can shoot, but neither of us got a perfect score today. Imagine someone who can't shoot like us."

We talked a little more, mostly about sports. I agreed to give him a rematch sometime, and we parted ways.

I headed out toward the door, but he called me back, and handed me a scrap of paper with an address scrawled on it. I raised my eyebrows and waited.

"Someone who wants the hardware we discussed would probably go there." He pointed at the scrap. "Don't go as a reporter, or start out by asking nosy questions. They won't give you the time of day. Go as a prospective purchaser. And tell them Kyle Fortz sent you. They won't tell you who bought the gun used to shoot at you. But maybe, if you have someone in mind as a suspect, you can use that name and see if they react. But you'll only get one chance at that. Pick a wrong name, and they'll think you're fishing and clam up."

"Why are you helping me?"

He paused. "You might not be ex-military, but the way you shoot, you could be."

I'm pretty sure that was the highest compliment he could give.

* * *

I reported the encounter to Zellie, who expressed surprise at Fortz' attitude.

"He was my number one suspect in the attacks against us," she said. "The first two attacks at least had military written all over them."

"He was mine, too," I said. "But it doesn't take an ex-military sergeant to acquire military hardware. It's all too available to every kind of nut out there." I held up the scrap of paper Fortz gave me. "Maybe from these people."

"He could be lying, and is just trying to divert us." Zellie mused.

"I don't know. Maybe. But he didn't seem defensive, and he didn't stonewall me. He described his post-military time without embarrassment and was grateful to Sterling for giving him a job. He sounded nothing like a nut job, or a guy with a vendetta."

"He could be setting a trap, because he's failed in his previous efforts to warn, or even kill us. And we gave him the perfect opportunity today to set it up."

"I suppose that's possible," I allowed. "But it may be our only chance to solve this case. Detective Johnson sure doesn't seem motivated to do so. Fortz said to pick someone who is our prime suspect to offer to the arms dealer."

Zellie scratched her temple, as if willing her brain to provide answers. Not Sterling, and not Mrs. Sterling, and not Fortz."

"What about Jennifer?"

"What's her motive? She was the one that brought us in to this case."

"True, but it's Jennifer. Need I say more?"

She didn't. Jennifer could have had one motive for bringing us in to the case, and another one to keep us from looking further. She had played many roles over the years. I could hardly reconcile the sweet, funny, free-spirited girl of my past with the mob-connected, conniving con-woman of more recent times. And now, she expected us to see her as the benevolent Jennifer, caring only for the old people. Wow. My head hurt just thinking about reconciling those three faces.

"What does she want?"

Zellie didn't hesitate. "Money."

I nodded. That was her usual motivation. "I guess freedom, too. She's ostensibly working for the FBI as part of her plea deal to stay out of jail."

"I wonder," Zellie said, and paused. "I wonder if we are going about this wrong."

"How so?"

"We're picking suspects before examining the evidence."

"Okay. Fair enough. Let's look at the evidence. Someone is freaking trying to kill us."

Zellie gave a nervous laugh. "One piece of evidence for sure. But why?"

"To stop us from finding something out."

"Who killed Tucker Ford and Bertrand Sterling?"

"Yes. And who stole the $108 million? But I think figuring that out is a job for the FBI. They have ways of tracing funds, and they have access to the firm's books and records. We don't."

"So, we focus on the two murders, and the attacks on us."

"Agreed. But before we leave following the money to the FBI, I have one thought."

"What?"

"Maybe it's a question. But isn't $108 million an odd figure?"

"Maybe that's what was in the account."

"Maybe. Or maybe it was an even $100 million, and someone else took $8 million."

"As a finders' fee?"

"Who knows? It may not have happened that way, and it might be something else entirely, but it struck me as a little strange."

"Maybe so, but we need to pick a name to give to the arms dealer."

We kicked it around a little longer, and decided on Roger Danish. The man just knew too much for a salesman, had a connection to both Sterlings, and had alienated both. He was a bitter man who we thought just might have been thirsting for revenge. Anyway, we took a guess as to the best name to present to the gun shop owners. Fortz had said we'd only get one chance before they'd clam up, but maybe he was wrong. Maybe my gun knowledge would convince them, and they'd ignore the name if we were wrong. I'd say Kyle Fortz sent me, as he'd suggested, and that might put me over the top. At least we hoped so. Anyway, I'd take a shot. Um, strangely appropriate choice of words.

***

It was time to go. With no small degree of trepidation, I drove to the gun shop, parked and walked right in the front door.

Kruger's Gun Shop was a classy place. Not what I expected at all. I bought my gun at a place like this, and it hardly looked the part as a front for illegal arms dealing. It had many hunting rifles on racks on the walls and assorted hunting gear. There were multiple display cases containing many hand guns. No automatic weapons of any kind. And a big sign near the cash register bore the words in large print "No identification, No sale. No exceptions. We do background checks here." I looked at the display case for a while, then signaled a salesman. He came over, and I introduced myself, and told him that Kyle Fortz had sent me. No reaction, just an inquiring look. Kind of a non-verbal "That's nice. I have no idea who that is. What do you want to buy?"

"I think I might need some specialized help. May I speak to the manager?"

The salesman shrugged and went into a back room. A tall, thin man with a wisp of mustache, and a pockmarked face came out of the room, nodded at his salesman that he would handle my business, and beckoned me to one side of the store, away from any customers or staff.

He spoke in a low voice.

"Kyle Fortz sent you? For what reason?"

I didn't hesitate, because I knew if I did, the man would go right back into his office and leave me standing there. So, throwing caution to the winds, I gave our pre-determined answer. "I'm interested in buying the same items you sold Roger Danish."

The man gave a slight nod and motioned for me to follow him to the office from which he'd emerged.

I did so, and entered a dark hallway leading to several offices on either side, all with open doors. I followed him past the first set of doors and felt a jab in my side. I became woozy, and stumbled, when two sets of strong hands kept me standing while someone pulled a dark sack over my head, and I blacked out.

CHAPTER THIRTY-ONE

Mrs. Minniefield hung up the phone after her conversation with her dear friend Hiram Towers, who was a high-ranking official in the Department of Justice. On an impulse, she'd called him to inquire about the FBI operation involving Goldback & Sterling, Special Agent Marilyn Magnuson, Jennifer Marquette and her friends Arnie Fischer and Zellie Morgan.

She expected him to confirm the existence of an operation, and decline to disclose the details, citing operational security. But he surprised her.

"We have no active investigation of Goldback & Sterling, and I know that right away, because we've discussed opening one due to the deaths of two members of senior management. But there's nothing active yet. What have Arnie and Zellie stumbled into this time, Mabel?"

"Nothing good, I'm afraid. Hiram, what do you know about this Agent Magnuson?"

"Give me a minute."

Mrs. Minniefield waited until he came back on the line.

"Now I remember her," he said. "We embedded her in the New York mob for two years and she blew their whole operation up. Got a commendation, and from what I can tell, it was well-deserved."

"What has she done since?"

"Nothing undercover, that's for sure. Mostly a desk job."

"Where she's no doubt chafing to get back in the action," Mrs. Minniefield muttered, half to herself.

"It wouldn't surprise me. I've seen this before. Undercover operatives never quite leaving the fantasy life they previously led. Tell me what you know," he added. And she did.

"I'll look into it and get back to you."

"Thank you."

She immediately picked up the phone again to call Arnie and got voice mail. So she tried Zellie and got through right away. Zellie listened without interrupting and told Mrs. M that she needed to get hold of Arnie right away.

"I tried just now and got voice mail."

Zellie explained where he was and said he likely turned his phone off.

"I'm going over there, Zellie said. "I'll pull him out in mid-conversation if necessary."

***

Zellie went into the gun shop and spotted a salesman. She described Arnie to the man, and he nodded.

"Sure. The guy came in here about an hour ago." He paused and narrowed his eyes. "What about him? You're not his wife, are you? He was only looking, he bought nothing."

"Don't worry. He's not in trouble. I just need to find him."

"He left. He told me he was a buyer for some military base I never heard of. Fort something. The only fort around here is Fort Monmouth, so I just looked at him and waited. He asked to speak to the manager."

"Did he talk to your boss?"

"No. He got a call from someone and hightailed it out of here."

"Did he say where he was going?"

"Nope. Um, I have customer over there, lady, if you don't mind."

"No, it's okay. I'll try to find him elsewhere. Thanks."

He gave a slight nod, and headed toward a man wearing camouflage fatigues, who stood gawking at some rifles on the wall.

Zellie stood for a moment, trying to figure out what to do next. She tried Arnie's cell again, and once again it went into voice mail. This was the last place she knew Arnie had been. The salesman seemed candid enough, but he could be lying his butt off for all she knew, and she had no way to verify his account.

She left the store and sat in her car. It was not like Arnie to stay out of touch, so something was wrong with his phone, or wrong with him.

Only one way to find out. She pulled out her phone, tapped the icon for finding a lost phone, typed in Arnie's password, and presto, she located his phone. And it was not in a good place at all. It was still in the gun shop. Zellie knew she couldn't just barge back in there and demand they tell her Arnie's location. She needed to be smart about this. Either the salesman was telling the truth, and Arnie somehow took a call, then dropped his phone before leaving, a sequence of events that was unlikely, or he was still in the store, maybe in the back, talking to the manager despite the salesman's denial. The salesman was lying, no question. Arnie needed help, and she was right in front of a gun shop, which may be engaged in illegal gun trafficking. They'd be heavily armed. She needed help. But who to call? Special Agent Marilyn Magnuson? Detective Johnson? Arms dealing and kidnapping seemed like FBI issues, but she didn't trust Marilyn. Detective Johnson was investigating the murders, but this wasn't really within his purview. And anyway, he had shown no willingness to pursue anything. He seemed a lot of talk, little action. It took Officer Yang to even get them protection. No, he was not the right choice. She could call Jennifer. Omigod, what was she thinking? She couldn't call Jennifer. How about Mrs. Sterling? That lady had good resources. She could think of only one trustworthy person, and called Mrs. Minniefield.

"It's not safe there," she said. "Come to my house."

As soon as Zellie pulled into Mrs. Minniefield's driveway, her cell phone exuded its familiar sound. She looked at the caller ID. Arnie, thank goodness. But when she answered the phone, it wasn't Arnie; it was a familiar voice that she couldn't place at that moment.

"Listen carefully. I will only say it once. We have your partner and are prepared to let him go if you follow our instructions to the letter. If you don't, you will never see him again. Instructions to follow." And the caller hung up.

Shaken, Zellie sat there for a moment. They had Arnie's phone, and could access it to make the call, which meant that they'd been able to use his face to open it. She looked up at Mrs. Minniefield's house.

She rang the doorbell, and Mrs. Minniefield admitted her. She saw Ted seated in the living room, and Zellie filled them both in on the latest set of events.

"What do you suggest I do?" Zellie asked.

"We wait for the next communication. What else can we do?" Mrs. Minniefield evidenced complete calm. "We can't just storm the place before we know what their plan is. And they might have moved him and kept his phone at the gun shop. Let it play out. Obviously, they want something, so Arnie is safe for the moment."

* * *

Special Agent Marilyn Magnuson considered her options, given the latest unfortunate turn of events. She'd taken the precaution of arranging wiretaps of both Arnie and Zellie's phones. Illegally. She had no court order, nor would any judge in his or her right mind have given her one.

But now she possessed important information, and she had to decide if and when she'd intervene to accomplish her goals.

* * *

I woke up unable to move. Still groggy, it took a while for me to understand someone had tied my legs and handcuffed me in a dark room. Another rope wrapped around my torso, holding my arms at my sides, with my handcuffed hands in my lap. I slowly remembered that I was at the gun shop and was a prisoner. the manager was crooked for sure, but was he the man in charge, or just middle-management?

The answer came soon enough, when a familiar face graced the doorway.

"You!" was all I could say. My captor's lips curled in an unpleasant sneer.

"You've pushed too much. Now you will pay. But not until after your partner handles some business for us."

"What business? She'd never do anything for you."

"I'm sure she wouldn't. But she'd do it for you. At least that's what I'm counting on. And your life lasts only as long as she's working."

I shuddered despite my attempt at bravado. I'd seen my captor's face. The intentional decision not to conceal an identity was a message — I wouldn't leave here alive irrespective of what Zellie did. I needed to find a way out, or at least to send a signal. But I wasn't going anywhere bound this way. First things first. I needed to loosen these ropes. If I could free myself from them, I could manage with cuffs on my wrists. I had experience with that. I wore handcuffs while evading a killer in our last case. I struggled with the ropes and made no progress. I stopped for a moment to catch my breath. I focused on my legs, and kept at it until I exhausted myself and needed to rest. But the ropes had loosened. I kicked them free and waited. As soon as the door opened again, I launched myself at the person who appeared, leaving a prone body in my wake as I charged into the hallway, heading for the exit.

My exhilaration at my daring escape was short-lived. I felt a hard object on my back and a jolt of lightning. Dazed, and tingling with inexplicable pain, I fell, my whole body wracked with uncontrollable twitching. Someone had jabbed me with a Taser. Even my addled brain knew I wasn't going anywhere.

CHAPTER THIRTY-TWO

The instructions came by text message. It contained instructions for accessing a laptop in Bertrand Sterling's office and wiring a huge sum of money to an account number provided in the text. Phone call to follow.

The phone rang as soon as Zellie finished reading the text, and before she could show it to Ted and Mrs. Minniefield.

That familiar voice again. "Listen carefully. You can access the building after 8 pm through the back entrance. Security will not stop you. There will be cameras watching you and recording every step you make from the entrance to Sterling's office. There are no cameras in the office itself. No one will stop you, but there will be a record of your movements. Complete your task by 10 pm, or Mr. Fischer dies."

"The police will arrest me."

"No doubt. But I assume you'll be able to explain yourself."

"I want to speak to him."

"No."

"Then I won't do it."

"Then Mr. Fischer will die. Your choice."

In a sudden revelation, Zellie knew who was speaking. "Why not just do it yourself? You have access."

"Very good, Ms. Morgan. I wondered when you'd figure it out. The reason is obvious. I wouldn't be able to explain myself to the police, and I have no intention of returning."

The line went dead. Zellie proffered her phone to Mrs. M, who read the text and passed it to Ted, while Zellie revealed the details of the phone call.

"You can't do that," Mrs. Minniefield said, with Ted nodding.

"You know I'm going to," Zellie replied, in a tone that brooked no disagreement.

Mrs. M sighed. "I do. But do it in consultation with the FBI."

"Do you trust Marilyn?"

"No. But I trust Hiram."

"I'm sure he's a good man, Mrs. M, but he is unaware of what one of his own agents is doing. I can't trust Arnie's life with that. I'll just do what I'm told, and Arnie will be released. She paused, while her two friends just looked at her, waiting.

"That's stupid, isn't it? Arnie's not getting released. As soon as I complete the assigned task, Arnie is a dead man."

Mrs. Minniefield's face reflected kindness. "The only thing keeping Arnie alive is that you have something his captor wants. Once given, you lose your leverage."

"There's only one thing to do. I follow the instructions, but transfer the money to a different account. One that we control. Then we negotiate Arnie's release with the exact fund his captor is after."

"Playing with fire to be sure, but I can't think of anything better," Ted said, stroking his chin as if willing a better answer from it.

"Let me be clear. I don't like it one bit. But I can't think of anything preferable. Even if we enlist the help of the FBI, they'll never let you go through with what amounts to criminal activity. And that could get Arnie killed. Okay, we do it your way, honey."

Zellie did a double-take. She couldn't recall another time that Mrs. Minniefield had called her, or anyone else "honey." She must be off the charts worried this time.

Mrs. Minniefield scribbled something on a piece of paper and handed it to Zellie.

"You can use this account number," she said. "It has special charac-teristics."

Zellie knew well enough not to ask questions.

***

Zellie parked down the street from the Goldback & Sterling Building, pulled her baseball cap down, and walked two blocks to the rear entrance as directed in the text. The back door was unlocked as promised, and no security personnel were in sight. She entered the building, and immediately spotted a security camera facing the door, filming her illegal entry. She was starring in a one-woman episode of "I Am a Criminal." And her cap would provide almost no help in shielding her identity. She'd considered wearing a ski mask, but rejected the idea. She needed to explain herself later, and how would that look?

Zellie eschewed the elevator and headed up the staircase to the third floor. She encountered no security personnel, or anyone at all. She wondered how Arnie's captor had managed that feat, but decided to just be thankful. She didn't want someone to shoot her before she carried out her mission. She placed her hand on the door, but heard a loud noise moving right toward her. She froze and continued to listen. The noise was right behind the door she'd started to open. Zellie crept forward and put her ear to the door and listened. And gave a quiet chuckle. She was listening to a vacuum cleaner. Probably that nice, nosy Harry Nickles, making his rounds on the night shift, or his compatriot Otis. Zellie didn't want to run into either of them. She waited, hoping that he didn't use the stairwell to travel between floors. She heard a rattling on the door, but there was nowhere to hide. She'd have to just talk her way out of it. But the custodian was probably just dusting the door, because the rattling stopped and there was no more noise. Zellie listened intently, and heard the familiar ding of an elevator, and breathed a sigh of relief. She opened the door a crack and was gratified to see that the floor was dark and empty. She knew the security cameras filmed every move, but she couldn't worry about that now. She had to accomplish her task, and communicate with Arnie's captor, or he'd be killed. The message his captor would receive would deviate somewhat from what was expected, but she hoped a desire for money trumped an impetus for vengeance. The whole plan depended upon it.

Zellie opened the door to Sterling's office and made her way to Sterling's desk. She tried the top drawer as directed, but it was locked. Fortunately, she had prepared for this possibility. Although not skilled by any stretch of the imagination, she pulled out a set of lock picks that Ted had given her, and followed his instructions. She wondered for just a moment why Ted had lock picks and how he had become proficient, but only for a moment. She had a little trouble at first, and panicked, but calmed herself by steadying herself with a palm on Sterling's desk. The lock opened with a click, and Zellie opened the drawer, pulling out a notebook computer. She quickly entered the passcode to open it, navigated to the correct spot, and entered the provided login and password. And nothing happened. She tried again, but nothing happened. Frantically, she double-checked the login and password, and knew she'd entered them correctly, but they didn't work. Now she really panicked. What to do? She tried once more, and received a "system locked" message, instructing her to speak to an administrator. She was screwed, and Arnie was in real trouble.

On impulse, Zellie grabbed the laptop, stuffed it into her pants, pulled her blouse out to cover it, closed the desk drawer, and hightailed it out of the office, down the stairwell, and out the back door, then awkwardly jogged to her car. She put the laptop on the seat, gripped the steering wheel tightly and sped away, while her mind roiled. What had she done?

CHAPTER THIRTY-THREE

Zellie's phone chirped as she pulled into her neighborhood. She looked down and saw it was from Arnie's phone again. In a near panic, she pulled over and picked up her phone and read the message.

"Advised you've left the building. No confirmation of funds transfer received. You have 30 minutes to effectuate transfer, or Mr. Fischer dies."

Zellie pulled into Mrs. Minniefield's driveway, entered the house, and handed Mrs. M the phone while explaining what had transpired.

"That was great thinking, Zellie," Mrs. Minniefield said, "And under extreme pressure."

She looked at Zellie for a moment and explained.

"We know you're worried, and so are we, but you've given us leverage, where none existed before. Far from putting Arnie at greater risk, you may have just saved his life."

Ted nodded. "His captor has to negotiate now. You're holding the money." He pointed at the laptop.

"Send a response," Mrs. Minniefield said. "That message doesn't reflect any knowledge that you have the laptop. Demand Arnie's release, or say goodbye to the big payday."

"What if it results in Arnie being killed?" Zellie asked, her voice cracking with pent-up anxiety.

"It's possible, and we have to steel ourselves for that, but I think un-likely. It's a lot of money. It won't be given up easily."

Zellie paused, fingering her phone with shaking fingers. She knew she had no choice. That decision had been made already, and she knew it. Why hadn't the login and password worked? If it had, then they would... be in the same position, holding the keys to release of the funds by having it in their own account. Would that have worked? She didn't know, but she knew what she needed to do now. She tapped out a text and sent it. And reached a state of sheer panic when there was no imme-diate response.

After what seemed like hours, but was only a few minutes, Zellie's phone chirped again. Another text.

"You win this round. But don't press your luck. Bring the laptop to Field 3 in Lincroft in one hour. Come alone, and no cops, or we cut our losses, and Mr. Fischer is a dead man."

"Will you bring Arnie?" Zellie texted back.

"Yes," was the terse answer.

"You can't go alone," Mrs. Minniefield said.

"I have to. You saw the text."

"We need to call the FBI."

"We can't. I'll turn over the laptop in exchange for Arnie, and we all go home safely with what we want."

Ted was quiet up to that point. "It's a trap, Zellie. Nothing stops someone with a gun from taking the laptop and killing you both."
Mrs. Minniefield nodded. "You need backup."

"But who? Not Marilyn. I know you trust Hiram, but he doesn't know what his own agent is doing."

"How about Detective Johnson? Maybe he can help."

"He seems okay, but ineffectual. After multiple attacks on us, he's done nothing. The only reason we got even temporary protection was Officer Yang."

"How about her, then?"

"It won't work. She works for him. And how can we explain to either of them I'm exchanging a laptop I stole? No, I go alone."

Ted and Mrs. Minniefield traded a look, and Ted handed Zellie a miniature receiver and earpiece.

"Stay in contact," Mrs. M said. "If there's trouble, we can try to help. But I'd prefer the involvement of law enforcement."

That preference was like a summons to unseen forces, as Zellie's phone rang. It was Officer Yang.

"We've had a tip, and we know you have a meet scheduled. I can't explain, but go ahead and do as you're told. You won't see us, but we'll have your back."

"How do you…"

Officer Yang interrupted. "Please don't ask questions. We know, and we have no intention of stopping you from getting Mr. Fischer back safely. Do your part, and we'll do ours."

Completely flummoxed, Zellie reported what Officer Yang said.

Mrs. Minniefield was thoughtful. "Strange. But I don't know how this changes anything."

"It could change plenty. If Detective Johnson and Officer Yang are spotted, they could get Arnie killed. All they care about is catching some criminals."

"I should call Hiram," Mrs. Minniefield said.

Zellie set her jaw. "No. The local cops are what we have. Calling Hiram and explaining the situation will take time we don't have. I need to get going."

* * *

The baseball fields used by the Lincroft Little League were quiet and empty this time of year. Field 3 was just beyond the fancy Field 2, which had a real home run fence and dugouts. Field 3 was less well-appointed, but served its purpose. Zellie drove up and parked about a hundred feet from a black SUV, which she hoped carried Arnie. She briefly debated whether to take the laptop out when she left the car, but left it in the trunk. She supposed Arnie's captor could just break in and steal it, but it could be stolen from her at gunpoint, anyway. Zellie didn't care if she had to trade it for Arnie. She just wanted Arnie back safely. She hadn't seen them, but was glad that Detective Johnson and Officer Yang were present to provide backup. Going alone would have been foolish. She thought of looking around for them, but realized the dumbness of such a move. It would spook Arnie's captor for sure.

She paused next to her car and waited for the person she expected to appear.

She didn't have to wait long. Master Sergeant Kyle Fortz popped out of the SUV and walked towards her. He held a nasty-looking Beretta in his right hand. Zellie shivered. She knew from Arnie that the man had uncommonly good skills as a marksman, and wouldn't miss at this range. She fought back her fear and held up her hand, palm facing him and said "Stop right now if you don't want the laptop turned over to the FBI."

She, Ted and Mrs. Minniefield had discussed this ploy, knowing full well that an unarmed Zellie stood no chance of stopping the criminals from taking the laptop from her. It was a bluff, for sure, but it worked. Fortz stopped.

"I could shoot you and kill Mr. Fischer," he said.

"And you'd never see your payday," Zellie said evenly, fighting against the terror she felt at that moment. She couldn't believe she'd intended to do this alone. Thank goodness Officer Yang had called. But where were she and Detective Johnson? Probably waiting for Fortz to produce Arnie, then they'd swoop in and arrest him. She had to maintain her bravado for a little more time.

"You release Arnie, and I'll get you the laptop," Zellie said.

"Is it here?"

Oh sure, she thought. Tell him it's right there in the car and he'll shoot me on the spot.

"It's close by. Now enough of this. Produce Arnie and get the laptop. We trade as agreed.

Fortz stared at her for a long moment, then nodded, returned to his SUV. He opened the hatch, and pulled out his handcuffed prisoner, holding his Beretta to his prisoner's head.

"Arnie!"

"Your move, little lady," Fortz said, "The laptop, please."

Zellie was in a bind. If she retrieved the laptop from the car, Fortz would shoot them both and take it. She needed a different idea, so she unlocked the trunk, retrieved the laptop, walked a few paces, and with all the power she could muster, threw the laptop at Fortz.

Fortz instinctively put up his hands to protect himself from the flying missile, and I darted away. My freedom was short-lived, however, as Fortz recovered and pointed the gun directly at me. I braced myself. No chance this guy misses. I'm a dead man. I called out to Zellie "I love you! Run!"

Fortz fingered the trigger, and I heard the gunshot just before I saw him crumple to the ground. I looked around to see what happened and saw Zellie pointing at a familiar face. Special Agent Marilyn Magnuson. Holding the weapon she'd just used to kill Kyle Fortz. And save my life.

CHAPTER THIRTY-FOUR

My relief was dashed almost immediately as Marilyn pointed the gun at me as she walked over and scooped up the laptop.

"I'll take this. Stay where you are, and you won't get hurt." She nodded at Zellie. "You, too. I have no intention of harming you. I'll just disappear, and no one will ever find me."

As she walked away, another female voice said in that infuriatingly calm voice, "Not so fast. That's mine. Now drop the gun and back away."

Jennifer was playing with fire. Marilyn was a trained FBI agent, more skilled in firearms than Jennifer. But I had to admit to a certain fascination with the standoff.

It didn't last long. Marilyn made a swift move and fired, as Jennifer did the same. Both fell at almost the same time.

Zellie and I looked at each other. This was too bizarre for words. I was just happy we were alive. I walked over, and we embraced.

After we disengaged, Zellie told me she'd fill me in when we went home, but was mystified about the call she'd received from Officer Yang that they'd provide backup.

"She and Detective Johnson?"

"That's what I assumed. Maybe others, but she didn't say. Where are they?"

"Right here," Detective Johnson replied, as he stepped into our view. "We waited for it all to play out. You were never in danger. It's all over now."

"Where's Officer Yang?"

"She's here. Just a little better hidden. Less possibility of being spotted. He nodded at the bodies. She'll arrange for CSI and cleanup of this mess. He pointed at the laptop which was on the ground in front of us and suggested that Zellie pick it up.

"It's evidence. We know your fingerprints are on it, so let's not disturb it."

He looked at us. "You're in shock, and I know you'll want to get home as soon as possible, but we have to stop at the station first. I'll drive you and the evidence there and get it checked in. We'll get some fast statements from you, and I'll have an officer drive you home. We'll be quick, I promise. Officer Yang and the other officers will secure the crime scene."

He looked it over. "And what a scene."

I nodded wearily. "Let's get it over with."

We followed Detective Johnson to his unmarked squad car, which he had parked in a nearby lot.

He ushered us into the back seat, making sure neither of us hit our heads.

"I'm sorry for ferrying you like captured criminals," he said. "But there really isn't room for all of us up front."

Detective Johnson put the car in gear, and we headed toward the familiar Middletown-Lincroft Road, which would take us near our neighborhood, and past the now infamous Poricy Park, where our current adventure had begun, although we didn't know it at the time. We passed our old elementary and junior high schools on opposite sides of the road, and as we approached Poricy Park on the right, Detective Johnson made a sudden turn into the parking lot.

"What are we doing here?" I demanded.

"I need to attend to something."

I reached for the door handle. Locked. We were in a police car.

"Hang on, I'll get that for you, so you can stretch your legs. I'm sorry for the delay, but this can't wait."

He opened one side door, and we both slid out. When I looked up, I saw the barrel of a gun pointed at my head.

"March," he said, and we complied. What could we do? Maybe in the park, one of us could find an opportunity to disarm him, or escape. Although I didn't see how, with us in front and a gun pointed at us. Maybe one of us could get away, but not both. And while I guessed both of us would sacrifice ourselves for the other, we had no way to coordinate. More likely, he'd kill both of us. Which would happen anyway. We were being led to the same spot where we found the body of Tucker Ford, the unfortunate Goldback and Sterling CFO.

We reached a clearing, and Detective Johnson ordered us to our knees. We both just looked at him.

"Now! Don't get any ideas. Or I pick one of you and shoot you in the knees. That would not be pleasant, I assure you."

I thought about just tackling him. We had nothing to lose, and even if he killed me, Zellie would get away. It was now or never.

CHAPTER THIRTY-FIVE

Jennifer moved first.

"They're gone."

Marilyn opened one eye.

"Yes. They bought it."

"Now what?"

Marilyn studied Jennifer's face.

"We hope like heck that the final piece of our plan is carried out to our mutual satisfaction."

***

As I was about to make my move, a clear, commanding voice, emanating from someone well-accustomed to giving orders, advised Detective Johnson he was surrounded, and demanded that he drop his gun, or be cut down where he stood.

Johnson froze, still pointing his gun at us. Then he lowered his weapon and dropped it.

"On the ground, face down," the voice commanded.

Johnson complied, as Officer Yang emerged from behind a tree.

"Officer Yang! Thank you!"

She motioned to other officers to secure Johnson and take him away.

"That's Captain Yang, actually. Internal Affairs."

***

To our surprise, Special Agent Marilyn Magnuson stood in the doorway as we entered a conference room in the separate building that housed the Internal Affairs Division of the Middletown Police Department.

"Um, aren't you dead?" I asked.

"Hello to you, too, Arnie. Hi, Zellie. No, I'm not dead, and neither is Jennifer. We staged that. Captain Yang will explain. But let me say this right away. We never intended to endanger you in this operation."

"Are you kidding? You did this to us again?" Zellie was hopping mad, and so was I. But I had an overwhelming curiosity about what had just happened.

"We had a joint operation," Captain Yang started.

"Not one authorized by the FBI," Marilyn interjected, "But I'll clear that up with my superiors." She grimaced. "If I still have a job at the FBI after this."

"I intend to speak to them," Captain Yang said. "I approached you, not the other way around."

Marilyn nodded at Captain Yang. "Catherine and I go way back."

"College. But enough of that. You are entitled to the whole story, and here it is. I knew Detective Johnson was corrupt, but he was a genius at concealing it. The guy was a war hero. He even won a Bronze Star for bravery in Afghanistan. And as a detective, he was decent. But somewhere he went astray. We don't know when or where, but we'll find out. Anyway, we had a bad apple and no proof of wrongdoing. I also didn't know who to trust. Not because there is widespread corruption in the police, but because we just didn't know the extent of Detective Johnson's loyalists. And by that I didn't mean corrupt cops, just friends who would never believe he'd do something wrong. So I went undercover as Officer Yang. We make a point of keeping IAD separate, and I'm a recent transfer from NYPD anyway, so I had a reasonable expectation that he wouldn't know me. I enlisted Marilyn to help me set a trap for him."

I couldn't help it. I jumped in. "How on Earth was Goldback & Sterling part of the trap? And why were we involved? And why was Jennifer a part of this scheme? And where is she?"

"All good questions. And Marilyn and I will answer all of them."

Marilyn coughed. "Except maybe Jennifer's location. I have no idea."

Zellie and I looked at each other. "Oh great," I muttered.

"She was a big help. Essential, in fact. But we're getting a little ahead of ourselves here. Let me go back and answer your question about the involvement of Goldback & Sterling.

"We knew Detective Johnson visited that place several times. He had a detective salary, and Goldback & Sterling primarily deals with wealthy people. Except the new annuity business. I wondered whether his visits were just related to a future desire to invest his police pension in an annuity, but it took almost no time to figure out it was something else entirely."

"He knew Kyle Fortz." Zellie interjected.

Captain Yang looked surprised. "War buddies. In the same unit in Afghanistan. Fortz commanded a unit that enemy fire pinned down. Both men received Bronze Stars. You knew that?"

Zellie smiled. "No, we saw the Bronze Star plaque in Detective Johnson's office, but didn't figure out that he and Fortz were in the same unit, or even knew each other."

Captain Yang continued, "We worried that Johnson and Fortz were up to something, and targeting that new annuity fund seemed like a juicy potential target."

Marilyn took up the story. "I had earlier viewed an FBI intelligence report specifying Kruger's Gun Shop as a suspected front for illegal arms sales, but there was no mention of Johnson and Fortz, and I had no reason to link it to the investigation Catherine proposed. We only realized it later. Breaking up that ring was an unexpected benefit."

"Catherine and I figured you could stir things up a little by investigating Goldback & Sterling, which might make them nervous enough to make a mistake. And to get them to avoid the annuity fund and target something that did not have the potential to harm a large proportion of retired and elderly people."

"When I first spoke to you about this, I told you the truth. Your mission was to investigate, and to help stop innocent people from being scammed. You should be proud of yourselves. You absolutely accomplished that goal. Make no mistake. If you hadn't been doing what you do so well, they'd have already stolen that money."

"How does Bertrand Sterling fit into this?"

"He was a man heavily into debt, divorcing his wealthy wife, and desperate for money. And Johnson and Fortz needed him for obvious reasons. The SEC required the company to show the security of the annuity fund, and the board of directors complied by putting into place some stringent protections. The provisions were effective, but not if you wanted to steal. To access any of the many funds G&S managed, he needed the approval of the Executive VP who was in his pocket; and the CFO, who presumably wouldn't agree, so they killed him; Fortz himself; and a senior analyst."

I spoke up. "Sterling told us he put the protections in place."

"In a way, he did, by complying with the security requirements of the SEC."

"Anyway, that procedure provided us with a perfect opportunity to set a trap. But unfortunately, and Marilyn and I both regret this deeply, I'm ashamed of myself for involving you at all. We exposed you to danger on multiple occasions. We didn't intend that.

"Detective Johnson predictably pursued nothing, and I had to make him feel like he was being obvious if he didn't allow me to assign an officer to protect you."

She paused. "An officer that I trust. Don Gleason is a good cop."

"Anyway, you know the rest. We had no way of knowing Arnie would visit the gun shop or be taken prisoner there, and no way to foresee that Zellie would have to retrieve the laptop. We knew the login and password Zellie put in wouldn't work, because we set it up so Jennifer would disable the code. And she obviously did, because you had to steal the laptop, instead of entering the login and password.

"You stealing the laptop provided an opportunity to draw Johnson out. We knew he'd be watching Fortz try to kill both of you, but as you saw, not only was I there but also Marilyn and Jennifer watching to keep you safe. If Fortz made a move to hurt you, Marilyn would take him down. Then they staged the mutual shooting to draw Johnson out, while I watched. Then I brought along my team to follow you. If he brought you to the station, the whole plan would go for naught. But he tried to kill you, so now he's in jail where he belongs."

"Why Jennifer?" Zellie asked.

"She's the perfect con-woman. And who better to convince Sterling that she was as crooked as he was?"

"But how can you trust her?"

"We can't. But we had a backup, and someone watching, just in case."

"Cindy Diamond," I said.

"Yes."

"Is she FBI or Middletown Police?"

"Neither. She's another friend, who really has an MBA, and who figured out a lot of the financial stuff for us. We hoped Sterling wouldn't choose her as his crooked accomplice. Jennifer is much more the part."

"How did you get Jennifer to agree to do this? It couldn't possibly be for altruistic reasons."

Marilyn laughed out loud at that. "No, that's not our Jennifer, is it? Although something she said made me think she had a grudge against cons involving the elderly. I told her I could keep her out of jail."

"Can you?"

"I have so far. My bosses think she's my confidential informant. And I had a lot of credibility built up from my undercover work. She did a good job here, and a promise is a promise. But if she's trying to disappear... I can't help her. And that promise would have been easier to keep if the FBI sanctioned this operation. I hope to get retroactive approval. We put a crooked cop in jail, and stopped the funding of illegal arms dealers. A good outcome. And you have a great story to write for the Clarion."

"We do, don't we?"

"And one more thing," Captain Yang said. "I have some influence in the New Jersey Attorney General's Office. And I intend to recommend to them that they waive the five- year waiting period for your licensure as private detectives."

"Thank you," we said together.

"I have one more question," Zellie said.

"What is it?"

"Were you able to recover the $108 million stolen from the Goldback & Sterling Global Fund?"

Marilyn smiled. "Yes. In fact, I just received confirmation. It hadn't left the country, and some smart forensic accountants worked night and day on it. They reversed the $100 million transfer."

"But the total theft was $108 million. What happened to the other $8 million?"

"I think the accountants assumed the original figure was in error," Captain Yang said. "And in that world, they don't seem to worry much about a figure as small as that. It's insured, anyway."

"I have a good idea on where it went," I said, "and so do you, if you think about it."

"Jennifer."

I nodded. "There's always a second scam with her. I bet she figured by not being greedy, she could walk away. And while it may not seem like much to the rich people investing at Goldback & Sterling, for Jennifer, it could enable her to disappear. She probably never trusted you to keep her out of jail."

"I'll put a BOLO out on her right now. She'll never be able to take a plane, bus, or train. And we know what car she's driving. She won't get far."

"She won't use public transportation. And she won't take that car."

"Do you know something?"

I grinned. "Maybe. We know Jennifer better than anyone. Lend us Officer Gleason, and we'll bring Jennifer to you."

Captain Yang pressed a button on her phone, and Officer Gleason stepped into the conference room.

"Go with them. You might make a big arrest."

"Can we take an unmarked car?" I asked.

She nodded at Officer Gleason. "Sign one out."

"Where to," he asked, after we got into the car. I gave him a location, and he started to pose a question, thought better of it, and drove us to a few blocks from the car dealership I'd named.

"Not the Mercedes dealer?" Zellie joked.

A Mercedes dealership played a significant role in our first case.

"Nope. Not this time. She'll be here unless she's already left."

"She has a weakness for foreign sports cars, and I know for a fact she's always wanted a Porsche 911 Turbo. And she must know that eventually Marilyn will figure out she isn't coming back, so she'll need new transportation to get her out of here."

The three of us walked down the street to a spot where we could see both the car lot and inside the windows. And there she was, sitting in front of a desk, talking to a car dealer.

I pointed her out to Don, and he walked over and said a few words to the two of them. Jennifer peered out the window at us and shrugged, as she rose and walked with Don to the squad car.

"I've done nothing wrong," she said. "We can clear it all up at the station."

Don put her in the back seat, and the three of us scrunched together in the front, while we returned to the police station, and they processed Jennifer, while we returned to Captain Yang's office.

While we walked over to the IAD building, Zellie turned to me and asked "Do you think she'll talk her way out of this?"

I smiled at her. "It's Jennifer. What do you think?"

Zellie stopped, and I stopped with her.

"You know," she said, "I don't care."

Captain Yang arranged for our transportation home and promised to have someone retrieve Zellie's rental car.

The officer dropped us off at Zellie's house just as two different Hondas pulled into her driveway — an older dark blue Honda Accord, and a gleaming new metallic green Honda CR-V.

"What do you think that's all about?" Zellie asked.

I tried to conceal my smile. "I wouldn't know. Let's find out."

Zellie looked at me. "You know something. Out with it."

I leaned over and kissed her.

"Happy Engagement. That green CR-V is all yours."

"Really? I've been ogling that one for a year. That color, too. How did you know?"

"I might have seen you ogling it for a year," I said. "But enough talk. Start her up and let's take a ride."

Zellie jumped into the driver's seat, fired the engine up, and with me manning the passenger's seat, we drove all the way to Red Bank and back, where Zelle took us on a tour of our entire neighborhood, culminated by pulling into my driveway, directly behind an older model black Chevy... Impala. In pristine condition on the outside, and without question, a 1966 model year. So definitely not Rupe's car. He had an inferior 1965 model, so who...? I looked over at Zellie, who was quivering, trying not to show her what? Nervousness at something? She answered my unspoken question by cracking up laughing.

"We both had the same idea," she croaked. "Happy Engagement. That 1966 Chevy Impala is all yours. I found it myself, and Rupe had his mechanic check it out for me. He said it's pristine inside. And yes, it has a 327 small block, just like Matilda. Not light blue like her, but I think you'll like a different look, anyway."

I was speechless. I mean, I tried to speak, but no words came out. And Zellie was enjoying every second.

"What are you waiting for?" she asked. "Let's take a ride."

I first had to pull up the hood and look. The mechanic was right. The engine was gorgeous. I put the hood down, hugged Zellie, beckoned to the front seat, and got behind the wheel of my new Chevy Impala. We drove all over the neighborhood again, and parked again, this time in my garage.

"You're not going to just leave it in the garage, are you?"

"Not a chance. If ever there was a car for driving, it's that one. But it's beautiful inside and out, and I'd like to keep it that way. I motioned at the other garage bay. Why don't you put your new Honda in here, too?"

"I think I will."

And our two cars nestled side by side as we walked, hands firmly clasped, into my house.

CHAPTER THIRTY-SIX

The sun's reflection on the brightly colored autumn leaves created the perfect backdrop for Zellie and I to traverse the few miles to the Molly Pitcher Inn, the site of our wedding. We drove together in my new classic Chevy Impala, while our parents rode together in Zellie's new Honda CR-V.

At Felicity's suggestion, we'd added a touch of formality to our nuptials, including renting a small ballroom with a veranda at the venerable Red Bank establishment. A fortuitous cancellation enabled us to slide right in to a time coinciding with our admittedly impetuous scheduling of our embarkation to matrimony.

Our party remained small, and included our parents, Mrs. Minniefield, Ted and Marla, and Rupe and Sarah. I'd moved up in rank, promoted to groom from my prior status as witness number two at Zellie's ill-fated prior marriage before a justice of the peace.

We asked a rabbi friend to preside this time, and the inn had fashioned a chuppah under which he'd perform the ceremony.

Upon arrival at the inn, we repaired to separate dressing rooms, where I donned my tuxedo, and Zellie changed into her wedding attire. I was not told what she would wear. Those in the know guarded the details more closely that the nuclear codes. All I knew was that Zellie's mother and Marla had helped her shop for the dress and had presumably bribed a dressmaker to finish it in record time.

My dad joined me in my dressing room after I'd completed changing. We'd had an awkward relationship, but he was warmth personified today. I don't think I'd ever seen him like this, but I could swear he had tears in his eyes.

He shook them off and clasped my hand.

"I thought this day would never come, son," he began. "Not only you getting married, but shedding that long line of temporary girlfriends for a true gem like Zellie. She's a rare pearl, son, and I can't tell you how proud I am of you, and how delighted your mother and I are in welcoming Zellie into our family."

He choked up again and covered it up by letting go of my hand and putting it over his mouth as if stifling a cough. He patted me on the shoulder and left.

Ted knocked on the door a few moments later, and my best man and I walked into the ballroom where all but Zellie and her parents, my mom, and Marla had already assembled. I shook hands with the rabbi. Mrs. Minniefield stood up and gave me a hug, as did Sarah. Rupe and I refrained from our usual friendly insults and exchanged a firm handshake.

The music started, and the rabbi, Ted and I took our places under the chuppah, watching and waiting for a door at the other end of the ballroom to open.

Being movie buffs, Zellie and I considered using the theme to Star Wars as our wedding music, but decided on a more traditional Canon D by Johann Pachelbel.

As the first bars of that music began, I froze. The moment of truth. I didn't panic, but I confess to a brief chest tightness, as the door opened and my parents, holding hands, strolled down the aisle and sat down in front. When the door opened again, all nervousness left me in a flash, as I viewed the love of my life, my best friend since childhood, emerge, walking, with her parents flanking her.

Zellie looked gorgeous in her floor-length snow-white wedding dress. She'd pinned up her golden-blonde brown locks, with a single slender, braided set of strands hanging from her left temple. She wore her grandmother's gold locket, which shimmered in the ballroom lights. As they approached, Ted shook my hand, pressing a ring into my palm.

Zellie's parents hugged her, walked her to her spot under the chuppah. Ted gave us both hugs, and sat down next to Marla, who'd quietly taken a seat next to Mrs. Minniefield.

The music stopped, and the rest was a whirlwind. The rabbi gave his spiel; we exchanged heartfelt vows, and time stopped as the rabbi pronounced us husband and wife, and invited me to kiss the bride.

Ignoring all present, Zellie and I locked lips in a magnificent kiss, one that marked both a culmination of the world's longest courtship, and the beginning of a different life together. A future we welcomed with all our hearts.

***

Dear Reader:

Thanks for reading my book! I hope you enjoyed Arnie & Zellie's latest adventure in Monmouth County, New Jersey.

Online reviews are much appreciated, so it would be great if you took a few moments to write a review on Amazon.com, BarnesandNoble.com, or any other review site. Thanks!

Just click on a link (or type it into your browser), and scroll down to where it provides for a review.

www.amazon.com/author/ericsmall
https://www.goodreads.com/author/show/19558925.Eric_Small

Eric Small

About the Author:

Retired government attorney Eric Small began writing a cozy mystery series featuring the investigations and adventures of Arnie and Zellie in their fledgling detective agency, set in the environs of Middletown, New Jersey. *Brazen Gambit* was the first in the series, and *A Tale of Two Freddies* continued fromwhere that left off. *Three Faces of Jennifer* is the third book in the series. Eric grew up in Middletown, and now lives in Florida with his wife, to whom he's been married for over thirty years.

Ordering and Contact Information:

At Amazon.com, Barnesandnoble.com, and other on-line   booksellers.

www.amazon.com/author/ericsmall

www.barnesandnoble.com

Contact Information:

Eric Small Books
P.O. Box 840003
St. Augustine, FL 32080
Eric@ericsmallbooks.com
www.ericsmallbooks.com